Murder B

Lizzie Bentham

Best Wishes

Lizzie Bentham

x x

Copyright © Lizzie Bentham 2024.

The right of Lizzie Bentham to be identified as the author of this work has been asserted by her in accordance with the Copyright, Designs and Patents Act, 1988.

First published in 2024 by Sharpe Books.

This inscription written by St Boniface to King Æthelbald of Mercia is found at the front of the *Boniface Psalter* – a book of psalms. It was written circa AD 754, just before St Boniface's death. This translation from Anglo-Saxon into English is by Miss Dorothea Roberts.

Boniface, Archbishop of Mainz in Germania, born in Crediton, once of Nhutscelle, had me made as a gift for Æthelbald, King of the Mercians.

Salvation, Æthelbald, is a precious gift from God that you as Lord of the Mercians, appear to hold lightly in your hands and ignore when it most suits your own lustful desires. You have been consecrated to be a light to the peoples of these isles but instead your life does not bear close scrutiny. I and my brothers in Christ, the honourable bishops of this realm, have admonished you previously for your laggardly desire to marry, your procuring of church funds, and your adulterous fornication with nuns. We have regularly beseeched you to repent and pray for forgiveness. You have not heeded our entreaties and have continued to consort with wanton women.

Fear the Lord God Almighty, repent and follow His decrees, or else you will be weighed in the balance and found wanting, like Belshazzar, and be replaced. Mene, mene, tekel, upharsin.
Heed this warning and change your ways.
Your Brother in Christ
Boniface

MURDER BY THE BOOK

CHAPTER ONE

The Legacy of Kings and Saints

Monday Morning, 25th February 1935

In a lecture theatre at the Victoria University of Manchester, rows of students, dazed from their weekend excesses, tried to concentrate. Female students in warm cardigans, wrinkled stockings, and curls ruffled by the wind, sat on the left. Male students in crumpled suits, smoking roll ups, sat on the right. Dorothea Roberts, a first-year English undergraduate student, listened raptly to what the silver-haired academic was saying.

'So, Æthelbald met an untimely death at the hands of men from his own bodyguard. It has been hypothesized by some historians, that the jagged gash to the leather back of the *Boniface Psalter* was sustained in that murderous attack when Æthelbald was at mass. According to Harrison's *A Concise History of the Curse of the Boniface Psalter*, not on the reading list but available from the library, throughout its twelve hundred year lifespan, many of its owners have come to rather gruesome ends. Some, including Dr Harrison, have called the high mortality rate of the owners of the *Boniface Psalter*, "The Boniface Curse".

'I am sure that St Boniface himself would have found this laughable, because he was merely quoting from the Bible. Specifically, from the book of Daniel, chapter 5 verses 25 to 28. If you remember from Sunday school, this is the story of the disembodied hand writing on the wall at a banquet. Daniel interprets the writing and warns King Belshazzar of Babylon, a terrible ruler, that he had been weighed by God and found wanting, that his days were numbered - he would die that very night, and that his kingdom would be divided between the Medes and Persians. A similar fate happened to King Æthelbald a couple of thousand years later.

'There does seem to be a correlation between the moral standing of the owners of the *Boniface Psalter* and the awfulness of their death. The psalter spent nearly eight hundred years in the care of various monasteries and they seem to have been less inconvenienced by a curse. Though it must be noted, that a 12th century source claimed that St Swithun's Priory in Winchester had so many civil lawsuits that the Bishop of Winchester gave the psalter into the care of Mickering Priory, near Ormskirk to distance themselves from it.'

A hand shot up from the middle of the lecture theatre.

'Who owns the manuscript now Professor Aldridge?'

'Good question. The *Boniface Psalter* was bequeathed to this university by the Quintrell family, thirty years ago, when the son of the 13th Baronet of Mickering died in rather tragic circumstances. An exhibition of the psalter was organised at the Ancoats Art Museum, around twenty years ago. A terrible occurrence happen on opening night and it had to close. A new exhibition is soon to be hosted at the museum, on Anglo-Saxon Art. It will include the *Boniface Psalter* on display properly for the first time. The exhibition is officially opening on the evening of Shrove Tuesday—'

There was a call of 'Rag, Rag, Rag,' from the back of the room.

'Yes I know that this clashes with your Rag Week events. I have managed to organise a private viewing of the exhibition, on the morning of Shrove Tuesday for my students. This is an exceptional opportunity for some Anglo-Saxon translation practice, so I am setting you all an assignment . . .'

There was a chorus of groans from within the ranks.

'At the front of the psalter there is an inscription in St Boniface's own hand to Æthelbald King of Mercia. He is also thought to have annotated the manuscript in a number of places, highlighting certain salient theological points, which makes it a fascinating document.

'By the end of term, I want a translation of that inscription. Go and see the manuscript for yourself in situ. The exhibition is free for students. For extra course marks, you can also write me an essay entitled, *The Curse of the Boniface Psalter - Fact or Fiction?,* to be given in on the same day.'

Professor Aldridge deliberately made eye contact with Dorothea. It sent a shock wave down her spine.

MURDER BY THE BOOK

Professor Aldridge wants me to write that essay. I wonder what he is up to. She thought.

'How much is the *Boniface Psalter* worth Professor?' asked a tall, young man with straw-coloured hair and brown eyes, seated on the back row.

'It is priceless Mr Tarleton, a piece of British history. There are a number of collectors I am sure that would pay a king's ransom to acquire it for their private collections.'

The clock on the wall struck the hour.

'Off you go to your tutorial groups. Don't keep your tutors waiting,' called Professor Aldridge as a hundred and twenty students surged out of the lecture theatre.

***

After her two hour tutorial, Dorothea popped into the Women's Union to check her pigeon hole. Since discovering a corpse at the Christmas ball, the building had lost some of its charm for her, so she tried to spend the minimum amount of time inside.

The pigeon holes were in the corridor outside of the committee office. Even from a distance, she could see a large, brown-paper package sticking out of hers. Feeling surprised, she quickly ripped off the outer wrapping to discover a copy of *A Concise History of the Curse of the Boniface Psalter,* recommended by Professor Aldridge only a few hours earlier. Inside the front cover was a university library sticker, with a return date stamp of after the essay deadline.

If this is the only copy of the book in the library, then none of my course-mates can write that essay, she thought.

Half of Dorothea's brain was screaming at her to take the book back to the library and walk away. The other half, the part that thought that this term was a lot duller than last term, told her to put the book quickly in her satchel and leave, which she did.

From a bench outside the Women's Union, a pair of keen hazel eyes watched over the top of a newspaper, as Dorothea exited the building. The watcher smiled to herself.

LIZZIE BENTHAM

A Concise History of the Curse of the Boniface Psalter by Dr M. Harrison – Æthelbald and Beornred AD 757

Two men crept through the forest, an hour before dawn. There were dark deeds to discuss. They met in the ley of the druid's oak and sat together with their backs to the trunk, for what little protection from the elements it afforded.

'What news Beornred on his Highness's movements?'

'We have spent most of the last fortnight kicking our heels at Tetbury. A godless place! King Æthelbald is bewitched by the Abbess of Boxwell. He brings her presents and sings her pretty songs. She in return simpers and lets the King share her bed. She has designs to be queen and if she can conceive a son, then perhaps she will succeed.'

'She will fail as others have failed. You, Beornred are the only child that Æthelbald has ever successfully sired, to a serving wench out of wedlock, when he was but a youth. This is a cycle that King Æthelbald goes through, as certain as the changing seasons. He finds a love, usually a married lady or a nun. They have their fun, then they part and no one wonders at the lack of children sired. Why do you think he has dawdled into wedlock when all his advisers, including myself, are advocating for an advantageous marriage? Because he is afraid that he won't be able to produce an heir and thus weaken his kingdom. By now a kingdom is usually littered with royal bastards but you are the only one.' Pendrod paused and looked at the younger man sat next to him, thoughtfully.

'You certainly look like him Beornred. His advisers have suggested that Æthelbald names an heir, to keep his cousin Offa from sniffing around the throne. It annoys his Majesty, because it makes him feel his mortality. He has never been the same since his row with Archbishop Boniface. The Archbishop's gift of a psalter did little to placate him, though I swear that Æthelbald was saddened to hear about Boniface's death.

'A date of midsummer has been set to name his successor. In the absence of any other heir, you are his best choice. You are a good soldier, a good leader of the king's bodyguard and you are

MURDER BY THE BOOK

King Æthelbald's natural son. He likes you too. Would you like to be king?'

'To be my father's acknowledged heir to the Kingdom of Mercia, of course I would!' The younger man looked thoughtful.

'Are you willing to fight for it? Æthelbald's great-nephew, Ælfnod, is sniffing around court looking for favours, the insolent pup.'

'Ælfnod would be disastrous for the kingdom. It would be better to give Offa the crown of Mercia now. My men are loyal to me. They will fight and kill for my sake.'

'I will use what influence I have with King Æthelbald. Await word from me,' said Pendrod.

***

At the midsummer feast, King Æthelbald addressed the whole court. 'I have decided to name my successor. I have thought long and hard. Ælfnod, my great-nephew, will succeed me as king. My scribes have drawn up the legal documents and I will sign them after mass this evening. I pray that you will be as loyal to him, as you have been to me.'

Beornred's face in the light of the braziers was white. He was not to be his father's heir. Pendrod whispered something in his ear. Beornred got up at once and called two of the king's guard to go with him. They exited the room silently and unseen.

King Æthelbald and Ælfnod left the table to go to the simple, wooden chapel to take mass together. They did not return.

Beornred re-entered the great hall holding Æthelbald's coronet. Men from the king's guard were stationed around the room and a frightened hush fell on the room. Everyone had noticed the blood on Beornred's hands.

Pendrod stepped forward. 'Æthelbald and Ælfnod are dead. It was a tragic accident. I present to you King Beornred, Æthelbald's son. I pledge my allegiance to him and I suggest that you do too.'

'Long live King Beornred,' cheered the king's bodyguard.

'Long live King Beornred,' chorused the frightened court in

response.

So Æthelbald was the first to fall prey to the curse of the *Boniface Psalter*. A little under a year later, Beornred was driven into exile by Offa, who became the greatest of the early Kings of Britain.

King Offa fearing the fate of his predecessors, very sensibly gave St Boniface's psalter to the Monastery at Nhutscelle, where Boniface had once studied. He made sure he married and kept away from nuns.

Primary Source: *The Chronicles of Mercia,* an illuminated manuscript currently in the private collection of the Vatican.

MURDER BY THE BOOK

The Worm
Edition 13 Academic Year 34/35, Tuesday 26th February 1935
Girls to Dress in Rag!
This Year's Shrovetide Rag Promises to be the Biggest and Best Yet!

Each year during Rag Week, male students put on a parade of comic floats, an epic review performance and take part in audacious stunts, all to raise money for good causes, including the University Settlement at Ancoats. Hundreds of students take to the streets with collecting tins, to extract money from the citizens of Manchester.

Up until now, women students have helped with collecting money.

After a mass protest, this year will be the first in which women will also wear fancy dress to hit the streets. Expect some spectacular new stunts from our female students! All costumes must meet the approval of the Appropriate Dress Committee run by the Women's Union.

The Lord Mayor and other civic dignitaries will watch the parade as it passes down Oxford Road, before attending the opening of a new exhibition on Anglo-Saxon Art, at the Ancoats Art Museum, later in the evening. Hopefully 1935 will be a record breaking year for raising money!

(David Simpkins Journalist)

LIZZIE BENTHAM

Sunday Afternoon, 3rd March 1935

Dorothea Robert's beloved Crossword Club had recently been put on hold. This was partly due to Dorothea and her friend Mary Long, a second-year chemist, having moved out of Grangebrook Hall after their ordeal at Christmas and partly due to Maggie Forshaw's upcoming nuptials. Instead, Wedding Dress and Bridesmaid's Dress Making Club met at St Bartholomew's vicarage, Lower Heaton-in-the-Marsh, on a Sunday afternoon. As Mary Long and Dorothea were now the Mosses' neighbours, it was decided that the vicarage was a more sensible venue to meet. Also Jinny Moss, the vicar's wife's and an alumna of the university, was lending them her sewing machine and it was not the easiest lump of metal to transport across the city.

The bride, Maggie, a postgraduate mathematician, and Mary Shor (known as Mary Short), a second-year medic, would motor out to the vicarage in an old Riley that Maggie's fiancé, Simon Culthorpe, had modified for Maggie's particular needs . . . mainly additional speed. She was an adept driver and even had her name down to participate in the next Le Mans race. Mary Short was the only person who would willingly accept a lift off Maggie, because her medical training had given her nerves of steel.

Maggie's bridal gown was going to be a simple, bias-cut wedding dress of white satin, with a long train and a tulle veil, provided they made it in time.

'I will look fabulous and if I end up tripping down the aisle, I can blame the train and not the callipers,' she said serenely.

Maggie had caught polio when she was a child and had been left with muscle weakness in her legs. Most of the time she used a wheelchair but for special occasions, including playing golf, she used callipers. Walking down the aisle would be a very special occasion indeed.

The bridesmaids, Dorothea Roberts, Mary Long, Mary Short and Jinny Moss would also be wearing simple bias-cut dresses, in a very pale, green satin, which had been a canny bargain by

MURDER BY THE BOOK

Maggie, but in reality did not particularly suit any of them.

While the young women were pinning, tacking, and sowing away, Dorothea carefully broached the subject of the textbook and the supposed curse, attributed to the *Boniface Psalter*.

'Did anyone else see the piece in *The Worm* about the Anglo-Saxon Art exhibition at the Ancoats Art Museum?'

There was a chorus of 'Yeas' and 'Nays' but no great interest was shown.

'Professor Aldridge has set my class a piece of work to translate the inscription from an old psalter, into English and there is meant to be a curse associated with the manuscript. He wants us to write an essay about the curse,' she began. Ears began to prick and suddenly Dorothea was being watched intently by four pairs of curious eyes.

'Down the ages the custodians of the psalter have prospered if they were good and died horribly if they were evil,' she continued knowing she had their rapt attention now. 'Someone put a book called *A Concise History of the Curse of the Boniface Psalter* into my pigeon hole, it's from the library. I checked and it is the only copy. Someone really wants me to write that essay and get interested in this "curse".'

'Dot have you stumbled on another mystery?' Jinny's eyes were shining. 'Please can we help?'

'It must have been Professor Aldridge who gave you the book,' hypothesised Mary Short. 'He set the essay. Why don't we invite him around for tea and quiz him?'

'We could invite Dr Hadley-Brown too,' chipped in Mary Long, with a sly dig at Dorothea.

Dorothea went red. Dorothea's friends thought she had "a thing" for Dr Hadley-Brown her tutor. Dorothea was adamant that she did not.

'Hang on ladies,' said Maggie. 'Remember what happened last time we investigated something. Dot and Mary Long almost got killed and Arabella was kidnapped by a maniac,' Arabella was Jinny's stepdaughter. 'Let me remind you that I am getting married on the 27th of April. I need all four of you, unharmed and unmolested, to walk down the aisle looking fabulous. If we investigate this, can you promise me that not one of us will sustain any physical trauma? Emotional and spiritual trauma I don't care about.'

'We promise to be at your wedding come hell or high water Maggie,' said Mary Long.

'We promise to look our best too,' added Mary Short.

'I am sure nothing bad will happen this time,' Jinny sounded positive.

'So shall we invite Professor Aldridge for tea?' Dorothea asked hopefully.

'Go on then, but do invite Dr Hadley-Brown too,' added Maggie as a caveat.

***

Mary Long and Dorothea walked home. Out of the front door, along the path around the side of the vicarage, through a rustic rose arch, then a few more steps and they were looking at what had once been an outbuilding. It had been clumsily converted into a small, rather dark cottage for a curate many years ago but in recent years it had stood empty.

Since Christmas, Jinny had helped the young women make Rose Cottage into a warm and cosy home. They had the freedom to come and go as they pleased without a hall of residence curfew hampering their activities. Mary Long could go out dancing until the early hours with impunity.

Mary was rather quiet as the two women were making bedtime cocoa. Dorothea suspected she was pondering the problem she had shared with her friends earlier, however she was soon proven wrong.

'Do you remember Dr Balvan Thakkar from dancing Dot?' asked Mary shyly. 'He is doing a postdoctoral fellowship at the Department of Chemistry until the end of the summer term. He is from Bombay in India and is the son of a physician. Well, he wants to travel up to Inverness to talk to my father to ask his permission—'

'He wants to ask your father's permission to marry you?'

interrupted Dorothea with a shriek. 'Do you love him? Will you say yes? Will you move to India?'

'Yes I do love him and he loves me. We have known it for some time now. Balvan is looking for a permanent academic job in a British university. He has applied for simply loads of them. They take one look at his skin colour at the interview, if he gets that far, and the job goes to a less well-qualified, British, white man. Considering we Brits are hugely proud of our empire, we don't seem to like our commonwealth citizens very much. If he can't get a job here, I'll move with him to India. Balvan says universities in India are very good and chemistry is very well taught, so I'll be able to graduate. I don't know what my father will say. He didn't want me to come to Manchester to study, so he won't want me to go to India.' Mary patiently answered Dorothea's questions, 'What do you think of him Dot?' her voice trembling slightly towards the end with apprehension.

'I think you are made for each other and I am so excited for you. Do the others know yet?' said Dot, giving her friend a hug.

'No, I haven't told anyone other than you.'

'Not even Shorty?' said Dorothea, trying to keep the surprise out of her voice. Mary Short was Mary Long's best friend.

Mary Long pursed her lips. 'No, she and David Simpkins are having issues with their own courtship, so whenever we get a chance to talk, she needs to unburden herself.'

Mary Short had been walking out with David Simpkins, the editor of *The Worm*, the university's magazine, for a few months now. As they were both busy people, they had not been able to see much of each other. When they did have a much anticipated dinner date planned, David would often have to rush off back to the office to meet a deadline.

'Thank you for trusting me with your news. I will help you in any way I can, including making you another cup of cocoa to celebrate!'

They spent a happy half hour before bed pouring over the well-thumbed pages of a children's encyclopaedia, to see what adventures were in store for Mary Long and her young man, in India.

LIZZIE BENTHAM

Monday Morning, 4th March 1935

Detective Chief Inspector (DCI) Kydd still had three more boxes to unpack, in his new, much larger office, at police headquarters. He had not used anything from them in the two months since his promotion. He wondered if he should ask Miss Grimstead, his very efficient and no nonsense secretary, to throw them out. He thought better of it. She terrified him more than any knife wielding assailant or mass murderer.

At least he was not on the hunt for a homicidal maniac at the moment. There had been a spate of jewellery thefts in the county over the past month, with some notable and priceless pieces being taken from stately homes, jewellers and museums. The thefts, while individually very different, were all characterised by their meticulous planning and daring execution. DCI Kydd suspected that they were all perpetrated by one particularly clever individual. The Pontefract Rubies had been smuggled out of Major Marshall's daughter's debutante ball in a strawberry trifle. The Turquoise Tiger belonging to the famous actress, Dolores Brambilla, had been dropped into her perfectly maintained swimming pool and then removed by a phoney pool cleaner. A Fabergé egg, rumoured to have once belonged to Tsar Alexander III, was swapped with a goose egg overnight in a jeweller's safe. In each case, a calling card had been left behind with a magpie on it, leading to the press naming the thief, "the Magpie".

No one had tried to sell the jewels to any of the usual suspects who touched hot property. DCI Kydd's men had tried all the usual fences, dodgy jewellers and collectors of the rare and beautiful. A watch had been put on the ports and the jewels had even been registered with the International Criminal Police Commission.

Miss Grimstead knocked primly and then popped her head around the door. She looked disapprovingly at the open case files strewn on the chief inspector's desk.

'Your ten thirty appointment has arrived DCI Kydd. A

representation is here from the university to talk about the plans for the forthcoming Shrove Tuesday Rag parade.'

The chief inspector sighed. He could ill afford distractions just at the moment but he was now seen as the university's police officer of choice, after helping to solve multiple incidents on campus the previous term.

'Thank you Miss Grimstead. Please send the young people through.'

CHAPTER TWO

The Shrovetide Rag

A Concise History of the Curse of the Boniface Psalter by Dr M. Harrison – The Destruction of Nhutscelle Monastery by the Danes in 878 AD

The monastery at Nhutscelle was on fire, so too were the living quarters and kitchen. Flames were slowly engulfing the prior's house. The prior himself was dead, killed by a single blow from a Danish raider's sword, while he was celebrating the Shrovetide Mass with his brothers.

The monks had scattered like sheep, when the armed Northmen entered the sanctuary. Some, the Danes slaughtered in cold blood for sport, others they let go. They took all the precious objects from the church then set it alight. They drove the monks' livestock away towards their ships and stole grain, mead, and salted fish from the monastery's larder.

Brother Luke, the infirmarer, was the only monk not at mass. He had sat with a dying brother all day, quietly reading to the old man words of comfort and hope from the scriptures. Brother John had taken his last breath before vespers and had died at peace. Brother Luke was finishing laying out the old man in a seemly fashion, when the church bell suddenly sang out a warning in the still evening air, then abruptly fell silent. Out of the window Brother Luke could see smoke in the distance and hear the shrieks of frightened men. A man in outlandish clothes, wielding a sword entered the north door of the church into the nave.

Brother Luke whispered a prayer committing his dead charge into God's care, all the burial service Brother John was likely to get.

Grabbing the poker used to stoke the infirmary fire, his scrip and cloak, Brother Luke headed out of the door towards the scriptorium where the monastery's library was kept. Once inside, he went straight to a reliquary made from rosewood, intricately carved with birds and flowers. Opening the precious box, he took out the book of psalms contained within and stuffed it into his scrip, unceremoniously dumping it's container on the floor.

A huge shape stooped to enter through the low door into the scriptorium and the evening light glinted off steel. Instinctively Brother Luke hit the Northman as hard as he could with the poker, aiming for his skull. All the while he muttered a prayer for forgiveness fervently under his breath. He heard a thud behind him but did not stop to look. He was already opening the shuttered window and climbing up on to one of the lecterns for a leg up.

There were footsteps and exclamations of wrath in an alien tongue behind him, as the monk climbed onto the sill and flung himself over, dropping lightly into an overgrown, drainage ditch full of noisome mud. Extracting himself, he scurried away using the undergrowth for shelter. The ditch, when it was full of winter water, emptied into a stream which crisscrossed the salt marsh and joined the River Test. He followed its course, keeping low.

Pausing to take stock from a safe distance, Brother Luke looked back towards the monastery as the wind fanned the raging inferno, consuming what had once been a thriving centre of Christianity on the south coast. Should he make his way to Reodford Monastery to seek sanctuary? It was an hour's walk through the salt marsh and if he borrowed a coracle from one of the local fishermen, he would be there in much less.

Then he thought of the Dane's long ships creeping up the sea channel at night. Reodford Monastery would have been a target long before Nhutscelle Monastery. Winchester it would have to be. The brothers there would take him in, but it was half a day's walk through the forest at night. If any of the brothers from Nhutscelle had survived, they would likely make for Winchester too, which settled the matter.

Brother Luke looked to the heavens, prayed a prayer of protection on himself and his scattered brothers, found the North Star and set a course towards Winchester taking the precious psalter with him.

Primary Source: *Tales of Danish Heroes* written in Old Norse in circa 900 AD and currently housed in a tiny kirk in Ballstad within the Arctic Circle.

LIZZIE BENTHAM

Shrove Tuesday Morning, 5th March 1935

Dorothea arrived at the Ancoats Art Museum early on the morning of Shrove Tuesday. It was based at Ancoats Hall, also home to the University Settlement, a social outreach project to the local community. It included a women's hall of residence in one wing which Dorothea had visited previously, meeting rooms, and a concert hall.

At the ticket desk she mentioned Professor Aldridge's name to the woman on duty and was waved through the barrier. The lady warned Dorothea that there might be some people coming in and out, to get the room ready for the exhibition opening that evening.

Dorothea was now sat on an uncomfortable, wooden bench that the museum guard had kindly obtained for her, in front of a large, glass cabinet containing the *Boniface Psalter*. It was a marginal improvement. She had been sat on the floor juggling an Anglo-Saxon vocabulary book, a clipboard, course notes, and pen. On top of which, she had to bob up and down every few minutes to read the front page of the ancient manuscript. She still had to bob up and down, but at least not quite as far.

Dorothea had decided to start work on her translation of St Boniface's message to Æthelbald, to get it over with. This would leave her free to focus on the essay about the Boniface curse, which she felt compelled to write, since the mysterious appearance of Dr Harrison's book. She was completely absorbed in her work, when a shadow loomed over her.

'Excuse me can I borrow your vocabulary book for a moment please? I appear to have left my own at home,' asked a deep, melodious voice from high above her head.

Startled Dorothea looked up, then up some more, into a handsome face, brimming with mischief. The newcomer had disarmingly frank brown eyes, straw-coloured hair framing an elfin face and a determined chin. She recognised him as Eric Tarleton, from her English Language course. He was the son of a notable archaeologist and was only taking the Anglo-Saxon and

Norse language modules to supplement his own archaeological degree. Dorothea had never spoken to him before because the set of young men that Eric called friends, thought very highly of themselves. The young women on the course were beneath their notice, except as the butt for smart Alec remarks and to crib skipped lecture notes from.

Now that he had her full attention, Eric smiled at Dorothea warmly and it was as if the sun had come out. Dorothea found herself smiling back shyly.

'Dot Roberts isn't it? We are on the same course. I am Eric. I have often wanted to make your acquaintance after the sensational events at Christmas.'

This wiped the smile off Dorothea's face. She still suffered from nightmares about being trapped on a rooftop with a killer. Eric saw the momentary spasm of pain cross her face and was appalled and apologetic over his gaff.

'I am so sorry, that was terribly gauche of me. Here let me make it up to you. When you have finished translating, will you let me treat you to tea and cake, to say thank you for lending me your vocabulary book?' He looked so contrite that Dorothea forgave him.

'Thank you that would be lovely,' she said.

They spent the next forty minutes balanced at either end of the wonky bench, with the vocabulary book in between them. They worked in companionable silence, except when warning each other that they were about to stand up for a closer look at the manuscript, to prevent catapulting the other to the floor.

Dorothea gave Eric Tarleton a surreptitious glance. He really was attractive, very different in type from any other man of her acquaintance. Eric looked like he never thought deeply about anything and did not have a care in the world, unlike the perpetually grumpy Dr Hadley-Brown, who seemed to be keeping his distance from Dorothea since the start of term. Reverend Moss, Jinny's husband, was kind and thoughtful, Simon Culthorpe, Maggie's fiancé, was laid back with a wry sense of humour, Balvan Thakkar, Mary Long's boyfriend, was sweet with oodles of common sense, and David Simpkins, Mary

Short's boyfriend, was intense, driven and sometimes quite hard work. A lot of the male undergraduates Dorothea had met were shy and tongue-tied in front of their female peers.

Eric resembled none of these and Dorothea was intrigued. At one point she looked up and caught Eric studying her intently. He grinned boyishly at her and went back to his translation.

At ten thirty Eric stood up without warning and catapulted Dorothea to the floor. He apologised profusely, helped her to her feet and picked up her paper and pens.

Offering his arm to Dorothea with mock seriousness he asked, 'Would my lady allow her humble servant to escort her to tea?'

Blushing slightly, Dorothea took the proffered arm and realised how tall he was, six foot three inches, if she was not mistaken. At five foot one, she felt like a child holding hands with an adult.

They caught a tram back to the university together, where they had tea and scones in the cafeteria. Eric regaled Dorothea with stories from his father's archaeological digs, which he had helped on during the summer holidays. The most recent dig was in Antioch. Eric was an interesting conversationalist and the allure of the East came through in all of his descriptions of the weather, souks, and ruins. Time ticked on. Dorothea realised that they had been talking for nearly two hours and if she did not run she would miss all of the fun of the Shrovetide Rag. She still needed to get changed into her fancy dress costume.

Eric too had to leave to take part in the planning of a Rag week stunt. She thanked her host with genuine delight and bade him a rushed goodbye. He stood in the street for some time looking after Dorothea thoughtfully.

MURDER BY THE BOOK

Shrove Tuesday Afternoon, 5th March 1935

Dorothea was lying on a mocked up bed pretending to be Sleeping Beauty asleep, in St Peter's Square, in the middle of Manchester. It had turned into a parky, bright spring day which looked a lot warmer than it actually was. Her thickest underlayers, her best voluminous nighty and a mob cap were not enough to keep her warm, though they had passed the scrutiny of the Women's Union Appropriate Rag Attire Committee.

Mary Short dressed as a fairy godmother in a tutu, ballet shoes, and wings looked half frozen to death but had also passed the committee's appropriateness standard, as ballet was considered an "art form". She waved her wand at passers-by asking them to throw a coin into the collecting tin to wake up Sleeping Beauty. When Dorothea heard the rattling of coins, she would yawn, stretch and thank the kind donor.

Mary Long would then jump out from behind the bed dressed as an evil fairy, to give the passers-by a fright and to extort a few extra pennies. What she was dressed in had certainly not been sanctioned by any committee!

After an hour or so they were freezing, so the trio disassembled the borrowed bed and took it back to the Drama Society's prop store. They got changed in the Women's Union, before retreating to drink cocoa in the cafeteria to warm up.

'What time does the parade start at?' asked Dorothea eagerly, looking forward to seeing her first Shrovetide Rag Parade.

'Four o'clock. Let's go and find a good vantage point now,' answered Mary Short.

There were crowds lining Oxford Road as they walked along and the atmosphere was that of a bank holiday. The three young women found a good place to stand with their collecting tins and cheered and clapped, as colourful floats built on the back of local brewery carts trundled along the predetermined route.

While everyone else was distracted by the Drama Society's float depicting a scene from *A Midsummer's Night Dream*, Dorothea felt someone jog her elbow. When she looked around, she noticed that an envelope had been stuffed into her collecting tin. She tried to stuff it in further, thinking it might be a generous donation, but it was too big to fit the opening. Instead, she wiggled it out and was surprised to see that it had her name on it. Prising it open, she found the folded page of an old newspaper clipping. Thoroughly bemused, she carefully put it away in her bag for future inspection.

As the parade was ending, the two Marys prepared to leave to get ready for the Shrovetide ball that evening in the Student Union buildings. Mary Long was being escorted there by Balvan Thakkar and Mary Short had persuaded David Simpkins that it was his duty as a journalist to attend, to record any momentous happenings.

'Are you sure you don't want to join us tonight Dot? Even Maggie and Simon are coming and they have attended three Rag Week balls already,' said Mary Long. 'I am sure that you can get in last minute as a member of the committee.'

'No thank you! I couldn't face it after last time. You'll have to find corpses without me.' Dorothea made light of her Christmas ordeal. 'Besides I want to look at my essay again before tomorrow's tea party and have an early night. Don't wake me up when you get in Longy.'

Dorothea also did not have anyone to go with. As all of her friends were pairing off, it brought home to her that the one person she really did want to go to the ball with, seemed to be advoiding her like the plague.

Drat you Dr Geraint Hadley-Brown, she thought crossly.

She said goodbye to her friends and caught a tram back home to the suburbs.

MURDER BY THE BOOK

Shrove Tuesday Evening, 5th March 1935

A very fashionable crowd had gathered at the Ancoats Art Museum to see the official opening of the Anglo-Saxon Art exhibition which included the *Boniface Psalter* as its star attraction.

'Geraint dear boy! Over here, I've saved you a seat,' called Professor Aldridge to his godson.

Geraint Hadley-Brown made his way through the throng of chatting historians, archaeologists, civic dignitaries, and the press, to where his godfather was sitting on the front row, directly in front of a red-velvet, draped display cabinet.

'I am so glad you could come. You have been very elusive recently. Do sit down, there's a good chap. I am sure something interesting is going to happen soon,' said Professor Aldridge.

'Why? What are you expecting to happen?' Geraint rapidly took his seat on a bench next to the professor which gave a hideous wobble in protest.

'"The Curse of St Boniface" to strike again obviously. I was at the launch event twenty years ago, when pardon the expression, all hell broke loose. It was just such an evening as this.'

'What did happen twenty years ago, sir? You have always been rather secretive about it . . . whatever "*it*" is.'

'All in good time Geraint. Let's wait and see what happens tonight.' The professor deliberately changed the subject. 'By the by, I have set my first-years the task of researching St Boniface's curse and producing an essay on it by Easter.'

'Really?' Geraint was non-committal.

'I am sure your Miss Roberts will write a really good essay and get her friends interested in the Boniface curse too.' Professor Aldridge was being deliberately provoking.

'She isn't my Miss Roberts sir.'

'Why ever not my boy? She is pretty, clever and brave. You are obviously smitten. Your mother will like her too. What more do you want?'

'For her not to be my student sir!' exclaimed Geraint crossly.

LIZZIE BENTHAM

'You know that staff-student liaisons are frowned upon.'

'I realise I am old fashioned Geraint, but she is a much better match for you than your last paramour.' Professor Aldridge ignored the fact that the lady in question was now the wife of Mr George, Head of U Division at MI5 and a very dear friend of his.

'Be that as it may sir, I wouldn't be comfortable with . . . walking out with one of my students.'

'Very noble Geraint. Very noble indeed. I'll stop teasing you now but do remember that she will not be your student forever. You do not teach the third-years for a start,' he added, sounding hopeful.

Geraint gave him an exasperated look.

'Very well but do not let some callow youth steal her heart because of your principles. Why do you think I am a bachelor? I was too slow telling the woman I loved that I had feelings for her and a rival suitor got there first. We'll say no more about it. Look, everyone is taking their places. It seems like we are getting started.'

Geraint tried to get comfortable on his wobbly bench but he could not concentrate. All he could think about were two blue-grey eyes, in a puckish face, with unruly fair curls, looking up at him and seeing a spark of gladness illuminate those eyes because it was him holding her safely.

Damn you Dorothea Roberts. You make me feel as insecure as a youth with calf love, he thought.

A glamorous, older lady took the podium, next to the velvet-draped display case. She was wearing the biggest pearl necklace that Geraint had ever seen. There were rows and rows of matching, opalescent balls with a much larger tear drop shaped pearl nestled in their midst. She was Mrs Geraldine Beaumaris one of the trustees of the museum and the widow of the late Professor Beaumaris. The necklace she was wearing was the famous Giant's Tear pearls.

'Thank you ladies and gentlemen for attending the opening of this important exhibition exploring different Anglo-Saxon art forms. This museum is very honoured to be hosting exhibits on loan from many other museums and I think you will all agree that

MURDER BY THE BOOK

our team of curators here have done a sterling job.' There was a spattering of polite applause.

She continued, 'The other trustees and I thought it was time that the *Boniface Psalter* was put on display. We are fortunate to have with us tonight, two very distinguished gentlemen. One is Sir Laurence Tarleton, the renowned archaeologist, who completed his doctorate on the *Legacy of St Boniface*, here at Manchester, quite a few years ago now and also famously discovered the burial place of King Offa.' There was some half-hearted applause.

'Secondly, the distinguished historian Dr Maximilian Harrison, whose book called . . .' She paused to look at a piece of paper, '*A Concise History of the Curse of the Boniface Psalter* was published ten years ago and is being re-released with new material for its tenth anniversary. It was very popular indeed, due to Dr Harrison's unique writing style, designed to appeal to the general public and academic alike.' There was more enthusiastic applause this time.

'They will each explain the significance of the *Boniface Psalter* throughout history and to us here today. Please join with me to welcome Sir Laurence Tarleton to the stage.'

During the applause Professor Aldridge nudged Geraint in the ribs. 'Stay awake my boy. This should be interesting. I have not seen these two gentlemen together in the same room, since *it* happened twenty years ago.'

'What is "*it*"?'

'Shhh, listen!'

Sir Laurence Tarleton droned through a brief history of St Boniface and the psalter's creation in particular, for nearly thirty minutes. Geraint felt he could have learnt just as much from the programme leaflet that he had been handed at the door. His head started nodding and his eyes fought sleep, until a loud and bombastic voice boomed from the podium, signalling a change of speaker.

Dr Harrison was not boring. He was a massive, bull of a man who fancied himself as an amateur thespian. His lecture entitled *The Curse of the Boniface Psalter* was enlivened with lots of drama and ham acting. He gave a whistle stop tour through the centuries including every murder, theft and affaire that the psalter had been associated with.

Dr Harrison was just working up to his big finale, when the studious atmosphere was shattered by a loud *BANG!* A firework exploded and suddenly the room was filled with smoke. Students dressed as highwaymen and highwaywomen appeared. They circled the room, brandishing cardboard blunderbusses and shaking collecting tins shouting, 'Rag, Rag, Rag!'

There were gasps of astonishment, rapidly replaced by disgruntled tutting and coughing fits as the acrid smoke ticked throats. Attendees began to search half-heartedly for coins in their purses and wallets.

A masked figure took Dr Harrison's place on the podium, much to the astonishment of the academic, who had never easily relinquished a podium in his life.

'In the spirit of Rag Week we are robbing from the rich to give to the poor. Anything you donate will be split between many university supported projects, including the excellent work done here at the University Settlement. Thank you for your generosity in advance.'

There was renewed grumbling and searching for coins in bags. Gradually the number of students dwindled, as they took themselves off to join the Rag ball.

Dr Harrison again took the podium and was about to plug the second edition of his book, when everyone present heard a muffled cry for help from the caretaker's cupboard at the back of the room. There were gasps from the audience and Sir Tarleton, who was the nearest, went with some trepidation, to open the door. A dishevelled and hysterical Mrs Beaumaris emerged. The Giant's Tear necklace that she had been wearing was missing.

She threw herself into the arms of her rescuer, Sir Laurence, who staggered under the onslaught and ineffectually pattered her on the back.

'There, there Geraldine, no need to fret. I am here now,' he muttered.

'My pearls have been stolen!' wailed the prostrated woman. 'I was held at gunpoint by a young ruffian dressed as a highwayman and told to, "Stand and deliver, my pearls or my life." Why aren't you ringing the police Laurence?'

'But my dear, they were only students and their blunderbusses were made of cardboard.' Sir Tarleton was confused and showed it.

'I know a real gun when I see it Laurence! I was held up by a pistol-wielding thug in a room full of people and no one did anything.'

'What did he look like?'

'He was tall, as tall as you Laurence, wearing a mask, hat, and a large cloak.' Geraldine Beaumaris wasn't going to be the best eyewitness.

'Did anyone here see the young hoodlum in question?' asked Sir Tarleton to the audience, who were now enjoying the drama immensely.

There was a chorus of 'No . . .' from around the room. Everyone's focus had been on the stage. Someone called out, 'The Magpie has struck again!' and chaos ensued.

'Now might be the time to give our friend, DCI Kydd, a phone call. He will be grateful to hear this first-hand from a reliable source. Sneak off now before the press get to the telephones first,' whispered Professor Aldridge in his godson's ear.

Geraint stood up so quickly that the mayor's private secretary, who was sitting on the opposite end of the bench, was catapulted to the floor. Not stopping to apologise, Geraint jogged to the foyer and managed to get the last telephone booth, before the reporter for the *Evening Trumpet* could get there first. In the distance he could hear Mrs Beaumaris crying hysterically. Geraint asked the operator to put him through to police headquarters and prayed DCI Kydd was working late that evening.

***

Professor Aldridge and Geraint Hadley-Brown were finally

allowed to leave the museum after giving their statements to a police constable. Professor Aldridge hailed a taxi to take them home.

'That was not what I was expecting Geraint but it was a fascinating evening all the same. How was it done I wonder?' commented the professor.

'Now will you tell me what is going on sir?' asked an exasperated Geraint.

'Tomorrow we have an invitation to afternoon tea at St Bartholomew's vicarage, where, if I am not very much mistaken, there will be a receptive audience. You know how much I hate repeating myself. Ah home already? I'll pick you up at three o'clock tomorrow afternoon Geraint. Don't be late. We don't want to keep the young ladies waiting.'

And with that, Geraint Hadley-Brown had to be satisfied.

MURDER BY THE BOOK

Shrove Tuesday Evening, 5th *March 1935*

"Dr Harrison gives multiple examples through the ages, where bad people receive their comeuppance and good people have prospered. There are fewer stories of curse like occurrences happening when the psalter has been in the safe care of a monastery or institute of learning. This suggests that theologians and academics do not have the necessary imagination, to believe in a curse which plagues less highly educated people.

There have been a higher than average number of murders, unexplained deaths, suicides, thefts, affaires, rapine and general pillaging, associated with this document, more so than any other of a similar age. The document and its associated curse, is in my opinion, being used as an excuse by normal people, to get away with all sorts of transgressions."

Dorothea was sat at home in Rose Cottage, trying to get her thoughts in order to continue writing her essay. She flicked to the end of Dr Harrison's book, to a story which had captured her attention about the search for King Offa's burial place. It was the last known occurrence of St Boniface's curse. She then studied the newspaper article that had been placed in her collecting tin. If the latter was true, then there was a much more recent example of the curse attributed to the *Boniface Psalter*.

She reread the stories again and was even more determined to ask Professor Aldridge about them the next day.

LIZZIE BENTHAM

A Concise History of the Curse of the Boniface Psalter by Dr M. Harrison – The Search for Offa's Burial Place 1904

Offa was unequivocally the greatest of the Mercian Kings and like his cousin Æthelbald before him, he reigned for a great many years, subjugated lesser kings and built the massive earthwork known as Offa's Dyke to keep out Welsh raiders.

For such an important monarch, his burial place has remained a mystery throughout the centuries. He died on the 29th July 796 AD and was then buried, according to contemporary sources, in a small chapel outside of Bedford, on the banks of the Great Ouse. On Offa's death, Cynethryth his wife, became Abbess of Cookham and had charge over the chapel. Over time the building was flooded by the river and its location was lost.

An archaeological team led by Professor Beaumaris and funded by Sir Joshua Quintrell the 13th Baronet of Mickering, started to dig on a site to the north of Bedford, in the summer of 1904. Finding Offa's tomb would be the pinnacle of achievement for any archaeologist's career and one that would lead to fame and fortune. It was known that some Anglo-Saxon burials, even Christian kings, were buried with expensive grave goods.

On Professor Beaumaris's team was Sir Joshua's son, Michael Quintrell and a young Laurence Tarleton.

The dig was unsuccessful and plagued with disasters, including the tragic death of Michael Quintrell, when a deep trench collapsed on top of him.

As well as losing his son and heir, Sir Joshua Quintrell lost a lot of money and was forced to retrench after this sad occurrence. He extended the mortgages on Mickering Priory substantially and sold off land that had been in the family for nearly five hundred years. Sir Joshua donated the *Boniface Psalter* to the Victorian University of Manchester, because he could not face any more of his family line being plagued by the St Boniface curse.

Five years later, Laurence Tarleton went back to the field next-door to where they had dug previously and almost in the first trench, found the remains of an Anglo-Saxon stone chapel. A week later, his team discovered a stone sarcophagus buried in deep river silt.

When opened, it contained the poorly preserved bones of the great Mercian king and silver and gold jewellery, armour and a sword with a bejewelled hilt.

The discovery was framed as "the find of the century" and Tarleton received a professorship, an unlimited research budget and eventually was knighted for his services to archaeology. His subsequent career to date has yet to match that early achievement.

Primary Source: *The Finding of Offa's Tomb* by Sir Laurence Tarleton published in 1910

LIZZIE BENTHAM

An Article from the Morning Mercury Newspaper, from 25th February 1914, placed in Dorothea Roberts' Collecting Tin

Murder at the Museum!

In Manchester, a leading academic in archaeology, Professor Beaumaris, was found dead on the opening night of an Anglo-Saxon exhibition, at the Ancoats Art Museum. On show was the notorious *Boniface Psalter* which is supposedly cursed, so that whoever owns it has to live a pious life or face terrible repercussions vested on them from on high. The cause of Professor Beaumaris' death has yet to be made public but a source, who wanted to remain anonymous, has indicated that the professor was found dead in the cabinet that the *Boniface Psalter* was being displayed in. In our source's opinion, the cause of death was not natural. There will be an update in our evening addition, when more information has come to light.

MURDER BY THE BOOK

The Early Hours of Wednesday Morning, 6th March 1935

In the middle of the night Dorothea was awakened by gusty sobbing coming from downstairs. She got up, threw on her dressing gown and crept downstairs to find a dishevelled Mary Long soaking wet, covered in rotten eggs and vegetable matter, crying her heart out next to the still warm embers of the dying fire.

Dorothea took one look at the state Mary was in, dropped to her knees next to her friend on the hearth rug and hugged her, while Mary choked out a distressing tale.

Balvan Thakkar and Mary Long, with David Simpkins and Mary Short, had enjoyed their time at the Shrovetide Rag ball and had left together before the end. Outside there was a gang of male students waiting for them, with eggs and rotten vegetables. These they threw at the group but specifically targeting Balvan. Mary Short managed to hail a taxicab and together they escaped. Then Mary Short and David Simpkins had a massive row, because David had started to write down their eye witness accounts of the event and wanted to go back to interview their attackers. Mary said if he went back, then their relationship was over. He stopped the cab, jumped out and shouted that he was not going to let Mary "silence the press". Mary Short then told David that he could not write for toffee. He slammed the door and walked off into the night. Mary Short then cried all the way back to Grangebrook Hall, where they dropped her off.

On the way home to Rose Cottage, Balvan wanted to break up with Mary Long because they had been targeted by a bunch of prejudiced thugs. He wished to protect Mary because he loved her. He thought it would be best if he booked a passage back to India as soon as possible.

Mary declared that she loved him too and she would do anything to be with him. She vowed to follow him to India and even to the ends of the earth.

They had danced on the vicarage lawn in the dark, kissed goodbye as doomed lovers on the cottage step in the rain and

Mary expected never to see him again.

All this, was snuffled into Dorothea's shoulder. Dorothea said nothing but mentally cursed the world and everyone in it, especially romantics. She stoked the fire, boiled the kettle for a cup of tea, then again for the bath and again and again, until there was six inches of tepid water in the tub. She found towels and a clean nightdress and left her friend with another cup of tea to soak her troubles away. Then, wearily she flung herself into her own bed and passed out after an exhausting and eventful day.

CHAPTER THREE

A New Case

Wednesday Afternoon, 6th March 1935

Six pairs of amused eyes watched as Geraint Hadley-Brown sat cross-legged on a picnic rug, in the middle of the vicarage parlour floor. He was surrounded by dolls and stuffed animals and was force-fed cucumber sandwiches, by a determined and obviously besotted six year old. Arabella Moss had taken a shine to Geraint and was not prepared to lose her uncomfortable, but politely persevering victim.

'Wouldn't you be more comfortable up here on a chair Dr Hadley-Brown?' Jinny inquired, despairing of her step-daughter Arabella but secretly impressed by Geraint's sticking power. The Bishop of Manchester had only lasted five minutes on the floor playing tea parties, before inventing a fictitious prior engagement that had slipped his mind. Perhaps Geraint was trying to impress someone in the room with his parenting skills? Jinny smiled and glanced over to Dorothea who was watching the performance raptly.

'Well actually—' began Geraint.

'No he wouldn't Mummy. He needs to eat his dinner like a good boy.' Arabella was adamant.

'Was there a particular reason that you invited us ladies?' Professor Aldridge asked.

All eyes turned towards Dorothea.

'Why did you set my year an essay on the *Boniface Psalter* and its curse?' she asked. 'Someone very helpfully placed the library's copy of Dr Harrison's book in my pigeon hole in the Women's Union. Was it you sir?'

'It is a subject close to my heart but I didn't give you the book.' The professor was amused and showed it. 'So Theodora is trying to get things moving,' he murmured to himself.

Dorothea pricked up her ears. 'Would this Theodora have

slipped a newspaper article into my collecting tin yesterday too?' She asked, handing Professor Aldridge the newspaper article in question. He nodded an affirmative.

'What has Mother been up to?' inquired Geraint Hadley-Brown from the floor.

'The newspapers this morning are saying that the necklace, stolen last night from the museum by the Magpie, is being attributed to St Boniface's curse,' Maggie butted in. 'Professor Aldridge please can you tell us all you know about the *Boniface Psalter* and we will try and help you.'

'Like consulting detectives? Excellent! I will employ your services to solve a most perplexing case that has troubled me for over twenty years. Geraint, this story involves your parents. I doubt you will have heard it before because it was all hushed up. I promised your mother that I would only tell you when I thought you could cope with the burden of the tale. I know that you are more than ready to hear about your family's past.'

Sat on the floor, Geraint was distracted enough not to notice Arabella's hand holding a cucumber sandwich coming towards his face, so he ended up with a mouthful of soggy, green mush.

Professor Aldridge settled back in his chair and began his tale.

'As a younger man I studied English as an undergraduate at the University of Liverpool, before moving to Manchester in 1912 for my doctoral degree. I was fascinated by everything to do with Anglo-Saxon culture, especially the language. I managed to secure a doctoral project in the joint History and Archaeology Department, under the supervision of the world renowned archaeologist Professor Beaumaris. My thesis was on the relationship of the *Boniface Psalter* to other better known examples of St Boniface's writing. I was not Professor Beaumaris's only doctoral student. Dr Harrison the bestselling author was also a doctoral student under Professor Beaumaris at the same time.

'Professor Beaumaris was also head of department. Like most university departments, we were short of space so the professor had an office in the Ancoats Art Museum. Maximilian Harrison and I shared an office there with another student, the now renowned archaeologist, Dr Lottie Ellis.

'Professor Beaumaris was considered a firm bachelor but around that time he rather precipitously married the daughter of one of the trustees of the museum, Geraldine, who was a lot younger than him. She regularly popped into the museum to see him and brought with her cakes for him, the doctoral students and other members of staff, including the newly appointed Chair of Field Archaeology, Professor Laurence Tarleton. He was Professor Beaumaris' protégé and was still basking in the glory of discovering King Offa's final resting place a few years previously. He had a large office in the museum on the first floor.

'Your father Geraint, Tristan Hadley-Brown, was head curator there and it was his job to collate and supervise all exhibitions that were hosted. Your parents were very happily married, even though your grandfather, Sir Joshua Quintrell, thought Theodora's marriage a mésalliance, a mistake, as your father was only the son of a grocer. He came around to it in the end, especially when you and your sister were born. He doted on his grandchildren.

'It was early in 1914 and the university had held the *Boniface Psalter* for ten years by this point and there were many scholars like myself, interested in the manuscript. The trustees of the museum thought it was about time to put the psalter on display for the public to enjoy. Tristan Hadley-Brown was charged with putting together an exhibition worthy of such a unique manuscript. That exhibition was also due to open on Shrove Tuesday, so you can see why I was eager to attend last night's opening of such a similar exhibition.

'On the evening before the exhibition was due to open, there was to be a small soirée in the museum for a few dignitaries and some eminent academics, who were all desperate to see the *Boniface Psalter* on display for the first time in modern times.

'The psalter was displayed on an ornate, wooden lectern inside a freestanding, cabinet in the middle of the South Gallery. A curator had to unlock and duck through a small door to get inside, to attend to the exhibits. As well as the psalter, there were some of the ornate grave goods found during Professor

Tarleton's archaeological dig of Offa's burial, on display.

'For the opening night, a heavy curtain of red velvet had been rigged up all around the museum case, the front of which could be drawn back with a cord and pulley system.

'Half an hour before the soirée was about to begin, Geraldine Beaumaris realised that her husband had not been seen for a while and he was meant to be the master of ceremonies for the event. Everyone scrambled around trying to find him and Laurence Tarleton volunteered to be master of ceremonies in his place.

'The dowager Baroness Quintrell, your grandmother Geraint, was due to open the exhibition as a representative of the Quintrell family. Your grandfather had died earlier that year, the title, but not Mickering Priory having gone to a very distant cousin. Laurence Tarleton welcomed everyone and invited Baroness Quintrell up to say a few words. She simply said, "Michael would have loved tonight and loved this exhibition." She was talking about your Uncle Michael, Geraint, who died on an archaeological dig many years before. Laurence Tarleton dropped all his notes on the floor at that point. Baroness Quintrell then yanked the cord so hard that the curtain rail toppled over with a crash, exposing a scene of carnage.

'Professor Beaumaris's body was in the cabinet, face and hands pressed up against the glass, blood splattered everywhere. The back of his head had been staved in by repeated blows with a heavy object, which turned out to be the *Boniface Psalter* itself. I remember that someone screamed and Geraldine Beaumaris fainted.

'On the glass someone had started to write the Persian symbols for "Mene, mene, tekel, upharsin," in blood, a reference to the Biblical passage from Daniel chapter 5 verse 27 which St Boniface mentions in his message to Æthelbald. Of course this brought the curse to the forefront of everyone's mind. There was even some silly talk in the press about an avenging, unearthly hand wielding the psalter as a weapon. Poor St Boniface was much maligned I fear.

'When the professor's body was examined later, there was

blood found on one forefinger as if it was him who had written those words. The pathologist however, said that would have been inconsistent with the injuries received.

'The door of the cabinet was locked and there was a key found in the dead man's pocket. The police were not inclined to believe in a vindictive curse. Their major suspects were those who had access to a key to the cabinet. The cabinet had been especially made for the psalter and there were only three identical keys in existence. One was with the master set of keys, kept locked in a safe in the main office. The second belonged to your father as head curator, and the third key Professor Beaumaris kept himself for his own research and for his students to borrow. Nothing else in the cabinet had been taken or even touched.

'When your father looked for his key, it was gone from his office so he naturally came under suspicion. He was also overheard having an argument in Professor Beaumaris's office earlier in the day. The master key was still in its rightful place in the safe. Presumably the key on Professor Beaumaris' body was his own, so the police thought it was Tristan's key that was used. It was not found during the investigation.

'Maximilian Harrison and I were also in the building that day and had access to Tristan's key so were under suspicion. Theodora Hadley-Brown and Geraldine Beaumaris were present to help with last minute preparations too. Laurence Tarleton was at work in the building all of that day. As was the museum watchman, Bertram Pickles.

'We seven were all under suspicion for Professor Beaumaris' murder. To this day we still are. No one was ever charged for killing him, as there wasn't enough evidence to convict anyone.

'It drove your father into a spiral of depression because he felt people looked at him differently. When war broke out, later that year, he volunteered to go and fight, against his wife's wishes. He was killed, near Ypres within weeks of being posted to the front. Some people whispered that it was a guilty conscious that drove him to enlist and that he wasn't careful of his own safety in the trenches – that he had a death wish. I do not believe this as I talked to men who served under him and they had nothing but praise for his courage and leadership,' said Professor Aldridge, finishing his story.

Geraint Hadley-Brown stood up stiffly, oblivious to the squeak of protest from Arabella and walked blindly out of the room. They heard the front door open and shut.

Dorothea's heart ached in sympathy. She knew how much Geraint Hadley-Brown had adored his father.

'Should I follow him Professor Aldridge?' asked Dorothea.

'Leave him with his thoughts. He has had rather a shock,' said the professor gently.

'Did anyone have an alibi for the time of the murder? Did you have an alibi?' asked Maggie breaking the tension that had built up in the room.

'Unfortunately no I did not. I didn't kill him by the way. However, don't take my word for it and draw your own conclusions. I was working in the doctoral student office on my own, for time period when the police believe that the murder happened. The body was found at seven o'clock in the evening and the police thought Professor Beaumaris had been dead for a couple of hours by then. His time of death was therefore between approximately three and five o'clock. The Hadley-Browns were together for some of the afternoon but not all of it. Geraldine Beaumaris was with Laurence Tarleton for part of the time and Maximilian Harrison spoke to Theodora Hadley-Brown at one point and he was with me for some of the time in the office. Oh dear I am not telling you this in any order.'

'Did Professor Beaumaris have any enemies Professor Aldridge?' asked Jinny.

'Professor Beaumaris was an astute man who did not suffer fools. He would not stay quiet if he saw something was wrong. He also had very little tact. There were many people in the university who had felt the sharp end of his tongue.'

'Did anyone benefit from his death sir?' asked Mary Long.

'Laurence Tarleton certainly did well out of Professor Beaumaris's death, in that he was promoted to head of department. Leading a department is a lot of work, on top of a teaching and research load. Killing to increase his work load would be an unusual motive for murder.'

There was some industrious note taking going on in the room.

'Did anyone else have a motive to kill Professor Beaumaris?' asked Mary Long

The professor looked uncomfortable. 'I am glad Geraint has gone for a walk to cool off because unfortunately his father did have a reason to kill Professor Beaumaris and they did argue on the afternoon of the murder. The position of museum director was vacant at that time. Tristan Hadley-Brown had been led to believe that his application would be most welcome. The week before the murder it was announced that a friend of Professor Beaumaris had been preferred above Geraint's father.'

'We need to see the original statements from each of the suspects to piece together everyone's movements on the day of the murder and have a proper look at the scene of the crime.' Mary Short, pink-eyed from crying herself to sleep the previous evening, was on the ball as ever.

'Seeing the scene of the crime will be easy,' said Professor Aldridge. 'I have some strings I can pull at the museum. With regards to the suspect statements, I suggest you have a chat with DCI Kydd. I did not realise it at first but I do believe he was a very young and eager police constable at the time. Police officers do tend to remember their first murder case, especially if it is still unsolved twenty years later.'

'Is there a way we can get an introduction to any of the other suspects without arousing their suspicions Professor?' Jinny was enjoying herself immensely.

'Yes there may well be.' The professor had a twinkle in his eye. 'I think Theodora Hadley-Brown would love to meet you all. It is time she stopped playing at intrigues and met you for real.'

LIZZIE BENTHAM

An Extract from The Worm's Famous Alumni Series - Dr Lottie Ellis

This week we are focusing on an alumna of the university who has contributed greatly to her chosen discipline of archaeology.

Dr Lottie Ellis graduated in 1909 with a Batchelor of Arts in Archaeology from the Victoria University of Manchester. She then studied for a postgraduate doctoral degree conducted under the supervision of Sir Laurence Tarleton, the famous archaeologist who discovered King Offa's burial site.

Dr Ellis graduated from her doctorate in 1915 *in absentia,* as the Great War prevented her from returning from Damascus where she was running a dig at Douma.

She is now considered to be the foremost expert in the post-Roman to early middle-ages period for the Middle East and has excavated at many sites including at Douma, Mosul and Tarsus.

Dr Ellis has always managed to find funding for her digs throughout her long career, when more experienced archaeologists have struggled to secure backers. When asked the source of her funding success by this reporter, she credits hard work, an ability to problem solve and being willing to break the rules, as the route to acquiring finance for her digs.

Dr Ellis includes excavating a Coptic church which had been abandoned since the 8th century in Egypt, finding a 7th century sword in a latrine in Mosul and finding a figurine of the goddess Asherah in Douma, as some of the most memorable moments of her career.

She will be visiting the university on the 18th of April to give a lecture on *Victorian Treasures – The First Female Archaeologists* at four p.m. in the History Department.

David Simpkins - Journalist

CHAPTER FOUR

The Game is Afoot

A Concise History of the Curse of the Boniface Psalter by Dr M. Harrison – The Monks of Mickering Priory

When the weary messenger arrived on horseback, he was taken to the chapel where Alun, the Prior of Mickering, was to be found in private prayer. The prior was old and a little bit stiff but astute of mind. He got unsteadily to his feet and greeted the stranger warmly.

'Greetings friend, what brings you to us with such haste? What news from the South? Nothing calamitous I hope. Come to the refectory and one of the brothers will bring mead, bread, and cheese to refresh you, while you tell me what is afoot.'

'Father I cannot tarry with you even one night. I promised my lord, the Bishop of Winchester, that I would carry a message to you with all due speed. He asks a special favour from this priory, that is a sister house to St Swithun's Priory in Winchester. They have had charge of St Boniface's own psalter, for three hundred years and it has caused no end of woe for the priory and for the city. In that time there have been more fallings out with the townsfolk, more rebellions over appointed priors and more legal wrangling with the nobility, that have all costed time and money, more than in any other diocese in England. The Bishop of Winchester has heard of the piety of this house and entreats you, for the sake of peace in Winchester, to become guardians of the psalter. He has even obtained an audience with the Archbishop of Canterbury and they are in agreement. They think it would be best for the whole country, that the book be kept under a prayerful guard, well away from kings, nobles, bishops, and the grind of politics. He asks for an answer from you to be brought back to him forthwith. What shall I tell him Father Prior?'

The old monk seemed to have aged in front of the messenger's eyes. He looked like he was carrying an unimaginable weight upon his shoulders. Yet there was a spark in his eyes and he would not be rushed.

'My son, this is a momentous commission to accept lightly. I am familiar with St Boniface's psalter and the curse that it bestows on those who care for it. I will tarry here awhile in prayer, asking God for His help and fortitude. There will be large implications for this house going forward. Go get refreshment and rest. I will be here some time.'

In fact, the prior spent all night in the chapel in a vigil of prayer and worship.

On appearing at chapter next morning, he called the messenger to him. 'I have sought God's will in this matter. Go back to the Bishop of Winchester, your master and say, "Alun, Prior of Mickering near Aughton, accepts the commission placed upon this house. We will take the psalter off his hands and protect it from the world and the world from it."'

To his brother monks in the chapter house the old prior said, 'My brothers this is no small undertaking and will change the way our daily lives run. The psalter will be brought from Winchester and will be placed on the altar of the chapel. Day and night, two brothers will be on watch in the chapel, singing psalms, reading scripture, and praying. We shall lead lives of great spiritual purity, for if we do not, the curse will strike us down, but if we do, then God will honour our sacrifice.'

From the moment that the saint's psalter was placed on the altar of the chapel, the monks of Mickering Priory were known to be the most holy and humble in the whole of Christendom. They lived simple, prayerful lives, looked after the poor and sick and bar one prior in the 13th century who came to a rather sticky end, never fell out with their neighbours or entered into any disputes. This continued until King Henry VIII's dissolution of the monasteries hit the little community hard. Mickering Priory had grown rich under the careful stewardship of many priors, so was a prime target for the money grubbing king. The monks were turfed out of their home and the priory church was demolished. The priory land and ruins were acquired by the newly created 1st Baronet of Mickering, Timothy Quintrell, a crony of King Henry, at a knock down price.

Primary Source: *The Journal of Alun Prior of Mickering Priory* now in the private collection of a Japanese Business man in Kyoto.

LIZZIE BENTHAM

Thursday Morning, 8th March 1935

In his office, DCI Kydd finally opened one of the boxes that he had been too busy to sort through. He was sure that there were some of his old notebooks in one of them, from when he had first joined the force. There had been a case that had made a connection in his brain to the theft of Mrs Beaumaris' pearl necklace, his very first murder case but those notebooks did not seem to be in this box. The phone rang in DCI Kydd's office and he answered it.

Miss Grimstead's prim voice enunciated clearly, 'A Miss Dorothea Roberts to speak with you Chief Inspector.'

'Hello Miss Roberts this is a nice surprise. How can I help you?' asked DCI Kydd.

The void responded in Dorothea's familiar country tones.

'Hello sir. My friends and I were wondering . . . I don't know quite how to say this, so here goes. We seem to have stumbled across another mystery and it is one that we think you will know all about. Do you remember the murder of Professor Beaumaris at the Ancoats Art Museum, the first time the *Boniface Psalter* was to be exhibited? It is still an unsolved murder investigation. We think it might have a connection with the theft of the pearl necklace the other night. Well we want to have a go at solving it.'

The chief inspector inhaled deeply. He was dumbfounded that Dorothea was talking about the same unsolved case that he had been thinking about only moments before.

'Professor Beaumaris' murder has been unsolved for the last twenty years. Even Detective Inspector "Daring" Dawlish couldn't solve it and he was the best detective on the force,' was all DCI Kydd could bleat.

'Yes we know, but we want to try. It was your first ever murder case as a police constable wasn't it? We know that we won't be able to see the police's original witness statements, as civilians but we did wonder if you happened to make your own notes, maybe to try and solve the case before DI "Daring"

Dawlish. Would we be able to see them please?'

'Hang on a minute Miss Roberts. This is all highly irregular. A murderer has managed to escape justice for twenty years and then you and your friends, (I assume all the old gang are involved, please give my regards to Dr Hadley-Brown), want to start digging up the dirt again. It could be very dangerous indeed.' DCI Kydd made his voice sound stern.

'We wanted to ask if you could oversee us as amateur detectives. We'll do the leg work but share what we find out with you. Professor Aldridge has a wizard idea about re-enacting the crime at the museum. You could come and supervise.'

So Professor Aldridge is behind this is he? He thought. *Interesting . . .*

DCI Kydd looked at the pile of work on his desk related to the Magpie's robberies and then at the three boxes still to be unpacked and made a decision.

'I'll let you see my old notebooks, if I can find them, on the promise that you and your insane friends keep me up to date with all your enquiries. I mean all of them! If I tell you to stop and let the police take over, then you must back off with no arguments. If you continue to investigate I'll have you all arrested. Do you understand?'

'Perfectly Chief Inspector, thank you, you are an absolute lamb. I'll drop past and pick them up later,' said Dorothea smugly.

LIZZIE BENTHAM

Police Constable Kydd's Notes on the Murder of Professor Beaumaris Shrovetide 1914

Who was Professor Beaumaris?
Professor Beaumaris was an eminent archaeologist and Anglo-Saxon scholar. He was head of the joint History and Archaeology Department at the Victoria University of Manchester and one of the trustees of the Ancoats Art Museum. He was married to Geraldine Beaumaris, née Rigby, daughter of a trustee of the museum. Professor Beaumaris was a softly-spoken man and well-thought of by his contemporaries. He was also a very fair man and would not stand by and let an injustice go unnoticed. He was not known for his tact.

What Happened?
On Monday 23rd February 1914, Professor Beaumaris was found murdered inside a locked display cabinet containing the *Boniface Psalter* (possibly cursed). His body was discovered at a private soirée for academics and dignitaries to celebrate the opening of a new exhibition at the Ancoats Art Museum. The museum was closed to the public that afternoon to prepare for the festivities. There were only a limited number of people within the museum and the internal door to the women's hall of residence was locked.

When did the Murder Occur?
Professor Beaumaris arrived early at his office. His secretary confirms he had a number of meetings with colleagues during the morning including; Laurence Tarleton, Maximilian Harrison, Harold Aldridge, and Tristan Hadley-Brown. Professor Beaumaris was last seen alive just after two o'clock by his secretary, who had to leave early for an emergency dental appointment. She said that Professor Beaumaris seemed to have something on his mind and he mentioned that he wanted to have a look at the *Boniface Psalter* that afternoon, before the opening of the exhibition that evening.

He was discovered to be missing at around six o'clock by his

MURDER BY THE BOOK

wife, who visited his office and who instigated a search for him. This search became progressively more frantic, the closer time got to the start of the event (seven o'clock), due to the professor being the master of ceremonies. Laurence Tarleton had to step in at the last minute. The body of Professor Beaumaris was found at seven-o-five. The police surgeon reckons the professor had been dead for a few hours and placed the time of death to between three and five o'clock on the afternoon of Monday 23rd February 1914.

Where did Professor Beaumaris Die?

Professor Beaumaris was found locked inside a specially constructed display cabinet made for the *Boniface Psalter*. It was a cuboid shape, made of wood and glass, five foot, by seven foot, by seven foot and placed in the centre of the South Gallery of the museum. There was only one entrance into the cabinet, a small door through which a curator could enter to change the display. There were three identical keys for the cabinet (one found in Professor Beaumaris' pocket, the master key in the safe in the museum main office and one missing from Tristan Hadley-Brown's office). Only the first two keys have been found to date. Rails with large velvet curtains had been placed around the cabinet on the morning of the murder, which could be drawn to unveil the display.

How did Professor Beaumaris Die?

He had been repeatedly hit on the head with a blunt object which the laboratory has confirmed was the psalter itself. On the glass of the cabinet, someone had written the Persian symbols for "Mene, mene, tekel, upharsin," a quote from the book of Daniel in the Bible, in Professor Beaumaris' blood. There was blood on one of the deceased's fingers but the pathologist doubts that Professor Beaumaris would have been alive after the attack to be able to write it himself.

Who are the Main Suspects?
Sir Laurence Tarleton

He was in his first floor office all afternoon, working on an important paper to give to a learned society the following week. Geraldine Beaumaris called past at three o'clock and stayed to help him with some shorthand. Geraldine left around four o'clock on realising that she was late to help Theodora Hadley-Brown with the refreshments for the soirée later. Sir Tarleton was by himself for the rest of the afternoon. He took over master of ceremony duties when it was discovered that Professor Beaumaris was missing and could not be found.

Geraldine Beaumaris

She arrived at the museum just before three o'clock to deliver some homemade cakes for the exhibition opening. Instead of going straight to the kitchen in the basement, she dropped by Sir Laurence Tarleton's office with some of his favourite scones and ended up getting drawn into preparations for his upcoming lecture. At four o'clock she hurried down to the basement to help Theodora Hadley-Brown with catering preparations. There she stayed until it was time for the refreshments to be moved upstairs. Geraldine volunteered to go to the top of the dumbwaiter to haul food up as Theodora Hadley-Brown had cut her hand.

Theodora Hadley-Brown

She arrived at the museum at two o'clock after picking up programmes for the exhibition from the printers. She helped her husband to put out chairs and tables for the soirée in the South Gallery until half past two. She then went to the staff kitchen in the basement to sort crockery, glasses, and cutlery and cleaned out the tea urns. Maximilian Harrison stopped by at two forty five to make two cups of tea but was only there a few minutes.

Theodora left the kitchen for five mins to take her husband some tea in his office at three thirty. She said that he was in his office when she visited and he corroborates this.

At four o'clock she was joined by Geraldine who was an hour late, rather breathless and rumpled. Together they made sandwiches and cream teas. Theodora said she cut her hand while preparing sandwiches for the soirée. Geraldine Beaumaris confirmed that this accident occurred (there was blood on

MURDER BY THE BOOK

Theodora Hadley-Brown's skirt when I interviewed her later), and she had bandaged her hand with sticking plaster. Theodora had to leave the kitchen at four thirty to retrieve the first aid kit from the museum main office and was gone for five minutes (confirmed by Bertram Pickles the watchman and Geraldine Beaumaris). On returning at four thirty five, the two women started to move the crockery and food from the kitchen in the dumbwaiter up to the South Gallery. The two women worked together to lay the table and the first guests started to arrive at six thirty. They were behind the refreshments table when the murder was discovered.

Tristan Hadley-Brown

From two thirty Tristan Hadley-Brown was in the library of the museum for nearly an hour, hanging banners of Anglo-Saxon crosses made by local school children. He says he looked out of the library door and spotted an unknown woman walking away from him, down the main corridor. He called out to her that the museum was closed but she carried on walking. (No one else saw this unidentified woman. DI Dawlish thinks Tristan Hadley-Brown made her up to cast suspicion away from himself. I prefer to keep an open mind). This was prior to when he went back to his office at three twenty five and his wife brought him a cup of tea at half past the hour. Afterward he could not concentrate on work due to nerves related to the exhibition's opening, so went for a walk and returned to the museum at five thirty. He was seen by Bertram Pickles both leaving and returning through the main entrance.

Maximilian Harrison

He was working in the doctoral student office with Harold Aldridge cleaning some Saxon coins and using wax and plaster of Paris to take imprints of them, for his thesis. He states that he left at two forty five to fetch Harold Aldridge and himself a cup of tea which he brought back to the office, before leaving again to take a tea break with his girlfriend over in the women's hall of residence. He is courting Phyllis Peters, a Master's student. He says he returned at three twenty to find Harold Aldridge snoring, so he got on with his work and woke Harold up at five thirty because they had to help downstairs in the South Gallery.

Harold Aldridge

He was working in the doctoral student office on the second floor (shared with Maximilian Harrison and a third student, Lottie Ellis, who was away on fieldwork on the day of the murder), from lunchtime through to five thirty. He says he was working on a tricky bit of Anglo-Saxon translation which made him pretty sleepy. Aldridge states that Maximilian Harrison was there, except for five minutes, at two forty five when he went to the kitchen to make them both a cup of tea and that Maximilian brought it back promptly. He says that Maximilian Harrison usually takes his tea break over in the women's hall to spend time with his girlfriend. Harold Aldridge says he may have fallen asleep later in the afternoon, as the translation he was doing was quite hard going, but Maximilian Harrison was there when he woke up.

Bertram Pickles – Museum Watchman

He was sat in the main office next to the front door of the museum all afternoon, except for two tours of the museum at two and five o'clock. It is known that Bertram takes sneaky cigarette breaks. He says Maximilian Harrison left the building by the front door at two fifty to go around to the women's hall of residence. He says Maximilian Harrison complained that the internal interconnecting door to the women's hall which usually was unlocked was on this occasion locked, (on Professor Beaumaris' orders to stop anyone from the University Settlement borrowing anything or holding a spontaneous teddy bears picnic with local school children). He saw Tristan Hadley-Brown leave at three forty five and return at five thirty. He says he helped Mrs Hadley-Brown to apply a sticking plaster from the first aid box to her cut finger at four thirty. The master key remained in the safe throughout the time period in question.

MURDER BY THE BOOK

Wednesday Evening, 13th March 1935

Five shadows crept through the formal grounds to the back door of the Ancoats Art Museum. There the original shadows met with three more shadows, muffled up against the cold.

'Ah ladies, glad you could make it, I'll just ask Alfred, the museum watchman to let us in. He is an old friend.' Professor Aldridge was genial as always.

'A watchman? I thought you said you would smuggle us into the museum. We have been keeping a low profile all the way from the tram stop.' Mary Long was incredulous. 'Are you going to give him a sneaky bribe?' she asked hopefully. Mary had made the group wear black and flit from shadow to shadow, so that no one would notice them.

'I do apologise Miss Long, for misleading you on the level of my nefariousness. I do unfortunately have friends on the Board of Trustees and quite often do tutorials and lectures here after hours, as do many of my colleagues. I have an arrangement with Alfred that I book in any extra sessions with him. Tonight is down as remedial Anglo-Saxon grammar, in case anyone asks. So no, I won't be bribing him but every so often, we do go for a pint at the Crown and Cobbler,' said Professor Aldridge, in a conciliatory tone.

Mary Long sniffed, unimpressed.

One of the other shadows had, in the meanwhile, rang the doorbell and was talking quietly to an older man who had opened it.

'We can go in now sir. Alfred is ready for us and there should be no one else using the building tonight,' Geraint Hadley-Brown confirmed in a hushed tone. His face looked stern in the light spilling from the doorway, as if he wanted to be anywhere else in Manchester rather than playing detectives with them.

'Now then ladies let's get you all inside,' DCI Kydd's voice boomed and made them all jump but confirmed the identity of the third shadow. He helped Maggie and her wheelchair up a step and through the backdoor.

LIZZIE BENTHAM

Professor Aldridge ushered the group through the bowels of the museum, past cases of stuffed animals, coin collections belonging to dead civilisations, and walls of Turners and Constables. Once inside the South Gallery, he marked out in chalk a rectangle five foot by seven foot in the centre of the floor.

'Ladies and gentlemen, thank you for joining me tonight in a rather interesting experiment to recreate a crime from twenty years ago. It was in this room, that Professor Beaumaris was found dead inside a specially constructed case to house the *Boniface Psalter* and that crime has never been solved. Tonight, I propose we conduct a little experiment. Dr Hadley-Brown will hand out a part to play to each of you, representing the people who were in the museum on that fateful day. This has been constructed from their stated movements, kindly supplied by DCI Kydd. We will recreate each of their reported activities for the two hours leading up to the discovery of the body.'

'Two hours! It is ten thirty already. I've got a full day in the laboratory tomorrow, I need my beauty sleep,' grumbled Mary Long from the back of the group.

'For the experiment we will make thirty real minutes equate to two hours so you will need to transpose your suspect's actions accordingly. I am glad to see you are all wearing wrist watches. Now the main suspects will be played as follows:

- Sir Laurence Tarleton: Mary Long
- Geraldine Beaumaris: Jinny Moss
- Professor Beaumaris: DCI Kydd
- Mr Tristan Hadley-Brown: Geraint Hadley-Brown
- Mrs Theodora Hadley-Brown: Dorothea Roberts
- Professor Maximilian Harrison: Mary Short
- Professor Aldridge: Maggie Forshaw

'There will be three keys in play to "open" the pretend cabinet; one with Alfred in his office, one with DCI Kydd, playing the murdered man and one with Dr Hadley-Brown, playing his father. Please make a note if your character has the opportunity to procure one of these keys. There is a map of the museum with your character's information. Take five minutes to familiarise yourself with your suspect and find your way around the museum to your starting point. I'll blow a whistle at a quarter past the hour and we will recreate the events of Shrovetide eve 1914.'

'Why am I playing you?' asked Maggie, 'Why don't you play yourself?'

'A very good question Miss Forshaw and my answer is this. You don't know I am telling the truth. You must test my movements, like any of the other people associated with the crime. Besides, this is only the first run through. The second time, I will want every one of you to try and find a space in your schedule to attempt to murder DCI Kydd, aka Professor Beaumaris. You need to test my statement and see if I could have committed the murder. Now if you are ready to take your places ladies and gentlemen, we will begin.'

***

The young people took up their various places around the museum, each one busily reading their scripts and consulting their wrist watches. The professor blew his whistle and they jumped into action. Professor Aldridge and DCI Kydd roamed the rooms of the museum with clipboards, watching who past near to the South Gallery on their legitimate journeys and who past each other, desperately looking for any discrepancies between the physical movements of the suspects and the written accounts.

Dorothea, concentrating on being Theodora Hadley-Brown, discovered the staff kitchen in the basement which looked like it had not been updated in twenty years. Mary Short as Dr Harrison, ran in and then out again needing to be elsewhere. Getting into character, Dorothea made a cup of tea to take up to Dr Hadley-Brown, in what was now a tutorial room but which had once been his father's office. He was sitting at a table and moodily rocking back on a chair, something she was sure he would chastise his students for doing.

'I brought you some tea,' she said. His face lightened slightly as he took the cup and saucer from her hands. 'I am sorry if all this brings back painful memories for you.'

'Thank you. It isn't so much this re-enactment that is bothering me . . . I was thinking of a couple of incidents during my academic career, that made no sense at the time but with hindsight, I can see that the person I was speaking to knew more about my past than I did. I just don't know how my mother and godfather have managed to keep this from me, all this time.'

'Do you think it is possible that either of your parents—'

'Neither of my parents, are or were, murderers,' he interrupted angrily.

'I was going to say, might they have known who did it?' Dorothea responded indignantly, hurt that he should think her so disloyal.

Geraint wilted visibly. 'Sorry, this has got to me more than I realise. My mother is a very astute woman and a force of nature. I wouldn't be surprised if she has her own views on who killed the professor.'

'I should like to meet her very much.'

'She would like to meet you too . . . She wants to invite you to Mickering Priory for the weekend, the week after next.' A wry smile twisted his lips. 'I have been informed that I am to drive you over.'

'I would be delighted to accept!' Dorothea tried to keep her voice calm, but in reality she was thrilled with the prospect.

'Shouldn't you be back in the kitchen by now Miss Roberts?' asked DCI Kydd, popping his head around the door. He showed no surprise at finding Dorothea and Dr Hadley-Brown in a tête-à-tête.

'Oh crumbs! Sorry Chief Inspector.' She left hurriedly but the DCI Kydd noticed that her eyes were shining.

Play continued for another twenty minutes, until Professor Aldridge brought it to an end with two blasts on his whistle. The group congregated back in the South Gallery, while the professor and DCI Kydd conferred together over their notes.

DCI Kydd addressed the group. 'Settle down there ladies and gentlemen please. That was very educational. Professor Aldridge and I noticed certain pertinent points from that exercise. These were as follows:

1) Geraldine walked past her husband's office at both three and four o'clock to get to and from Laurence Tarleton's office. If there was anyone in there, she would have seen them. At the time she said the office was empty both times.

2) How did Maximilian Harrison return to the doctoral student's office from the women's hall without Mr Pickles seeing him? He was pretty vague about that at the time. Miss Shor ran around the outside of the building both times tonight because the interconnecting fire door was shut, as on the night of the murder.

3) Up until three thirty anyone entering the South Gallery through the library would have past Tristan Hadley-Brown hanging up banners, so this route to the South Gallery would be out for the murderer during this time period unless the Tristan Hadley-Brown is our man.

4) Why didn't Theodora, or anyone else, see the woman that Tristan Hadley-Brown saw in the corridor? Theodora must have just missed her when she took her husband a brew.'

Maggie put up her hand. 'I managed to liberate the key from Alfred's office on my way past. I think that Alfred must have gone for a fag break. If Mr Pickles had a similar tobacco habit then anyone could have easily stolen his key while he was outside smoking.'

'Bertram Pickles was a dedicated smoker. I don't know what happened to him, he wasn't here when I returned after the war,' said Professor Aldridge. 'DCI Kydd, do you know?'

'I'll ask PC Standish to look into Mr Pickles' whereabouts tomorrow. He was an old man twenty years ago, so may well be long gone by now. If he is still alive, it would be useful to see if the passage of time has jogged his memory. I thought at the time there was something he wasn't telling the police,' said DCI Kydd.

***

The whistle for the start of the second, "anything goes" game blew. DCI Kydd sat back in his chair within the chalk rectangle and smiled somewhat grimly at the young people's enthusiasm for playing murders. Being back in the museum and playing "the body" was bringing back some powerful memories from the night of his first murder investigation, as a very green police constable. He remembered that on viewing the corpse, his nineteen year old self had run away and thrown up in a convenient Grecian urn. He had been too ashamed to mention the fact to DI "Daring" Dawlish his superior. He was pretty sure he had past the same Grecian urn in the hallway.

Professor Aldridge sat quietly nearby, looking at his wrist watch at regular intervals, and making copious notes in his notebook.

There was a whirring noise in the corner of the room. DCI Kydd watched with some amusement as Dorothea (or Mrs Theodora Hadley-Brown), emerged somewhat ruffled and perspiring from the cupboard housing the dumbwaiter and dropped the three foot to the floor somewhat stiffly. She then proceeded to creep across the bare expanse of oak floorboards and pretended to open the imaginary door of the imaginary cabinet, with an imaginary key.

'The key had already gone from Mr Hadley-Brown's office so someone was ahead of me,' whispered Dorothea to DCI Kydd, while simultaneously pretending to hit him on the head with an imaginary book. 'Still presumably you/Professor Beaumaris could let me in with your own key.'

'How do you explain the locked cabinet and the key in the professor's pocket when he was found, if the murderer didn't bring a key with them?'

'Drat, I hadn't thought of that. Well maybe the door wasn't locked when the first person got there or maybe the murderer had the opportunity to place the key in Professor Beaumaris's pocket before the police arrived. Better dash, I think someone else is coming.'

The chief inspector watched as Dorothea clambered back into the dumbwaiter, closing the cupboard doors awkwardly behind herself. He heard a muffled shriek, as the dumbwaiter dropped suddenly, with the heavier than normal weight, but then the breaks kicked in and the descent of the little lift continued more slowly.

Next to appear almost simultaneously, were Mary Short (Dr Maximilian Harrison) wearing a suit of armour and Mary Long (Sir Laurence Tarleton); Mary Short through the main doors into the South Gallery from the hallway containing the grand staircase and Mary Long from outside in the grounds, by using a pen knife to lever up the sash window. When Mary Short realised she was not on her own in the room with the victim, she stood stock still in the suit of armour against the wall.

'I unlocked the window latch while you were giving us our instructions earlier,' said Mary Long, obviously very pleased with herself. 'I climbed out of Sir Laurence's study window on the first floor and shinned down the drain pipe.'

'Very ingenious both of you! How were you thinking of getting into the display cabinet Miss Shor, without being spotted, dressed in a clanking suit of armour? Miss Long I applaud your athleticism and head for heights, but the murder happened on a spring afternoon so it would have been light. Could you be seen from the road?'

'I did think of that Chief Inspector. There is an old oak tree that blocks most of the view.'

'Noted Miss Long. Did either of you manage to bring a key with you?'

'No Chief Inspector,' they chorused.

As the two young women were leaving, there was a noise again in the dumbwaiter cupboard. The doors opened and Jinny Moss (Geraldine Beaumaris) appeared. She extracted herself and sprinted across the room. She mimed knocking on the invisible cabinet door, hit her pretend husband on the head, then spirited back across the room and disappeared into the dumbwaiter. The squeak of pulleys and the whirr of ropes were a strange rear-guard.

'She only has one five minute window to whizz up in the dumbwaiter when Theodora, was being patched up after cutting her hand. Wow is she going to try it again? Ah here she comes. Well done Mrs Moss!' commentated Professor Aldridge.

LIZZIE BENTHAM

Jinny nearly fell out of the dumbwaiter cupboard, bright red in the face and panting. She repeated her sprint across the floor and then her fictional attack on DCI Kydd, before galloping back again towards the dumbwaiter cupboard yelling, 'I am trying to beat six and a half minutes.'

'If Mrs Moss is struggling to achieve a dumbwaiter trip in sub five minutes, then Geraldine Beaumaris wouldn't have succeeded either,' commented DCI Kydd.

Watching her disappear precipitously down the lift shaft, they almost failed to notice Maggie appear silently on rubber wheels through the door at the west end of the South Gallery, from what had once been the library. She had for a second time managed to liberate the watchman's key. She did a one hundred and eighty degree spin, stopped by DCI Kydd, pretended to clunk him on the head and then sped off again the way she had come.

The professor was about to blow his whistle to signal the end of the game, when he startled. Rising through the floorboards was Dr Hadley-Brown like a sardonic apparition, holding a key.

'Whatever have you found Geraint?' Professor Aldridge was visibly shocked. DCI Kydd looked thoughtful.

'My father showed it to me when I was a small boy. Before the new concert hall was built specifically for performances, they used this room for theatricals and recitals. Everyone from Titania Queen of the Fairies to the Archangel Gabriel made their entrance via this trap door. It has taken me most of the last half hour, to work out where it was and how to open it.'

'We didn't know about this during the previous investigation.' DCI Kydd was visibly ruffled. 'Where does the trap door lead to?'

'Like I said, it was obsolete well before 1914 and probably had a display case on top of it.' Geraint Hadley-Brown was a little too casual. 'It goes to what is now a cleaner's cupboard but which also houses the remnants of some amateur dramatic lighting switches.'

He pulled the trapdoor back into place and the three men gazed down at what looked like an unbroken section of wood flooring.

'It is remarkably well camouflaged. I'll dig out the photographs from the original crime scene and see what was over in that corner of the room at the time. Was your dad the only person that knew about this?' asked the chief inspector gently.

'I am sure it was a well-known piece of information,' said Geraint emphatically, however the look on Professor Aldridge's face told DCI Kydd that it was a new piece of information to him.

Well Aldridge didn't kill Beaumaris using this trap door, thought DCI Kydd, *But Geraint Hadley-Brown is worried that one of his parents might have done.*

The professor blew his whistle and the young people reappeared from around the building.

The next half an hour was spent playing with the trapdoor mechanism and racing each other up and down in the dumbwaiter. No one managed the journey in sub-five minutes but Mary Long beat Geraint Hadley-Brown hands down.

LIZZIE BENTHAM

CHAPTER FIVE

An Unexpected Detour

Friday Morning, 15th March 1935

PC Standish practically bounced into DCI Kydd's office, so momentous was the news he had to impart. The chief inspector looked up from rereading his old notebooks, surprised that his secretary had let anyone in. Since he had asked Miss Grimstead to type up his notes on the Beaumaris murder, she was suddenly being a lot less . . . well, a lot less like Miss Grimstead. She had even added some pertinent pencil notes of her own in the margins. DCI Kydd wondered if she had a passion for unsolved cases and vowed to dig out some of the most notorious ones for Miss Grimstead to peruse.

PC Standish was bursting with excitement. 'Sir, I looked into the present whereabouts of Bertram Pickles like you asked. I went to the address we had on record for him and it now belongs to his married daughter. She said that her father died in the December of 1914. He had gone to meet someone he knew at the pub on Christmas Eve for a tipple. On the way home he was assaulted and died of knife wounds. No one has ever been convicted for his murder. His daughter said that she wasn't expecting her old dad to leave her any money but she was shocked to discover he had a tidy sum put away, in a bank account that had only been opened a few months before. She said no one in her family had ever had a bank account before, or that amount of money. Pretty telling don't you think sir?'

'Good work Standish! Blackmail! How did we miss the link to the Beaumaris case at the time? If it had come through headquarters then surely we would have made the connection?'

'The murder happened in Salford sir, quite a long way from his usual stomping ground, so Salford police investigated it. I have requested a copy of their case notes.'

'The end of 1914 you say? Hmm . . . we lost a good few men

to enlisting in the armed services around that time and were short staffed. No doubt Salford police were short too, almost as if someone planned the murder for when they knew manpower was scarce,' said DCI Kydd thoughtfully.

Miss Grimstead knocked on the door to the inner office. 'Chief Inspector you need to leave now for your meeting with the chief superintendent about the Magpie's jewel thefts,' she said disapprovingly.

Brought back to the present forcibly, DCI Kydd made his apologies and left at a sharp trot.

LIZZIE BENTHAM

Tuesday Morning, 19th March 1935

A note surreptitiously made its way across and down the lecture theatre, from the back row, to where Dorothea sat with her course-mates near the front. The sniggering and whispering by her immediate colleagues caused the timorous Romantic Poets lecturer, to admonish the class in his loudest whisper. Dorothea hid the note under her desk, until he regained his flow and continued to drone on about Blake.

Unfolding the message, she read, "My fairest lady, would you bestow the pleasure of your smiles tonight, on one who would like to know you better? A trip to the picture house on Oxford Road is called for. Would you care to join me at six o'clock today to see *The Carbuncle Caper?* I have heard it is really good. Say you will. Your devoted servant Eric."

Dorothea rolled her eyes at Eric's flamboyant penmanship but was secretly delighted. Quietly as possible she ripped a page from her note book and scribbled a reply.

"Good sir, thank you for your kind invitation. I would be delighted to accompany you tonight. I will meet you outside the cinema at ten minutes to the hour. Dorothea."

Lectures seemed to be interminable that day and once they were finished Dorothea went to the Arts library to study but could not concentrate. She found herself daydreaming about a pair of brown eyes and a cheeky smile. She wondered how well Eric moved on the dance floor.

At five forty she powdered her nose, added a touch of lipstick to her lips and ran a comb through her curls to create a more ordered coiffure. Feeling a mixture of excitement and trepidation, she left the library and walked to the cinema.

Eric was already waiting and greeted her with an affectionate bear hug which lifted her off her feet. Her heart did a little wobble, he really was rather handsome.

'Dot you came! You look marvellous! I have already purchased our tickets. Let me escort you to your seat, my lady.'

Linking arms they went inside together, Eric keeping up a

running flow of chatter. They were shown to their places by a bored attendant. Eric had not stinted on price and they were right in the middle, in the best seats. He was obviously trying to make a good impression. They chatted and giggled like old friends, before the auditorium lights dimmed and the film reel started.

The feature film was a light hearted affair about a female South American Raffles – a jewel thief, outsmarting the police and her male British, Rafflesesque rival who was also the love interest.

On the film finishing, Eric suggested that they get something to eat at a little place he knew. It turned out to be a jazz café. They ordered the house special, lemon sole and hanky panky cocktails. They talked and laughed together over their meal. Dorothea felt like she had known Eric all her life. He was excellent company and was going all out to impress her. While discussing the film over dessert, there were obvious parallels to be drawn with the real-life spate of thefts by the Magpie.

'What do you think about all this hoo-ha with the Magpie?' asked Eric.

'Well I don't own anything valuable, so I am not in danger of a visit from him,' laughed Dorothea.

'Or her. After your adventures at Christmas, you more than anyone else know first-hand that women can be master criminals.'

'True, but for some reason I just get the feeling that the Magpie is male.' Her brow creased in thought. 'I think it is the level of daring involved in each of the crimes and *the joie de vivre* he seems to take in baffling the police.'

'I must disagree with you. I think the Magpie shows the very feminine characteristics of subtly and finesse in all her crimes. Maybe you and your clever friends should investigate her. What does your friend DCI Kydd think on the subject?'

'I have never talked to him about the Magpie case,' said Dorothea, aghast.

'But you have seen him recently,' stated Eric. His directness unsettled Dorothea even more.

'Well yes, we are working on an historical case together but its early days yet.'

'I should be fascinated to hear all about it. Do tell Dot.'

Dorothea hesitantly started to tell the story of Professor Beaumaris' murder, full well realising that Eric's father was one of the prime suspects, but not knowing how to avoid revealing this to his son. She need not have worried. Eric was enthralled and at the end threw back his head with a burst of laughter.

'How funny! My cautious, boring father is a murder suspect in an unsolved case. Why did I not know this before? I hope you nail it on him Dot. He is such a goody two shoes that he would be mortified to be caught up in such a scandal. If you have finished eating let's dance and you can tell me all your theories about whodunit. You do have the most super adventures Dot.' There was a boyish wistfulness in his voice.

They danced to the lively jazz music. Eric had to accommodate an unusually flamboyant dance style to his partner's petite frame because Dorothea could not keep up with his galloping strides. It caused Dorothea to compare Eric with Geraint Hadley-Brown, who was a much more considerate dance partner, though, not necessarily as much fun.

They called it a night well before the last bus home, as they both had nine o'clock lectures the next morning. Dot said she did not mind getting the bus home by herself but Eric would not hear of it. He bought a bus ticket and escorted Dorothea all the way home to Rose Cottage. Mary Long was still up and the light from the little cottage looked inviting and homely.

In the vicarage garden, under a sweetly scented arbour, with daffodils and hyacinths around its base, they kissed goodnight.

Dorothea in a happy daydream, watched as Eric walked back up the garden path with a spring in his step, to find a bus to take him back to his hall of residence. Blushing and somewhat breathless, Dorothea entered the cottage to be greeted by Mary Long all agog at Dorothea's new beau.

'Poor Dr Hadley-Brown, your Eric has quite cut him out,' teased Mary over a cup of cocoa a little while later.

'Don't be silly Longy he isn't my Dr Hadley-Brown. He isn't even interested in me,' said Dorothea, with a hint of regret in her voice.

MURDER BY THE BOOK

The Worm
Edition 15 Academic Year 34/35, Wednesday 20th March 1935
Mayhem at the Manchester Hotel
The Magpie steals the show as famous ballerina's bracelet goes missing

Yesterday evening while the company of the Lancashire Opera Ballet were getting ready to perform the opening night of Swan Lake, at the Manchester Opera House, the Magpie struck again!

An emerald bracelet belonging to Susanna Koning, the prima ballerina and the third wife of the American multimillionaire Herbert Koning, was stolen from the safe in the couple's suite in the Manchester Hotel. The room was locked and on the fifth floor of the hotel. The hotel also has an efficient security arrangement. The Magpie's signature card was found in the safe by Mr Koning later that evening, on returning from the ballet.

Police are baffled at how the Magpie pulled off such a feat of cat burglary. There have been no arrests as yet, in regards to the spate of jewel thefts attributed to the Magpie and the police have no leads.

Are the North West's jewels safe from such a deadly predator as the Magpie?

David Simpkins (Journalist)

LIZZIE BENTHAM

Thursday Morning, 21ˢᵗ March 1935

Miss Grimstead knocked discretely on DCI Kydd's door. 'There is a man to see you Chief Inspector, a Mr Gritty. He says he is a private investigator currently employed by the Dinkworth, Dinkworth and Small Insurance Company.'

DCI Kydd noted the lack of the word "gentleman" in Miss Grimstead's description. Miss Grimstead called every male person over the age of fourteen, a gentleman.

He must be really dreadful to have offended Miss Grimstead in such a short time period, thought DCI Kydd.

When Mr Gritty entered the office, DCI Kydd was surprised to find him to be a personable young man in his late twenties, with a broad Liverpudlian accent.

'DCI Kydd, thank you for seeing me on such short notice. I may have information that is pertinent to your investigations into the jewel thefts by the Magpie. My clients have authorised me to disclose certain information to you, on my current investigations into insurance fraud.'

'Please continue Mr Gritty,' said DCI Kydd intrigued.

'Do you remember that the first crime attributed to the Magpie was the theft of the Pontefract Rubies last year from the Marshalls? I think the theft of the Evergreen Emeralds at Tottingley Hall a month earlier might have been the Magpie's trial run, as it shows all the hallmarks of his ingenuity. My clients are interested because the Asquith-Joneses had insured the Evergreen Emeralds with Dinkworth, Dinkworth and Small, a month before the theft and they have now made a claim for ten thousand pounds. My clients are also the insurers for Miss Brambilla's Turquoise Tiger, the Pontefract Rubies belonging to the Marshalls and Mrs Beaumaris and her Giant's Tear necklace. All have made similar claims in a very timely manner. After last night, we are expecting the Konings to follow suit. It could be coincidental, however on investigation all of these families are currently undergoing financial difficulties. Miss Brambilla is a gambler, Mr Asquith-Jones lost all of his money when his business went under, Major Marshall's estates have been crippled by death duties and Mrs Beaumaris collects expensive artwork that greatly exceeds her means.'

'I know all this from our own investigations Mr Gritty. What is your point?' asked DCI Kydd.

'My point is this; I believe that the Magpie is working a massive insurance fraud in cahoots with the victims. That is why he can get away with such daring deeds . . . because he has inside help from the victims. As the Magpie was as yet unknown, Dinkworth, Dinkworth and Small paid the Asquith-Joneses their ten thousand pounds on the 14th of February, straight into Mr Asquith-Jones bank as requested. My clients were a little suspicious and I was employed to investigate. On the 21st of February, two weeks later, I witnessed Mr Asquith-Jones depositing five thousand pounds in cash into his bank account. This is half of the amount that the Evergreen Emeralds are worth and that my clients paid out.

'I think that the swindle goes like this, the victim claims on their insurance and the Magpie sells the original, then gives the owner half of the money from the sale and keeps half for himself. Understandably Dinkworth, Dinkworth and Small are reticent to pay out any further claims until I have gathered more evidence.'

'My men have found no evidence of jewellery sales using any of the normal routes for selling hot goods,' commented DCI Kydd.

'No, I think the jewels are being smuggled out of the country by some method, but as yet I don't know how,' said Mr Gritty.

'This is all very logical Mr Gritty and I agree with your reasoning, but what you lack is solid evidence,' said DCI Kydd.

'I know that sir but I am determined to find it!' said Mr Gritty.

LIZZIE BENTHAM

Friday Evening, 22nd March 1934

The Crossley automobile, a cocoon against the freezing fog that had descended on the north, purred along country lanes and ate up the miles between Manchester and the mosslands near Aughton. The car's inhabitants physically close, knees and shoulders almost touching, were politely skating around the gaping chasm that lay between them emotionally.

Dorothea carefully stole sideways glances at the handsome, taciturn man sat next to her, his profile hard to discern in the dim light.

'It is very kind of you to drive me all the way to Mickering Priory, to meet your mother, Dr Hadley-Brown.' Dorothea commented. An awkward silence had descended almost as soon as they had stowed their suitcases in the car after lectures on Friday afternoon. 'It is very kind of her to invite me to stay over the weekend. I hope I am not putting her to any trouble.'

I wish she would stop calling me Dr Hadley-Brown. The way she says it, it sounds like I am a middle aged man who collects stamps and has halitosis. Dr Hadley-Brown the philatelist, with bad breath, no one could love you, Geraint thought to himself wistfully.

Out loud, he said, 'It is no trouble at all. I often visit Mickering Priory, which is where I grew up and I am very fond of the drive, though not so much in this weather. Mother lives a quiet life now, but adores company, so is greatly looking forward to meeting you.'

Geraint failed to mention that both his mother and godfather had suggested that he should drive Dorothea to Mickering Priory, rather than her getting the train. He tried to ignore their blatant interference in his love life.

The silence resumed. Dorothea reflected how different this evening was, to her recent date with Eric Tarleton, where they had chatted away like old friends.

'I had a postcard from Mrs George this morning, from Monaco. It seems that Mr and Mrs George are currently holidaying on the

French Riviera with her son Luca. They were finally reunited last week, after nearly twenty years and she sounded so excited. Luca seems to be a very pleasant person, despite all the troubles he must have gone through. It was kind of her to think of me while she was abroad,' Dorothea said, as she tried to restart the conversation again.

This news drew a spark of interest from Geraint. Mr George was head of MI5's U branch that Geraint secretly worked for, when he was not teaching English Language undergraduates Anglo-Saxon verbs.

'I wondered where the boss had disappeared off to. I thought he was on one of his golfing trips to St Andrews, with his ministerial chums. He hasn't read my latest report.'

'Have you been active as an agent since Christmas?' Dorothea asked curiously.

'Unfortunately that is classified Miss Roberts and I can't possibly tell you.'

Silence descended again. Geraint was trying to concentrate because they had come to a crossroads, in a fog hollow, and the visibility had deteriorated. The junction safely negotiated and the freezing fog abating slightly, he let the Crossley accelerate for a stretch.

A deer startled by the noise of their progress, leapt out in front of the car, eyes wild and staring, before it skittered away into the bracken on the far side of the road. Geraint had to swerve on the icy road and slam on the breaks to avoid hitting the creature. The car skidded dangerously. Dorothea was thrown across the front seat into Geraint, as they slewed on the frozen road. His left arm shot out and held her tightly pinned to his side, as he tried to regain control of the car. Dorothea heard a loud *CRUNCH* as they bumped over the verge, before coming to an undignified stop.

'Are you alright?' He looked down, concern showing in his face.

Heart pounding and disconcerted by being embraced so tightly but also not wanting it to end, she nodded into his shoulder.

'Yes, thank you Geraint,' she said sitting up, pushing her hair out of her eyes and taking stock.

'She said my name,' thought Geraint with something resembling glee. *'Pull yourself together man. You are behaving like a romantic schoolboy.'*

'I am going to have to take a look at the car. We hit something, possibly a milestone and it was quite a bump. I need to check the old bus over for damage.'

He opened the door letting in frozen tendrils of air and a temperature drop of sixty degrees Fahrenheit, before disappearing into the night with the starter handle. Even cocooned in the car, she could hear him swear, as again and again, the starter handle turned but there was no corresponding roar from the engine.

'It's a dead duck I'm afraid,' he said, gratefully returning to his seat to rub some warmth back into his hands. 'The front-axle is bent out of shape and the transmission is severed. We are going to have to abandon the car, walk to the nearest village and see if we can get a lift to Aughton. We are still about eight miles away from Mickering Priory. We passed an inn about half a mile back. They may have a telephone so we can ring ahead to my mother and they should be able to recommend a mechanic. We might still be in time for dinner.'

After some debate, they picked up their suitcases and set off the way they had come. In seconds the car disappeared from view, consumed by the fog. They retraced their journey back to the crossroads. It was not such a long walk back to the Bull Inn but it was not one that either of them wanted to repeat. Dorothea was soon chilled to the bone and could feel her extremities start to prickle with the cold.

They arrived in the bar a quarter of an hour later, crisp with frost and shivering. There were the usual regulars in the bar, so a newly arrived, dishevelled, young couple made a bit of a stir. The landlord on hearing their plight ushered Dorothea to a cosy nook next to the fire to warm up and took Geraint off to use the telephone in the inn's cramped office.

The landlord's wife kindly brought Dorothea a cup of coffee, laced with brandy, while she was waiting. Geraint was gone for some time and when he returned he looked thoughtful.

'The landlord is going to bring us some dinner. I managed to get through to my mother and have told her what has happened. I said we might be stuck here a while. Then I rang the local garage and when I got through, the mechanic said that they won't be able to take a look at the Crossley until tomorrow morning, as their tow truck is out on a job. There doesn't seem to be any alternative transport to be had, this side of Bickerstaffe tonight.'

A couple of locals got up to leave. The main door opened and closed behind them with a waft of chilling air moving in the young people's direction.

'Urgh,' shuddered Dorothea.

'Quite.' For the first time Geraint Hadley-Brown sounded a little unsure. 'I took the liberty of asking if there were any rooms available for the night and apart from a motorcyclist who didn't fancy continuing his journey, they have space, so if you agree I will book us two rooms for the night.'

'Yes that is an excellent idea.' Dorothea wondered if she would have enough money in her purse to pay him back but then decided that was a worry for a different time.

'The landlord's wife started asking questions about us, she was only going to make up one room at first and I got a bit flustered. The truth sounded a bit unbelievable, that you are my student and I am taking you to meet my mother, to investigate a twenty year old murder mystery. Instead, I said that we are a soon to be engaged couple on the way to meet my mother and that was why we needed two rooms. I am terribly, terribly sorry.'

His colour had heightened and he looked so sheepish that Dorothea laughed out loud. She looked at him coyly and deliberately placed her hand on his sleeve.

'Darling, this is all so sudden. I am obviously delighted about our sudden engagement . . .' in a lowered voice she hissed, 'that explains why the landlord's wife has been staring at us intently for the past five minutes. Quick, look like you actually like me. Give me both of your hands.' Dorothea had a much better view of the bar than Geraint whose back was towards it.

Obviously ill at ease, Geraint fidgeted with a signet ring on his littlest figure and shuffled around the table a bit to place both hands tentatively into Dorothea's. He drew one hand away for a moment to take the signet ring off his finger and very deliberately for anyone watching, slipped the ring on to Dorothea's finger. Dorothea gave a dramatic little shriek and an, 'Oh Geraint!' which drew every eye in the bar towards the couple. She hugged Geraint tightly before giving him a light kiss on the cheek. She waved her now be-ringed finger to all the regulars in the bar. The landlady had been watching this performance intently. She smiled indulgently, now seemingly satisfied that their engagement was bona fide.

'How was that?' asked Geraint trying to keep a straight face.

'Convincing, it definitely did the job but needs some work. I'll give you a C plus Dr Hadley-Brown, as I am more generous with my marking than you are. Don't they teach you amateur dramatics at MI5?'

'Needs some work . . . C plus . . . I was in the Footlights at Cambridge I'll have you know and they still talk about my Hamlet!'

Half laughing, half enraged, he carefully drew her hand to his lips and kissed it for a lot longer than was necessary but which made the bar regulars cheer and one, who had imbibed a little too much ale, cried 'Hip hip hooray!' and then fell off his stool.

'Much better Dr Hadley-Brown, we'll make an actor out of you yet.'

Fortunately the landlord brought them their meals at this point, so they could drop their pretence. They applied themselves to a hearty Lancashire hotpot with fresh bread and red cabbage.

Dorothea found that she was enjoying herself hugely. Geraint Hadley-Brown was excellent company when he relaxed, the food was tasty and the brandy had gone to her head somewhat. The situation they were in tickled her sense of humour too. Geraint looking across the table noted the sparkle in her eyes, her laugh and the blush on her cheeks, and thought that he had never seen a more beautiful woman.

After dinner they inspected their bedrooms, which were small and cosy, with a shared bathroom with doors that could be locked on both sides.

While getting ready for bed, their ability to lock and unlock the bathroom door was sorely tested. They spent an embarrassing half hour, each trying to use the bathroom while the other one was using it and having to retreat, rapidly averting their eyes and apologising profusely.

Before getting into bed, Dorothea locked both the bathroom and bedroom doors. Crawling under the warmed sheets, she found that her bed enveloped her in comfortable, lavender smelling eiderdown and she soon nodded off after an eventful day.

***

Dorothea woke up suddenly knowing something was wrong. There was a presence in the room with her. She kept her eyes shut, kept her breathing even and pretended to still be asleep while she gauged what was happening. There were small movements over by the chest of drawers, where she had placed her suitcase, too tired to unpack properly before bed. It sounded like someone was going through her belongings very carefully and quietly. Dorothea cautiously opened one eye. In the gloom she could imagine a darker shape amid the shadows, crouched down on the floor. Her hand slowly and silently moved towards the bedside cabinet, desperately trying to find a weapon of some sort. Her fingers closed on the handle of a water jug.

The shape slowly stood up and moved closer to the bed. Her nose detected a whiff of petrol, as the intruder moved towards the bedside cabinet and began to inch open the drawer.

Dorothea saw her opportunity. She swung the water jug at the figure and was satisfied with the guttural 'Umph' as it made contact. She let out a whooping, war cry at the top of her lungs in both elation and fear. Jumping out of bed, she headed towards the bathroom and locked herself inside. The door through into Geraint Hadley-Brown's room was locked so she banged and shouted loudly.

Geraint was woken from a deep sleep by a manic knocking

coming from his bathroom door and his name repeatedly shouted by a familiar, female voice. He got out of bed wearily, put on his dressing gown and sauntered over to the door before opening it. Dorothea shot in like a cat through a kitchen door. She banged it shut behind her, slamming the bolt home.

'Whatever is the matter Dorothea?' asked a sleepy Geraint Hadley-Brown, yawning, 'You can stop hiding behind the bed now.'

'There is a man in my room. He was looking through my drawers. I clobbered him with the water jug,' said Dorothea poking her head above the bed sheepishly.

'Really? Remind me never to wake you up suddenly.' He started to turn the bathroom door handle.

'What are you doing? He might be armed . . . have a knife or a gun . . . be a killer.'

'Or be bleeding to death. I have seen you in action before and I feel sorry for the fellow. I am going to hold his hand and bandage his head, if he actually exists and you didn't dream him.' Geraint Hadley-Brown opened the door and slipped through.

Dorothea held her breath and listened.

'You can come through, there is no one here,' called Geraint, 'You didn't lock your door last night.'

'I did too!' Momentary distraction caused Dorothea to forget her fear and she marched back into her bedroom. 'I definitely locked the door. I remember doing so quite distinctly!'

She inspected the door closely while Geraint Hadley-Brown closed a wardrobe door that was swinging on its hinge, exposing Dorothea's coat.

'Look at these scratches. Someone has picked the lock. I knew I had locked the door properly.' She relocked it again. 'What did he want I wonder?'

'Do you have any valuables with you? Is your jewellery and money still here?'

Dorothea checked her purse which was untouched. Her gold wristwatch and Dr Hadley-Brown's signet ring were where she had left them on the nightstand before bed.

'Where are Dr Harrison's book and my essay notes?' Dorothea

rummaged in her suitcase, 'I made notes about our reconstruction in the museum too and a detailed drawing of the museum's layout. I definitely put them in here and they are all gone!'

'Why would anyone want to steal your essay notes Dot? I have read your essays and they really aren't worth pinching—'

'Oi!' She threw a pair of woolly socks at him, which he dodged easily. 'Be serious for a moment. Those things have definitely gone and they are not something that one can go to the police about at this time of night. A very odd thief don't you think?'

'Mmm . . .' Geraint was non-committal. He was still unconvinced that her phantom wasn't the fancy of a nightmare. 'Since there is nothing more that we can do tonight, I am off back to bed. See you in the morning.' He moved towards his own room.

'Oh . . . right . . . Goodnight then.' Dorothea looked rather crestfallen.

Geraint closed the bathroom door and got into bed and waited. Five minutes elapsed before there was a knock.

'I can't sleep. I keep imagining someone is sneaking through my door again,' said Dorothea plaintively.

Geraint Hadley-Brown turned on the light by his bed and looked at the sheepish figure wrapped in a demure dressing gown that nearly swamped her.

'Look why don't we change rooms. I'll sleep in your room and you can sleep in my room,' he suggested.

'The burglar hasn't tried your room yet. What if he comes back?' asked Dorothea with some trepidation.

'We can leave the door open between and you can shout for me.'

'But I might be dead by then. Can I sleep on the sofa in your room? You won't even know that I am here and I would feel safer.'

'Very well then. I will protect any more midnight assassins that come calling, from you.'

Dorothea lugged her bed clothes and pillows through from her room and made a bed up on the sofa and tried it out.

'It's not very comfortable,' she commented. She turned over

causing the old sofa to squeak alarmingly. *SQUEAK.*

The squeaking went on for five minutes while Dorothea tried to settle. *SQUEAK.*

'That is it. I can't cope any longer,' called out Geraint in exasperation. He jumped out of bed, pulled the covers off Dorothea escorted her to his bed, tucked her in, then took her place on the couch.

There was a sleepy, 'Thank you,' from Dorothea who fell asleep immediately and then started to snore loudly.

SQUEAK. The sofa really was very uncomfortable. Geraint gave up, picked up all the bed clothes and trudged back into Dorothea's recently vacated room and climbed into her bed with relief.

Heroes in books and on the silver screen have it easy, thought Geraint. *Why is being a gentleman such hard work with so few rewards?*

MURDER BY THE BOOK

CHAPTER SIX

Mickering Priory

A Concise History of the Curse of the Boniface Psalter by Dr M. Harrison – Sir Timothy Quintrell 1st Baronet of Mickering

The newly ennobled Sir Timothy Quintrell, 1st Baronet of Mickering, richly attired in black velvet and ermine, viewed his purchase with pleasure. The bones of the chapter house and refectory could be stripped back and would make the basis for the east wing of the grand house that he could see in his mind's eye. The priory building, already without its roof to prevent the now homeless monks from returning, would make an excellent quarry of high quality stone for his build. The priory land was rich and fertile, the fish ponds well stocked and the animals fat and healthy.

Yes, this was a good use for his hard earned gold. He would build a house that would stand for generations. That his children, grandchildren and great-grandchildren would be born in and where they would live out their days.

It would be an ornate house filled with oak, stained glass, colour and light and there would be a library. A beautiful library filled with all the books that he had bought belonging to the priory. He was illiterate but he appreciated the look, feel, and smell of a solid book. There would be many more educated men than he, who would be jealous of his library and he would hire the best tutors to teach his children to read, so they could entertain him in his dotage.

It took four years for the new house, Mickering Priory, to be habitable. The 1st Baronet of Mickering had only been living in it for three weeks with his young family, when he was killed in an accident during a jousting competition at King Henry VIII's court.

His heir, an eighteen month old toddler, Sir Henry Quintrell (named for his royal godfather), the 2nd Baronet of Mickering, bumped down the grand staircase on his bottom and used the library books as teething toys, under the benign watch of his doting mother and her much younger, second husband, an expert jouster.

Primary Source: Correspondence held by the Crown, between His Majesty King Henry VIII and his friend Sir Timothy Quintrell 1st Baronet of Mickering.

MURDER BY THE BOOK

Saturday Afternoon 23rd March 1935

Mickering Priory rose up out of the low-lying coastal mosslands, atop a slim ridge of ground, abandoned by retreating glaciers. In past times it would have been a beacon to the souls of the nearby villages, when the mosses were underwater and ships were said to be able to navigate all the way to Clieves Hill.

Nowadays approaching from the road, the oldest wing with remnants of the medieval priory architecture still visible, looked like something from a gothic novel. Turning onto the driveway and following its bends, the main wing of the house appeared as a regency box, that had replaced the Tudor structure, burnt down by an accident-prone, eighteenth century baroness with a candle.

It had taken the whole morning to recover and mend the Crossley, so it was nearly three o'clock in the afternoon, when the young couple drew up, in front of the imposing façade. While awe-inspiring, Dorothea noticed traces of decay. There were weeds in the drive, cracks in the mortar, and the formal gardens had a wild, overgrown feel, as if they had been neglected in recent years.

Remembering Geraint's signet ring, Dorothea took it off and handed it back to him.

'It should have diamonds and sapphires anyway,' he said cryptically, pocketing it with a smile.

Geraint suggested that Dorothea go on ahead while he sorted out their luggage. Timidly, she knocked on the massive, oak door, a relic from the original priory. After a dramatic pause . . . it creaked open slowly. In the doorway stood a ram-rod, straight figure dressed in black, her face in shadow. The one drop of colour on her person was a pair of sapphire blue shoes, which marred the somewhat sinister presence. Drawing closer, Dorothea saw an older woman who was wearing glasses and had her silver hair pulled back into a neat bun. She had buck teeth and a wart on the end of her nose.

The stranger beckoned Dorothea to venture inside into a grand hallway, which she did nervously, with a backwards glance towards Geraint.

'Miss Roberts I presume. Please come this way. The mistress is expecting you,' lisped the stranger.

Geraint, following with the suitcases, stood on the doorstep with a sardonic smile on his face. He rolled his eyes.

'Not this again Mo—'

The old women cut him off abruptly by shutting the door in his face.

'Young Master Geraint will see to your bags. Come on now, quickly please.'

With trepidation Dorothea followed the decrepit retainer, who had suddenly developed a hunched back and a doddery gait, along thickly curtained corridors which effectively kept out the weak March afternoon sunshine.

Coming to a long gallery, Dorothea saw portraits of long dead Quintrells hung on the walls, most with a passing resemblance to Geraint, all with creepy eyes that followed one down the room. She had a vague recollection of a Quintrell family tree in Dr Harrison's missing book.

'Master Geraint looks most like the 10th Baronet don't you think? He was one of the few moral Quintrells. He died in his bed at a ripe old age and the curse didn't get him,' the old lady said, chattily.

Dorothea murmured in agreement. The 10th Baronet did look like a rather forbidding Geraint in a grump. She stood on tiptoes to get a better look, before standing back on to a creaky floorboard and making herself jump. She realised that she was now alone in the long, dark gallery and all the portraits were staring at her. Dorothea gave a squeak and hurriedly headed in the direction that the old retainer had taken.

Catching her up, they came to a panelled chamber in the old part of the house. The old woman beckoned Dorothea to sit down in a chair on one side of the fire. She lit a lamp and directly pointed it in Dorothea's eyes.

'I'll see if my mistress is ready to receive you, Miss Roberts.' The servant hobbled out of the room, leaving Dorothea sat uncomfortably shielding her eyes against the dazzling light.

MURDER BY THE BOOK

Five minutes passed. Dorothea could hear strange noises coming from the next room, before the door opened and a woman entered. She sat down opposite Dorothea. Dorothea straining to see, got the impression of chestnut hair, a youthful tread, and an imagined hint of blue at the woman's feet.

'It is so nice that you could join me Miss Roberts.'

'Oh hello, is that you Mrs Hadley-Brown? I can't see you because there is this light in my eyes—'

'Never mind that, tell me what sort of family do you come from?' The disembodied voice was urgent. 'Any scandals, hereditary madness, skeletons in the closet, bankruptcy, bigamy, gambling addictions, could you possibly have been exchanged at birth?'

'My dad was a farmer,' was all Dorothea could bleat under this onslaught.

'Farmers? Oh well, could be worse. What about diet and exercise? How fast can you run a mile? Do you eat your greens? Are your bowels regular?'

Dorothea was saved from answering this final question, by the main light switch being flicked. When her eyes had adjusted, she could see Geraint Hadley-Brown stood by the door glowering.

'Not this again Mother! You cannot interrogate every young woman I bring to visit. It is not *de rigueur*. What will Miss Roberts think of us? You still have a wart stuck to your nose by the way.'

Theodora Hadley-Brown was not at all abashed at being told off by her offspring and chuckled wickedly, while peeling off the fake wart from her nose.

'My apologies Miss Roberts, you must indulge a mother's anxieties about who her only son and heir, is running around with. That last woman you brought to see me Geraint was far too old for you.'

'Yes and you subjected her to an equally silly performance. Kindly remember Mother that Mrs Adams is now Mrs George and the wife of my boss. You weren't nearly so dramatic when my sister Kitty brought Desmond to visit for the first time.'

'That you know of dear,' said Theodora smugly, with a little wink at Dorothea. 'Miss Roberts, I am very sorry for my behaviour. Do let's start again. I really am so pleased that Geraint has brought you to visit. He has told me all about your investigations at the museum.'

Thoroughly befuddled Dorothea clung on to what she knew.

'Did you give me the copy of Dr Harrison's book and slip a newspaper clip about Professor Beaumaris' murder into my collecting tin?'

'Call me Theodora dear and yes I did. I may have interfered just a teensy bit but in my defence how else was I going to meet you? Geraint kept talking about one of his students who had solved a series of murders. I had to pump Harold Aldridge for all the details, because Geraint just clammed up as soon as I took an interest. Anyway, it was so nice to have a virtuous excuse to visit the big city, rather than just shopping and theatres.'

'I live in Manchester. Don't I count as a virtuous excuse to visit?' Her son was mildly offended.

His mother ignored the interruption. 'I thought it was about time to stir up all the old business again. Harold Aldridge agrees with me. Someone killed Professor Beaumaris, who for all his faults did not deserve to die and his murderer has never been brought to justice. Miss Roberts, I want you and your friends to clear my husband's name.'

'But Mrs . . . I mean Theodora, your husband was never charged,' said Dorothea, confused.

'No dear but only from lack of evidence. DI Dawlish, who thought himself such a big noise, fancied Tristan in the role of chief murderer from day one. Tristan had an argument with Professor Beaumaris that day you see, due to the appointment of an outside candidate for the role of museum director. Professor Beaumaris's secretary overheard part of the argument and Tristan did use some very wild language. No other witness saw the unknown woman in the corridor that he swore blind he saw. Tristan's alibi was weak, though fortunately everyone else's were pretty shoddy too,' said Theodora, a wave of sadness past across her face. 'The police could not charge Tristan, so the crime was left unsolved but people pointed and whispered unkind things. The museum trustees politely gave Tristan the push. It nearly killed him to leave the job he loved so much. When war broke out, he enlisted immediately and perhaps wasn't as careful of his own safety as he could have been. He died at Ypres on the 3rd November 1914, trying to rescue a group of his men who had become separated and were under attack.'

Geraint who had been listening intently asked a question.

'Mother why are you so sure that Father was innocent? What do you know that we don't?'

'Because I knew him and loved him Geraint. Your father would never have killed Professor Beaumaris. He was an honourable man.'

'Still, you are keeping something from us Mother.'

'It is only a little thing darling,' Theodora had the grace to look sheepish. 'Only, that when I took your father's tea to his office that day . . . well he wasn't there.'

'You lied to the police!' Geraint Hadley-Brown was shocked. 'You said you had seen him.'

'I wasn't going to tell that pushy DI Dawlish that your father had popped out to use the lavatory, was I? He told me so later.'

'Mother I think you need to tell us exactly what happened that day,' said Geraint, trying to remain calm.

'If you think it would help dear.' Her brow furrowed in concentration. 'I went to the museum early to give your father a hand. He was feeling really despondent that morning at breakfast, unappreciated, after being passed over for promotion. I wanted to check up on him. Make sure he was doing what he was meant to do, rather than sit in his office letting everything go to hell in a handcart.

'When I arrived, I helped him to put out chairs for that evening. He told me that he had argued with Professor Beaumaris that morning over the appointment and had handed in his resignation in protest. I was very worried by this. Tristan was the bread winner in our family and you and your sister were only very small. Then I went downstairs to the staff kitchen but I went via Professor Beaumaris' office first, to see if I could catch him alone. I wanted to ask him not to accept Tristan's resignation.

LIZZIE BENTHAM

This was at around two thirty. Professor Beaumaris was in his office but he was just leaving and was very brusque with me.'

"'I can't stop Theodora," he said. "There is something I must do."'

'I asked him what was so important that he couldn't stop and talk with common courtesy.'

'He called back down the corridor, "A case of intellectual fraud!"'

'I didn't tell this to the police. In the kitchen I started preparing refreshments. Max Harrison called in at two forty five to make tea for himself and Harold Aldridge. He seemed inclined to stay and chat, as is his want, but I was really busy so I shooed him away. At three thirty I took Tristan up a tea tray. I went via Professor Beaumaris' office again. He wasn't there, so I went along to my husband's office. He wasn't there either, so I left the tray and went back to the kitchen. I was only gone five minutes. I was expecting Geraldine Beaumaris at three o'clock but in reality I wasn't. She was always late but four o'clock was pushing it, even for her. When Geraldine finally arrived I noticed she was flushed and flustered. Also, her skirt was tucked into her stockings at the back, which I pointed out to her but I didn't mention that to the police either.

'We made sandwiches together until I cut myself when slicing bread. I still have a scar on my finger from it. I left Geraldine and went to find the first aid kit in the museum's main office.'

'Why didn't Geraldine get it and you stay? Surely that would have been more sensible,' asked Dorothea.

'Geraldine hates the sight of blood dear. She closed her eyes and wouldn't open them until I could guarantee there was no blood around. The police surgeon kindly stitched it for me after the police were called in. I think they were checking it was real.'

'Was Bertram Pickles in his office?'

'Yes dear, he stuck sticking plaster on my finger and told me I should see a doctor. There was far too much still to do, so I couldn't possibly leave. I asked him to stick an extra piece of plaster on it and I carried on.

'When I got back to the kitchen, Geraldine was where I had left her with her eyes closed. I cleaned up the work top and we started moving crockery and food upstairs using the dumbwaiter. It was quite a job. I was at the bottom and Geraldine was at the top. I know what you are thinking; Geraldine could have killed the professor because she was alone in the room with the cabinet. The thing is, we were talking to each other all the time and she had to pull the dumbwaiter up when it was full. We must have sent it up and down fifteen to twenty times. Geraldine said no one entered the South Gallery while she was there. The police thought Professor Beaumaris was dead by the time we started to move the refreshments in. Ugh, makes you think. He was in the cabinet by the time we were setting up.'

'Mother, have you told us everything? You haven't left out anything this time?' asked Geraint sternly.

Theodora looked like she wanted to say something more but changed her mind.

'Geraint darling, do show Dorothea the gardens while the sun is still shining. I'll go and see what Mrs Barns is making for dinner,' she said changing the subject.

***

Dorothea still speechless from Theodora's bombshell, followed a glowering Geraint out onto the veranda.

'How can she believe Father was innocent after that? He wasn't where he should have been at the time of the murder and she covered for him. Ahhhh she is insane!' The usually urbane Dr Hadley-Brown was really rattled. 'If DCI Kydd knew about this, it would be a cut and dried case.' He paced up and down beside an overgrown, herbaceous border, while Dorothea sat down on a nearby bench. 'What she doesn't seem to realise, is that by suppressing Father's movements, she is now an accessory to murder!' He threw himself discontentedly on to the bench next to Dorothea.

'Stop being melodramatic and think for a second. Our reconstruction in the museum was helpful but inconclusive. The position of chief murderer is still open. Your mother and father may have missed each other by seconds. Don't forget the woman that your father saw. If we knew who she was, we would probably find our murderer. Maybe your father thought it was your mother and was covering for her. He only caught a glimpse of her from a distance.'

'He was short sighted too,' Geraint added grudgingly.

'Your mother had blood on her skirt from cutting her finger. Maybe he jumped to the wrong conclusion. She was the only person that did have blood on her.'

Geraint groaned again. He distractedly ran his hand through his hair before realising it was covered in brilliantine and wiped it on a hanky.

Dorothea had an idea. 'We are learning about this crime second-hand. We have access to primary sources in your mother, godfather and DCI Kydd but we don't know how reliable or biased they are, or what time has done to their recollections. Also we don't have the full set of suspects amongst our sources. What we need to do is to bring this crime into the modern age and generate new information.'

Geraint looked confused.

Dorothea tried again, 'Let's get all the suspects back together again for the first time, in one place and see what happens. The guilty party might let something slip.'

'This sounds dangerous,' Geraint was worried but intrigued.

'It could be fun,' Dorothea said, briefly explaining her audacious plan.

***

Geraint discontentedly knocked some coloured balls around the billiard table, after the ladies had retired for the night. On his way upstairs, Geraint saw that there was light still spilling from under his mother's bedroom door. Geraint knocked and waited for the faint, 'Come in.'

Inside Theodora was propped up on a mountain of pillows in bed, sporting a very fetching bed jacket and curlers, and was scribbling away in a notebook.

'Geraint darling, I am so excited about Dorothea's plan. There are a lot of variables but it might just work. She is a clever young lady with such a good heart. She has volunteered to help me with all the preparations and to ask her friends to help too.'

'So do you like her then Mother?' he asked somewhat nervously.

'Yes Geraint. Why is there something you want to tell me?' His mother looked hopeful.

'No, no, no . . . no. Goodnight Mother.'

'Goodnight dear.'

Theodora smiled wickedly after her son's fast retreating figure.

LIZZIE BENTHAM

The Telegram Received by DCI Kydd from Mr Gritty, Private Investigator, 12th April 1935

DCI KYDD POLICE HQ MANCHESTER 12TH APRIL 1935

GIANTS TEAR SOLD IN ANKARA 8000 POUNDS STOP PRIVATE SALE TO DEALER STOP WILL INVESTIGATE FURTHER STOP CONTACT ME AT THE CENTRAL STOP

R GRITTY
CENTRAL HOTEL ANKARA TURKEY

CHAPTER SEVEN

A Weekend Party with a Difference

Maundy Thursday Afternoon, 18th April 1935

'Why am I the kitchen maid?' moaned Mary Long. 'Kitchen maids have the worst costumes, they work the worst hours, and are stuck in the kitchen away from the action!'

'Because you are the best cook out of all of us,' hissed Mary Short. 'Besides cooking is basically chemistry, which you are very good at. Shhh now Longy! They are here!'

The newly acquired "staff" of Mickering Priory was assembled into two lines outside the main door, to greet the guests to the priory, for an Easter weekend house party. Over the past few weeks, Dorothea's friends had spent every weekend at Mickering Priory helping Theodora sort out the rooms, tidy the gardens, learn their roles and their way around the house and grounds. Today, everything was ready for the big performance.

The Reverend Clarence Moss's battered, old Ford returned from meeting the three fifteen train into Ormskirk. They watched, as the ancient car laboured ponderously up the drive, away from the waterlogged fields, under heavy, foreboding skies. There was more rain forecast for later that day. Reverend Moss looked the part in his chauffeur's uniform. He deftly pocketed a tip from Sir Laurence Tarleton, as the great man alighted, with a little touch of his cap and a deferential, 'Thank you sir!' He avoided eye contact with his wife Jinny, who as housekeeper was stood on the steps with the staff, giving him daggers.

Mrs Hadley-Brown's new butler, Balvan Thakkar, looked impressively exotic in his traditional sherwani and churindars. He smoothly helped Mrs Geraldine Beaumaris alight and passed her jewellery case to ladies maid, Mary Short, for safe keeping.

Geraint Hadley-Brown's Crossley drew up next, containing himself and Professor Harold Aldridge. The professor had been prepared by Geraint for the theatrical carnage he was about to witness, however, was overwhelmed by a coughing fit when he beheld the French chef, DCI Kydd, in his chef whites with a glued on miniature moustache. The parlour maid, Dorothea Roberts, had to run inside and procure him a glass of water.

Theodora was enjoying herself enormously as hostess, greeting everyone with enthusiasm and kisses. She hadn't yet slipped up by calling her new staff, "her darlings".

A taxicab pulled into the drive, followed closely by a motorcyclist in full leathers, riding a motorbike and side car. The taxicab deposited Dr Maximilian Harrison and his luggage on the doorstep.

'Absolute hoodlums these motorcyclists,' he complained loudly, as he paid off the driver who obviously agreed with him. 'Theodora!' He boomed turning to his hostess. 'You haven't changed a bit but the priory is looking smarter than last time I was here,' he shot the old house an envious look. 'And this is new too, how can you afford such a large staff my dear? Post war prices are extortionate. My offer still stands you know.'

'You haven't changed either Max. My answer is still the same too. Do let Rev— I mean Moss, take your bags up to your room. I have put you in the Honeysuckle room as normal,' said Theodora, quickly recovering from her near slip and expertly palming Maximilian Harrison off on to the Reverend Moss.

'What offer is that?' whispered Geraint to his mother.

'Max offers to buy Mickering Priory from me on an annual basis. He loves this building and all that rot about St Boniface's curse.'

'Would you ever consider selling this house Mother?'

'Over my dead body,' she replied.

While this exchange was happening, the motorcyclist slowly took off his leather gloves, goggles, and helmet. Dorothea helping Mary Short with Mrs Beaumaris' twelve cases, gasped as she recognised his face. It was Eric Tarleton! He had not been invited but was gate-crashing the weekend on his father's coat-tails. He was bound to recognise her if they came face-to-face. She grabbed two cases and headed for the stairs while gesturing a warning to Mary Short.

MURDER BY THE BOOK

Another car drew up fashionably late, as the other guests were leaving to freshen up before afternoon tea in the drawing room. The undergardener, Simon Culthorpe, ran around to the car's boot to wrestle a wheelchair out of it. He tenderly helped out of the car and into the chair, the most beautiful starlet that Hollywood could only have dreamed of producing. Simon then realised that an undergardener probably would not do this and went red in the face.

Balvan stepped in, 'Allow me Miss Maggie to show you the easiest route to your room. Culthorpe please bring Miss Maggie's bags.'

The kitchen staff, not needed at this time, watched the spectacle with delight and awe.

'Oh why does Maggie get to be an actress, she looks fabulous!' Mary Long complained wistfully.

'But my petite, you get to aid the greatest chef in the whole, wide world. Who could ask for more?' said DCI Kydd in a diabolical French accent, stroking his little moustache.

'Can you even cook French food DCI Kydd?'

'No.'

'Can you cook at all?'

'No . . .'

'It's going to be a long weekend,' sighed Mary. 'I had better get started on the canapés for later.

Downstairs

Professor Aldridge shook Dorothea's hand warmly. They were alone in the corridor.

'This is a capital idea of yours Miss Roberts. Geraint kept it a secret and only told me on the drive here, a little payback for the tea party.' He chuckled.

'I am glad you approve sir. I hope it will be fruitful.' Dorothea had something on her mind regarding her English coursework. 'I am sorry my essay on *The Curse of the Boniface Psalter - Fact or Fiction?* wasn't very good. I had to start from scratch when someone stole all of my notes and Dr Harrison's book.'

'Don't worry my dear. Setting the essay served its purpose to spark your curiosity in this case. Of the handful of essays that were handed in, one very well written one was submitted by Eric Tarleton. He is usually not the most diligent of students and it surprised me somewhat.'

'Yes that is odd—' Dorothea broke off, as Dr Maximilian Harrison rounded a corner and came along the corridor towards them.

'Thank you young lady I have everything I need in my room. You have done an excellent job,' said Professor Aldridge adlibbing beautifully. 'Ah Max! Are you going to the drawing room for tea too? Then let's go down together. What a lot of catching up we have to do.'

MURDER BY THE BOOK

A Concise History of the Curse of the Boniface Psalter by Dr M Harrison – Piracy, Smuggling and the Lost Quintrell Treasure

In an attempt to recoup some of the losses that his ancestors faced after the civil war of the previous century, the 7th Baronet, Sir Philip Quintrell, fell into company with a band of smugglers who worked out of the Isle of Man, a notorious haven for smuggling. They landed goods on the sandy beaches of the Lancashire coastline and brought tea, coffee, tobacco, and French wines by pack pony across the salt marshes, in an attempt to escape the duty imposed at Liverpool's docks. There were many landowners in the county who looked the other way, if contraband was taken across their land, or stored overnight in a barn, cellar, or church, especially if they were reimbursed with a case of port.

Sir Philip Quintrell allowed smuggled goods to be kept in Mickering Priory's cellars. He even had tunnels constructed in secret, from an old priest hole, into the grounds as an escape route for any smuggler too closely followed by exercisemen. His eldest son, married to an heiress and middle son, a clergyman, nervously condemned his involvement but drank his sherry and smoked his tobacco.

His youngest son followed in his footsteps. Giles signed up as a privateer sailing the seven seas and acquired a fortune in looted treasure, which he kept in an old sea chest. Sometimes he helped transport goods for the smugglers and landed them on the beaches at Formby and Ainsdale. This continued until he fell in love with a gentlewoman of impeccable birth and respectability. He swore to leave his former life behind.

Sir Philip, deep in debt, convinced Giles to do one last lucrative contraband run to Mickering Priory and to bring his sea chest with him.

The weather was foul, the journey arduous and the excisemen had wind of a run that night and were out in force. The young man led his small band of men and ponies carefully through the salt marshes and fields, avoiding all potential ambushes and eventually unloaded the goods at the prearranged drop off point, a barn belonging to Mickering Priory.

Saying a fond farewell to his men, Giles picked his way carefully through the priory grounds, struggling with his heavy sea chest and found the entrance to the secret tunnel. He entered the dank space, closing the door behind him, thus locking himself in. He followed the twisting passageway up some steps to a room in the oldest wing of Mickering Priory and into the back of what had been a priest hole. He knocked on the rear of the panelling, a coded *Rata-tat-tat,* but got no response. He tried again. This time the panel moved slowly across at shoulder height to reveal his father holding a duelling pistol pointed directly at him.

'Pass me your sea chest Son,' said Sir Philip Quintrell. The younger man kept hold of the chest suddenly very wary.

'It is very heavy Father. I'll need a hand to raise it over the ledge. Why don't you come in here with me and help me lift it?'

The older man and gun did not move. 'The excisemen are downstairs son. They know that you moved contraband tonight and they are waiting for you. Leave your gold here. Be away to the coast and to Ireland or Man, before they catch you and hang you.'

The younger man was chilled by his father's words. Mechanically he asked, 'But what about you? Do they suspect you? Will you be safe?'

'Don't worry about me. They don't suspect me yet. Fly as fast as you can and leave the gold. I'll look after it for you.'

While he was talking, the door of the room which had been left ajar, opened fully and a woman entered quietly. In her hand she carried a duelling pistol, the twin of the one held by her husband.

'Philip, why are you brandishing a pistol at our youngest son? Why do you lie? There are no excisemen in the house. Jem Todd has led them away to lose them on the mosses. Put your pistol down sir and explain yourself.'

Sir Philip's gun hand dropped gradually to his side as he turned to face his furious wife. He licked his lips nervously. His eyes flickered between his wife's face and the gun that she was

MURDER BY THE BOOK

handling expertly.

'My dearest Fanny, you misunderstand the situation—'

'Don't you dearest Fanny me. I see the situation quite clearly. I talked to Dearsby today. He told me that you have extended the mortgages on Mickering Priory. I know of your losses at cards and of the high stakes you play for. Now you think that you will replace the family coffers, by stealing a fortune from our youngest son and frightening him into hiding. Enough, sir! I shall not allow it.'

Whilst Fanny Quintrell was talking, Giles extracted himself with some difficulty from the priest hole, on to the sofa underneath the gaping hole in the wood panelling, then down to the floor. Giles had left his treasure chest behind in the secret passageway. He stood between his warring parents.

'Father is this true? I would have given you all my treasure if you had asked. Would you really have had me banished with a price on my head, to pay your debts?'

'Don't believe her my boy. Your mother has these funny turns,' said Sir Philip, looking shifty.

'I am saner than you are, you deceitful devil. I am not the one who has lost a fortune at the faro table. Giles disarm him please. We don't want anyone shot accidentally. These pistols have hair triggers.'

'Father please put down your weapon on the floor.'

Sir Philip Quintrell had been backing towards the priest hole and stepped onto the sofa. He lost his temper and aimed his pistol at his wife.

'I'll shoot you here and now you meddling witch. The treasure is mine. I need it.'

Their son leapt to intercept but a shot rang out and a red rose bloomed on Sir Philip's temple. He was straddling the priest hole opening and toppled backwards into the void. The mechanism of the secret door must have been knocked in his fall, because it closed silently after the exiting 7th Baronet.

Giles Quintrell banged on the innocent looking wood panelling frantically.

'Father is the only one who knows how to operate the secret

passage. My gold is in there with him. Did you kill him Mother?'

'He is dead Son. I never miss. Your grandfather taught me to shoot.'

She looked weary but like a great weight had been lifted off her shoulders. This drew the young man up short. His parent's marriage had never been cordial. He looked at his mother with new understanding.

'No word of tonight's happenings must get out for your sake Mother. Let us make it known that Father was in league with the smugglers and that he escaped to Man with my gold, for fear of the hangman's noose. We need never go looking for his body. In death he can keep my gold. It was his for the asking and I give it to him now with my whole heart.'

Mother and son embraced.

'Thank you my dear. I'll make sure you do not lose out by this act and can still marry your lady. I have been hiding away anything precious that I own, from your father, for years as his gambling got worse. My father wisely left the estate in Ireland solely to me and I have made sure your father could not reach any of the profits from it, though he has tried on many occasions. He even attempted to convince the doctors and lawyers I was insane but they knew me too well. Let us leave this place. It is the source of all unhappiness in my life.'

Richard Quintrell, the eldest son, had to wait for seven years to inherit the baronetcy. In the interim, his good financial management meant the mortgages on the priory were paid off gradually, so that when he did inherit the title, Mickering Priory was an asset and not a mill stone. Giles Quintrell married his lady and turned his hand to farming in Ireland. No one ever discovered the entrances to the secret passage or the chest full of treasure, nor the skeleton guarding it.

Primary Source: Correspondence between Fanny Quintrell as a nonagenarian and her great-granddaughter Josephine Buckleigh, found under the floorboards of a farm in Ireland.

MURDER BY THE BOOK

Maundy Thursday Evening, 18th April 1935
Upstairs

'Do tell Theodora, how have you managed to keep on a whole staff. Domestic servants are so hard to find and a drain on one's income?' asked Geraldine Beaumaris with a hint of jealousy in her voice.

The guests were sitting around the vast table in the freezing dining room, in the oldest part of the house. Balvan and Jinny entered with the soup course.

'Yes Theodora, last time I was here there was only your old housekeeper, Mrs Barns, and a couple of dailies. If I am being honest, the whole place seemed to me to be mouldering into rack and ruin. You have certainly done some sprucing up. A butler all the way from India and a French chef . . . Very natty,' commented Maximilian Harrison.

'I am so pleased that you have noticed. I have had a little bit of unexpected luck since you were last here,' murmured Theodora truthfully. She was relieved she had persuaded Mrs Barns to visit her daughter in Formby. Mrs Barns would have given the game away.

'I am looking forward to eating what Monsieur Jean has prepared for us. Escargots perhaps or possibly cuisses de grenouilles,' said Professor Aldridge with a twinkle. 'What is on the menu tonight please Balvan?'

'Cream of leek and potato soup, sir. Followed by roast beef and horseradish with all the trimmings and apple pie and custard for dessert.'

'Very Gallic,' murmured Professor Aldridge under his breath.

'Monsieur Jean has obviously looked at the weather and realised that we all need hearty food. I must say this soup is delicious,' intervened Geraint giving his godfather a reproving stare, 'Maggie, please tell us about some of the movies that you have been involved with. I was so sorry to hear about your sad accident last year.'

This was a prearranged signal. Maggie launched into a

colourful monologue of the fictitious films she had starred in and the events surrounding her invented car accident, which had supposedly left her in a wheelchair. No one seemed inclined to question her silver screen credentials. This, together with anecdotes about Mickering Priory's more colourful historical characters from Maximilian Harrison, kept conversation flowing until dessert.

***

Downstairs

Once dinner for the house party was over and Mary Long had been given a stiff drink for cooking the biggest meal of her life, enthusiastically but somewhat inexpertly, aided by the chief inspector, the staff sat down to eat their own meal. Between mouthfuls, the young people updated DCI Kydd on what they had discovered so far.

'Mrs Beaumaris has a lot of jewellery with her Chief Inspector. I helped to unpack her bags and she has brought her jewellery box with her for a weekend. It is full of very expensive pieces. You would have thought that she would have learned from the loss of the Giant's Tear neckless to the Magpie,' said Mary Short. 'She says it will be safer here than being left at home.'

'Laurence Tarleton has a revolver in his luggage. He placed it in the drawer of the bedside table in his room,' stated Balvan calmly. 'I noticed that there were cartridges too.'

'That's good to know. I'll ask Dr Hadley-Brown to remind the guests to put anything of value or of potential danger, in the safe for the duration of their stay. We don't want to tempt fate.'

'Once I had finished helping Eric Tarleton with his bag, he basically shut his bedroom door in my face. I think there may have been something he didn't want me to see amongst his luggage,' suggested Simon Culthorpe.

'Tomorrow morning when you make up the rooms Dorothea and Jinny, see if you can get to the bottom of why he was being so coy,' said the chief inspector. 'What about Maximilian Harrison?'

'He has brought reference books, a typewriter and a whole host of personal items too, like some very odd pieces of art. It nearly killed me lugging it all up to his room,' said Reverend Moss. 'I'll have to leave early tomorrow morning to make it back to Manchester for the Good Friday services and to relieve Mrs O'Neil our housekeeper, who is looking after Arabella tonight. I'll be back on Easter Monday to take the guests back to the station.'

'We are extremely grateful that you could join us at this busy time of the year vicar. Send little Arabella our best regards,' said DCI Kydd, making a note. 'Everyone please keep your eyes and ears open this evening for anything pertinent to our inquiries and report back in the morning at breakfast. Thank you to everyone who is keeping a watch tonight. Now I want you all to appreciate the apple pie for dessert which I helped to make.'

'All he had to do was keep stirring but he got distracted and let the custard go lumpy,' muttered a slightly tiddly Mary Long from the other end of the table. 'Oh and he licked the spoon.'

***

Upstairs, Downstairs

After dinner the ladies withdrew to the drawing room and were soon followed by the gentlemen, who were not inclined to linger in the draughty former refectory. There, in more temperate conditions, Geraldine Beaumaris discovered the gramophone and bullied Laurence Tarleton into dancing with her. Eric gallantly asked Theodora Hadley-Brown to dance and the two couples whirled effortlessly around each other, like odd mirror images.

Geraint and Harold Aldridge had gone off to play billiards, leaving Maggie to make polite conversation with Maximilian Harrison by the fire.

'Dr Harrison, just before we sat down to eat you tapped on the wood panelling in the dining room. Does it have wood worm?'

asked Maggie curiously.

'Probably my dear but I didn't do it for that reason. You may know that I have written a little history book about the *Boniface Psalter* and the curse associated with it. Some people say it is rather good. If you are interested I can send you a signed copy of the second edition when it is published. This house plays a huge part in the history of the psalter. The manuscript was housed in the library here for nearly eight centuries. Theodora's father gave it to the university, when his son and heir, Michael Quintrell, died tragically young. I have made it my life's work to be the psalter's chronicler, a modern day Bede . . . but possibly less venerable.' He laughed at his own joke.

'The reason I tap on the woodwork, is that there is some evidence that in the 18th century, the son of the 7th Baronet lost a fortune in treasure acquired by piracy in a secret passage built for smuggling, somewhere in the old part of this house. I know of the whereabouts of one priest hole, unusually in the pantry, very convenient for passing the reverend his vittles, but have not yet found this other passageway.

'After my own wife died very young, Theodora Hadley-Brown very kindly let me stay here to conduct some research. I usually come back once a year on a sort of pilgrimage. Theodora tolerates my whimsy, for which I am eternally grateful.'

'How thrilling!' said Maggie. 'Have you any idea where the secret passage might be?'

'One end must come out in the park, to have allowed the smugglers to bring in contraband to the priory cellars for safe keeping. I employed a surveyor to look at the earthworks in the garden and there does seem to be a ditch, which could be a collapsed tunnel. It ends near the ice house, another potential place that smugglers might stash their goods. The other end could be anywhere in the old part of the priory. I believe that it might be hidden by the panelling in one of the rooms on the east side of the building, so the library, dining room or the blue parlour. It could just as easily be in one of the cellars or up in one of the first floor bedrooms on that side.'

'A secret passage you say? What fun!' Eric and Theodora had

finished dancing. Eric had been shamelessly eavesdropping for the past few minutes. 'Let's go and have a look!'

'Leave it until tomorrow morning dear. You need natural light for searching for secret passages,' suggested Theodora mildly.

Geraint and Harold Aldridge returning from the billiard room caught the tail end of this conversation.

'I am not sure there will be a lot of light tomorrow. It's lashing it down outside. The forecast for the next few days is pretty ropey. I can show you the priest hole in the pantry now,' offered Geraint. 'My sister and I used to hide in there as children and jump out to scare the cook.'

'You were absolute scamps the pair of you,' said Theodora nostalgically.

In the end, all of the party descended into the nether regions of Mickering Priory, to see the priest hole. It was a hidden cavity the size of a wardrobe at the back of a pantry cupboard, in front of which, goods could be stacked to hide it.

The staff were surprised to find their sanctum being invaded by, "them upstairs". Dorothea had to quickly duck under the table to avoid Eric catching sight of her.

'Give us some warning next time,' whispered DCI Kydd to Professor Aldridge at the back of the group, 'I had taken off my moustache to eat and I think I may have just stuck it on upside down.'

Suddenly, there was a clamorous ringing of the main door bell. When no reply was instantly forthcoming, there was a loud pounding on the ancient knocker.

'Balvan dear, can you get the door please,' asked Theodora, forgetting that her staff weren't actually her "dears". 'I think we have another visitor.'

There was some shocked whispering amongst both the upstairs and downstairs priory inhabitants.

'There aren't any more suspects left to arrive.'

'Theodora didn't mention that any more guests were due.'

'Mother has got something up her sleeve. She has been like an excited child since the phone rang mid-afternoon,' whispered Geraint to Dorothea.

There was a mass exodus from downstairs, up into the entrance hall. Balvan drew back the creaky bolts to let in a gust of wind, rain and a woman wearing serviceable waterproofs. She walked into the hallway carrying a battered suitcase and surveyed the assembled, eclectic welcome party dispassionately. There was a stifled gasp from Professor Aldridge.

'The old gang is back together I see. Damn. I could murder a stiff scotch,' said Dr Lottie Ellis.

***

Downstairs, Upstairs

With the distraction of a new and unexpected guest arriving, DCI Kydd quietly detached himself from the gaggle of staff and headed for the drawing room where there was a telephone extension. He asked the operator for police headquarters and waited anxiously while the call was put through. He was relieved to hear PC Standish's chirpy tones on the line.

'Evening sir. How is your culinary weekend away going?'

'Interesting so far. Listen Standish, I want you to do me a favour. Get on to Somerset House please and look up a marriage certificate and a death certificate for me.'

He told Standish a name and a reason and Standish whistled.

'Alright sir I will get on to it—'

The telephone line went dead. DCI Kydd pressed the hook switch a number of times but the instrument remained silent.

'What do you think you are doing?' Geraldine Beaumaris had come up behind him remarkable quietly on the parquet floor. 'Does your mistress know that you are using the telephone? No trunk calls to Belgium I hope?' She gave a little laugh.

Checking that his moustache was firmly affixed, DCI Kydd calmly spun around on the balls of his feet.

'I am from France madam, not Belgium. I regret to inform you that the phone line appears to be broken. I will not now be able to order kippers from the fishmongers, for madam's breakfast tomorrow. Excuse me please.' With a click of his heels and a bow, he swept out of the room rather pleased with his performance.

'Is the fishmonger still open at nine p.m. on Maundy Thursday?' asked Geraldine in bemusement, to Monsieur Jean's retreating figure. She gingerly picked up the telephone receiver and listened for the dialling tone but there was none.

***

Upstairs and Downstairs

'Hello Lottie, I am so glad you could come,' cooed Theodora, kissing the new comer on the cheek while trying to avoid getting wet from her dripping sou'wester. 'Do come on through. Balvan will fetch you a drink and Moss my chauffeur, will see to your car.'

Theodora guided the newcomer into the drawing room where the other guests had congregated. On divesting her outermost garments, it could be seen than Lottie was a wiry lady of indefinite age, with a somewhat weather beaten complexion and a tan even in April.

'Do you all know Lottie Ellis?' asked Theodora. 'Maggie and Geraint you may not. Lottie is the foremost expert in what we in Britain would consider as the Dark Ages period but for the Middle East. She spends most of her life flitting between digs in Baghdad, Damascus and Beirut. She was a doctoral student of both Professor Beaumaris (God rest his soul) and Sir Laurence here. She used to share an office with Harold and Maximilian.'

'Hello Auntie Lottie,' Eric came forward to give his godmother a hug.

'Hello Eric, full of mischief as always, I see. When are you coming to Tarsus to work on my dig?'

'This summer, if you and my father permit it,' he glanced over at Laurence Tarleton.

Laurence looked worried and murmured, 'We'll see'.

'Dearest boy, you are always welcome to come,' said Lottie enthusiastically.

'We need to pump Lottie Ellis for information. Presumably she is the one doctoral student who wasn't there on the day of the murder twenty years ago,' hissed Maggie to Geraint.

'It would be interesting to get her take on what happened. Maybe that is why Mother invited her,' replied Geraint.

'Lottie! I haven't seen you in twenty years. You look well my dear!' said Maximilian Harrison jovially, kissing her on both cheeks.

'Dr Ellis,' Harold Aldridge's acknowledgement was uncharacteristically curt. He hid behind a newspaper in the furthermost corner of the room.

'Harold,' the newcomer nodded. 'I am afraid that I am rather late Theodora, because I was held up giving my lecture at the university. I am glad I set off when I did, as all this rain has caused the River Alt to burst its banks. The road from Maghull is now a couple of inches under water and large swathes of the moss are flooded. With more rain forecast for the next few days, we will soon be an island.'

On hearing this news, Geraint slipped quietly out the room and raced back downstairs to the kitchen, where the last lot of washing up was being started, with much hilarity and chatter.

'Reverend Moss please can I borrow you? Grab some waterproofs and gum boots and come with me,' Geraint called.

Together, the two men wrapped up against the storm that was coming down in torrents and ventured outside. They followed the driveway until they reached the main road and gazed out at a scene of Biblical desolation. The road petered out after two hundred yards or so, deluged by murky waters. Turning clockwise, they followed Mickering Priory's boundary wall and traversed the edge of the small estate in a loop, keeping the house in the fulcrum of their circuit. For as far as they could discern, in every direction, there was water. Mickering Priory was once again an island, as it would have been centuries before when the monks lived there, surrounded by salt marsh.

Reaching the road again they beat a tactical retreat to the warmth of the kitchen just as DCI Kydd was returning from using the telephone.

'Lottie Ellis is correct. Mickering Priory is now an island. The mosslands haven't flooded this badly since I was at school and we were marooned here for a week,' said Geraint.

'I won't be able to get home for Easter services,' bemoaned Reverend Moss. 'I'll need to telephone my curate. Mrs O'Neil won't mind looking after Arabella a bit longer but we need to let them know we are safe.'

'You can't,' interjected DCI Kydd, looking worried. 'The phone line is down too, so we are cut off from "the mainland," indefinitely. What with a potential murderer in our midst, it is going to feel like a very long Easter weekend . . .'

CHAPTER EIGHT

Players on a Stage

Maundy Thursday Evening, 18th April 1935
Downstairs, Under the Stairs

DCI Kydd had drawn up a night watch rota. Each night was split into four watches of two hours each, between the hours of ten o'clock in the evening, until six o'clock the following morning, with two people on duty at any one time. Geraint, Maggie and Professor Aldridge had clamoured to be included. They were rostered on either the first or last watch, to give the impression that as guests, they were staying up late playing cards or getting up early to watch the sunrise.

It was the second watch of the night and Dorothea and DCI Kydd's were on duty. DCI Kydd was positioned on the first floor, at the bottom of the stairs up to the staff quarters, where he could see the majority of the guestrooms without being seen himself.

Dorothea was positioned in the entrance hall, in the shadow of the grand staircase. She settled down for a tedious watch, taking over from Maggie who had a bedroom on the ground floor. Maggie had reported that Lottie Ellis and Harold Aldridge were both still awake in different rooms downstairs, the professor in the library and Lottie in the study.

The clock struck half past midnight and Dorothea was struggling to stay awake. She heard doors opening and footsteps in the distance. Suddenly she was very alert.

Professor Aldridge appeared out of the library carrying a pile of books and papers. Simultaneously, Lottie Ellis came out of the study with an identical pile of books and papers and they collided at the foot of the stairs, in a shower of academic works.

'Oh Harold! Why can't you look where you are going? Lottie sounded exasperated. She scrabbled around on the floor for her belongings.

MURDER BY THE BOOK

'I am sorry for inconveniencing you madam,' said Harold Aldridge, strangely stiff and formal, even though he had crawled all the way to the fireplace to rescue one of his sheets of paper.

'Don't be silly Harold, we are old friends. Surely you are not still mad at me for leaving, after all these years? We would have driven each other mad.'

'You broke my heart disappearing off like that,' said the professor. 'I was about to pluck up the courage to ask you to marry me and you knew it. I had even bought a ring on the morning of Professor Beaumaris' murder. I was greatly looking forward to you returning from your fieldwork but you didn't.'

'Pooh! I would have had to wait until doomsday for you to propose.'

'I heard the news from Max. He enjoyed telling me too, that you and Laurence were having an affair and that you weren't coming back. I went to ask Professor Beaumaris if it was true. He confirmed that you had accepted the position of second-in-command of Laurence Tarleton's Damascus dig, that Laurence would be taking over as your thesis supervisor, and that you weren't coming back to Manchester.'

'Laurence was a useful tool in my career. He was still the golden boy of archaeology back then, before his career hit the doldrums of middle age.'

'He was a member of staff and you were his student. He had a duty of care towards you!' Harold exploded.

'He did care, rather a lot actually.'

'He was married and you knew it!'

'Don't be such an old maid Harold. Nobody cares a fig for those conventions,' She wrinkled her nose. 'Besides, I sent him back to his wife afterwards and because of me he never strayed from Rosamunde again. In fact, I helped their relationship.'

'You are completely impossible!' Harold Aldridge spluttered in rage.

'That is not the real reason, you are still mad at me, though is it?'

'You didn't even say goodbye to me. If nothing else, we were friends,' Harold looked desolate.

She could see the pain in his eyes and asked more gently, 'Harold have you been carrying a torch for me all these years? You could have married and had children yourself.'

'She wouldn't have been you and those children wouldn't have been ours,' he said sadly, turning and walking slowly up the stairs.'

'Harold, I wouldn't have made you happy,' she called after him.

He half turned towards her, 'I know,' he said and continued upstairs.

Lottie stood staring after him for a long time as if in a trance. Then she shrugged and picked up her papers and continued up to bed.

Poor Professor Aldridge, thought Dorothea, *No wonder he didn't mention what his interview was about with Professor Beaumaris on the day he died. Lottie and Laurence were lovers too! What a mess. I had better report all this to DCI Kydd but it feels rather disloyal to Professor Aldridge . . .*

MURDER BY THE BOOK

Good Friday Morning, 19th April 1935
Downstairs

At staff breakfast the next morning, DCI Kydd updated the young people on the tangled relationship between Professor Aldridge, Lottie Ellis and Laurence Tarleton.

Mary Short and Simon Culthorpe had taken the third watch of the night.

'We saw a rather interesting thing sir, at around about three o'clock in the morning. Maximilian Harrison left his room, went downstairs and spent an hour sounding the panelling in the drawing room. I watched through the gap under the door,' said Simon.

'Interesting, so Mr Harrison is pretty sure that there is a secret passage to find and it is worth his while being discovered in nocturnal panel knocking. Anything else? No? Then please do continue with your breakfast.'

***

Upstairs

Maggie an early riser arrived at breakfast before the rest of the house party. She helped herself to a heaped plate of bacon, eggs, and sausages which Mary Long and Dorothea had got up even earlier to cook and took her place at the breakfast table. She was soon joined by Maximilian Harrison with an equally loaded plate.

Maggie cast around for a topic of conversation and hit upon Max's favourite subject.

'I was wondering Dr Harrison, why you find St Boniface's curse so interesting and why it is pertinent today?' began Maggie as her opening gambit. Her prey took the bait.

'My dear Miss Maggie, of course the curse is pertinent today! Didn't the Magpie steal Geraldine's jewels, only a month ago, when the *Boniface Psalter* was on display? The previous time the psalter was going to be exhibited, Professor Beaumaris, my PhD supervisor, died in an extraordinary way. All through history, there have been examples of the curse wreaking havoc on those who didn't take it seriously enough. I know young people today don't have a proper appreciation of the supernatural, but time after time things happen that cannot be explained by science alone. What I find fascinating is the sheer versatility of the curse. Each story is different. There is always a twist.'

'I was thinking about what you told us last night at dinner about St Boniface's inscription. Surely he was a kindly, Christian man with an ardent missionary fervour. Why would he let loose a curse that would rampage down through the centuries?'

Max settled back in his chair and gave his beautiful, attentive audience a paternal smile and launched into his favourite lecture.

'Why indeed? The letter to King Æthelbald at the front of the *Boniface Psalter* is a fascinating insight into the relationship between Boniface, Æthelbald and Æthelbald's personal life, as well as being the primary source for the conception of the curse. What is less well known is that Boniface wrote some shorter annotations, within the psalter. There are fifteen annotations ranging from corrections of spellings and grammar, to theological comments, even some making reference to the curse. These have been rather passed over by other scholars and miss-assigned to more junior monks. I believe they give us a small window into St Boniface's own personality—'

Professor Aldridge had quietly entered the room and was helping himself to breakfast from the hot plates on the sideboard, when he accidentally dropped a serving spoon.

'Sorry, don't mind me.' Harold Aldridge was apologetic.

'In my doctoral thesis,' Maximilian Harrison continued, 'I showed that the handwriting of the inscription at the front of the book and the annotations were identical. I also identified three inscriptions that I believe pertain to the curse—'

'How many annotations did you say there were Max?' interrupted Harold Aldridge. 'I thought that there were twelve but then my memory isn't what it was.'

'Fifteen Harold. There have been some breakthroughs in the

past twenty years since you last studied the manuscript. You are quite out of date old chap.'

'Remind me Max, which are the annotations about the curse please? said Harold Aldridge.

'Gladly Harold, 1) Psalm 69 verse 24 is underlined with a note in the margin that translates as, "This means you Æthelbald." 2) Psalm 89 verse 23 is also underlined with a note in the margin which translates as, "Take heed Æthelbald." 3) Psalm 109 verse 8 is very faintly circled with a note in the margin of the Persian symbols from Daniel chapter 5 verse 7, "Mene, mene, tekel, upharsin," - that God had numbered Belshazzar's days of ruling, weighed him and found him wanting and was going to divide his kingdom between the Medes and Persians.'

'I remember now. My work was focused on the initial letter from St Boniface to Æthelbald. I struggle to remember what I had for dinner last night; never mind what my doctorate was about.'

Max patted Harold Aldridge sympathetically on the shoulder. 'Never mind old chap. It happens to the best of us eventually.'

Maggie marvelled at Professor Aldridge's portrayal of a doddery academic, when she knew he was as sharp as a tack.

'This is absolutely fascinating Dr Harrison. If you have finished, do come with me into the drawing room and tell me more about St Boniface's curse,' she tittered. 'You make it seem so real!'

Harold Aldridge was left alone in the dining room with his thoughts.

One, two, three, four . . . five, six, seven . . . eight, nine . . . ten, eleven, twelve . . . There were definitely only twelve annotations. So useful to have a photographic memory, Professor Aldridge thought. *What is Max up to?*

***

Downstairs, Upstairs

'Psst Dot and Mary, come and see what I've found,' called

Jinny across the hallway to where Dorothea and Mary Short were efficiently making up Sir Laurence Tarleton's room.

'What is it?' asked Dorothea, abandoning her task of straightening the bed clothes.

'Look what Geraldine has got in her knicker drawer,' whispered Jinny, carefully moving some flimsy undergarments to one side, to reveal a wad of used pound notes, held together with string and a little label with a picture of a magpie on it.

'It wasn't here yesterday when I unpacked her gear,' Mary Short leant over to see.

'Why would Geraldine Beaumaris receive money from the Magpie? How did it get here?' pondered Dorothea.

'Dot and Jinny, look at the bed,' called Mary Short noticing something amiss.

'I am looking. What am I looking for?' asked Jinny.

'The bed hasn't been slept in. It is exactly as I made it up before the guests arrived.'

'Sir Laurence Tarleton's bed has been well and truly slept in,' said Dorothea pointedly. 'I thought he must dream of wrestling pythons, the state it was in this morning but maybe him and our Geraldine were "together" last night.'

'An intrigue, how thrilling,' said Jinny, the staid vicar's wife.

'Excuse me ladies, have you tidied my room today?' asked Maximilian Harrison sticking his head around the door and making them jump.

'No sir, we haven't made up your room yet. We started at Dr Hadley-Brown's room and have turned out Mrs Hadley-Brown's, Mrs Beaumaris's and Sir Laurence's rooms. Mr Eric's and your rooms are next,' answered Jinny.

'Someone has been messing about with my book proofs and some of the pages are missing. I am going to get to the bottom of it!' The usually gregarious academic stomped off to complain to his long-suffering hostess.

Dorothea and Mary finished making up Laurence Tarleton's room, while Jinny dusted Geraldine's room. Together they moved on to Eric Tarleton's room, which they found was locked. Jinny tried to unlock it with the master key. She wiggled the lock and put her shoulder to the door but it would not budge.

'What has he done to this door? It was opening fine yesterday.'

'There are scratches next to the lock Jinny, see here and here. I think it might be a new lock, it looks so shiny, yet your master key is tarnished.' Dorothea touched the marks experimentally.

'Why would anyone change the lock Dot?' asked Mary Short perplexed.

Dorothea's face creased with worry. 'I really don't know. What has Eric got to hide?'

LIZZIE BENTHAM

Good Friday Afternoon 19th April 1935
Upstairs

All morning it rained and rained. From Mickering Priory's upper stories the expanse of flooding could be seen to its full extent. The priory was now an island, in a silty muddy coloured sea.

After lunch, Maggie decided that some entertainment was called for, so enlisted Maximilian Harrison's expertise for some secret passage hunting.

Geraldine Beaumaris and Sir Laurence Tarleton refused to join in. Geraldine declared it to be a "childish game". When Harold Aldridge saw that Lottie Ellis was amongst the secret passage hunters, he pointedly decided to mark some essays in the morning room.

Max suggested that the party start tapping the panelling in the drawing room. Maggie borrowed a dressmaking tape measure off Theodora and set Eric and Geraint to work surveying the proportions of the room, inside and out. While the two young men were at their task, Theodora, Lottie, Max and Maggie sounded the wooden panelling, listening out for any hollow spaces. They pressed the wooden carvings and plaster mouldings that stood out too, searching for a mechanism that would release a hidden door.

At three thirty Theodora rang the bell for tea. Balvan and Mary Short brought in refreshments for the intrepid passage hunters.

Geraint nipped downstairs to the kitchen in the hope of finding Simon Culthorpe, who was there helping Mary Long peel potatoes, while the chief inspector snoozed in a rocking chair by the fire.

'Shhhh Dr Hadley-Brown, DCI Kydd has just nodded off. He has been working very hard on the Magpie case recently,' said Mary.

'Please will you cast your eyes over this? It is a very rough plan of part of the ground floor. Simon, as an engineer, you must do technical drawing. Is there anything we've missed?'

MURDER BY THE BOOK

'You could do with the corridor dimensions. If you give it to me afterwards, I will check all your calculations. I am on the second watch tonight, so might do some panel tapping myself,' said Simon.

Returning upstairs, Geraint found that the search party had moved to the study. Eric had the carpet rolled up and the guests were energetically sounding the floor boards. Geraint tried not to chortle at the sight. He got down on his hands and knees to help. It was in this posture that Laurence Tarleton and Geraldine Beaumaris found them all ten minutes later.

'Absolute slander! What is the meaning of this Harrison? I know your flamboyant writing style when I see it,' shouted Laurence Tarleton apoplectic with rage.

'Calm down Laurence, you will make yourself ill,' implored Geraldine, following closely behind, wringing her hands ineffectively.

Sir Laurence backed Dr Harrison into a corner. He repeatedly hit a wodge of closely typewritten papers with his hand, gradually scattering them to the floor. Geraint, with great forethought kicked the nearest ones under a sofa for perusal later.

'I don't know what you are talking about Laurence.' Maximilian Harrison spoke slowly and calmly, as if to someone who had lost their grip on reality. 'Really old chap, have you been having a sneaky afternoon sherry?'

Unsurprisingly, this only antagonised Sir Laurence further.

'These are the proofs for the new addition of your dreadful book. In this document you accuse me of murder, ME A MURDERER! And not only a murderer . . . the murderer of our good hostess's only brother. Have you no scruples man? I AM NOT A MURDERER . . . You have absolutely no evidence. There was a tragic accident.'

'Laurence, you need to calm down darling,' bleated Geraldine.

'Of course my dear fellow,' said Maximilian Harrison reassuringly. 'We know you are not a murderer.'

'I know what I know. If any of these lies are ever published, I'll print what I know too.'

'Of course these were not for publication. I am writing a novel purely for my own pleasure, as well as the second edition of my book. Perhaps the two got muddled up. Wherever did you find them? I think one of the staff might have moved them by mistake.'

'Don't try and con me. Of course these are for publication. Someone had left them on the bed in my room. Just watch your step Max or your flaccid, dead body will end up floating in the flood waters outside, in the very near future.'

With that gruesome threat he turned on his heel and stormed out of the room. Geraldine tried to follow him but he slammed the door behind him, hitting her in the face.

Maximilian was white around the gills and his jaw was clenched hard. He knelt down to gather up as many of the pages as he could.

'You must excuse me, Theodora, ladies and gentlemen. I may have some work to do sorting out this mess.' He left hurriedly too.

Theodora, ever the hostess, fluttered around her guests making sure they had not been upset by this odd scene and rang the bell for cocktails as a distraction. While Balvan expertly mixed cocktails, Geraint surreptitiously lay down on the floor and reached under the sofa for the papers he had hidden which had got right to the back. Maggie scooted over and they divided them in half, to skim read quickly, before Maximilian Harrison realised some were missing and came back.

'I have got it, read this,' cried Maggie excitedly.

Geraint leaned over and read the following:

MURDER BY THE BOOK

The Search for Offa's Burial Place 1904 (Revised Version) by Dr M. Harrison

One young archaeologist pawed over old maps looking at past river courses of the Great Ouse. He took a great many auger core samples and studied soil specimens from up to a mile away from the main archaeological site. He was often found lying flat on his belly in a field, studying the topography of the land, or up the local church tower trying to spot earthworks from crop marks.

A colleague found him digging a small test pit in the farmer's field next door to the main excavation during the lunch break.

'What are you doing Michael? You do like to disappear off on a whim. I thought that Professor Beaumaris wanted you to excavate trench 3b another foot. It is pretty deep already and will need shoring.'

'I will do that this afternoon. I persuaded Professor Beaumaris to let me dig a test pit here. I am convinced we are excavating in the wrong place. By my calculations, the field we are digging in hasn't been truly underwater since the ice age. Five hundred yards this way, it is a completely different story. I found this in one of my core samples.'

He reached into his jacket pocket and pulled out a small box containing a bent, silver coin baring the profile of Cynethryth, Offa's queen consort, which the other young archaeologist inspected.

Michael pointed to the trench. 'I think I have hit a substantial stone foundation. See, there is a hint of pointed stone here and there are a few shards of Saxon pottery coming out from the same level. I will show Professor Beaumaris tomorrow when he gets back from giving his lecture at Cambridge. I hope he will let me extend it.'

'That looks promising . . .' There was an unusually calculating tone in the other man's voice, 'Much better than anything we have on the main site. Here let me give you a hand.'

An hour later they had uncovered a further three worked stones and some Anglo-Saxon floor tiles from a high status building, like a chapel or a manor.

'Very promising indeed,' said the calculating-sounding man again. 'Michael let's record this trench, then there was something in trench 3b that I spotted on the way here and in all this excitement I forgot to show you.'

They finished recording the archaeology together and went off to see trench 3b.

When Professor Beaumaris returned next day, he discovered the site in uproar. The evening before, Michael Quintrell had been excavating by himself in trench 3b, until late into the night. The walls had collapsed in on him, killing him. The disaster had only been found the next morning in the dewy light of dawn. The test pit in the next field had been filled in. No one could find Michael's drawings of it and in all the commotion, no one looked very hard.

Soon afterwards the excavation closed down due to a lack of results and a lack of funding because Michael's father pulled out as sponsor, due to financial troubles of his own.

Five years later, the other young archaeologist went on to make one of the major archaeological finds of his generation – the discovery of Offa's burial place in the field next door.

Primary Sources: Eyewitness accounts of members of both archaeological digs.

Upstairs

'Wow,' Geraint whistled. 'The implication that Uncle Michael was murdered in this is clear. Anyone who reads this will know that Max means "the calculating man," to be Laurence Tarleton. It is almost certainly libellous.'

'DCI Kydd should see this Dr Hadley-Brown,' said Maggie. 'Quick take it to him and Mary Long in the kitchen and ask her to photograph it. Then Jinny or Dot can take the whole lot back to Dr Harrison and pretend they found them while cleaning in here.'

'Good idea!' Geraint sped off to do what he was told.

***

Downstairs, Upstairs

To the south side of Mickering Priory there was a sheltered veranda where any of the guests that had both a tobacco craving and who wanted to blow the cobwebs away, went to smoke in the relative dryness of an overhanging cupola. It was still bone chillingly damp but at least the lashing rain did not venture far underneath.

DCI Kydd, in his chef whites, had crept away from the kitchen for ten minutes to find somewhere to smoke his pipe. He wanted to reflect on what his "spies" had gleaned so far about the inmates of Mickering Priory that had any bearing on the Beaumaris murder case.

Laurence Tarleton may or may not have caused Michael Quintrell's death all those years ago on the Offa dig. Geraldine Beaumaris was up to her eyeballs in the Magpie's insurance fraud scheme. Eric Tarleton was definitely up to something in his room but DCI Kydd was not sure what that might be. Why would Maximilian Harrison, a very odd man admittedly, write such libellous material and leave it around for someone to find and make mischief with? Theodora was lovely but erratic. Professor Aldridge was a jilted lover. Lottie Ellis was an unknown quantity. Was there any way that she could have been the unknown woman that Tristan Hadley-Brown saw in the museum? He needed to check the exact date she had left for Douma, but how with no access to the outside world?

The door through to the billiard room clicked open suddenly and with surprising speed DCI Kydd threw himself behind one of the pillars conscious that his alter ego, Monsieur Jean, should not be found smoking a pipe. On the windward side of the pillar he could hear very well but see poorly. His back was also getting soaked. Laurence Tarleton exited the billiard room onto the veranda to have a cigarette. He dragged on the butt angrily.

Lottie Ellis wearing her full oilskins came around the side of the house.

'Hello Laurence! I have been checking the old bus over. The spark plugs don't like this sort of weather even under cover.'

'What have you been up to Lottie?' asked Laurence Tarleton, suspiciously.

'Just what I told you Laurence, checking my spark—'

'No not that. A friend from the Turkish Archaeological Society contacted me recently. Someone, I won't say who, tried to sell a tenth century brooch to a local museum in the south of the country. The only provenance the brooch had was that it had been found "nearby." You are the only archaeologist who is currently excavating in that area and you are far too organised to let your dig staff steal any finds—'

'Looters do get everywhere Laurence. It is a sad part of the discipline we work in.'

'I know that Lottie. Remember I taught you . . . You always seem able to finance your digs when others of us struggle. Just how do you get funds to finance your excavations?' Laurence Tarleton laid a restraining hand on Lottie's arm.

'I am just exceptionally good at getting backers Laurence and I don't like your tone.'

'I think you skim off some of the choicest finds from your digs and sell them to private collectors for vast sums, so that you can continue digging, but academia loses out on valuable knowledge and beautiful artefacts,' he said accusingly.

'Very noble Laurence but you have absolutely no proof whatsoever.'

'My voice still carries weight in our discipline Lottie. People will listen to me.'

'It's sweet that you think that, but you haven't discovered anything major since Offa's burial place. After the revelations of this afternoon, even that seems to be thrown into disarray . . .' she taunted him.

'I did not kill Michael Quintrell.'

'Yes dear, so you say, but there is no smoke without fire as the old saying goes.'

'I could say the same about you.'

'You could Laurence but everyone knows we used to be lovers. They will just say you are being spiteful because I am now more successful than you. Your student has surpassed you.'

'I discovered Offa's burial. I am the greatest archaeologist of my generation, no matter what you say,' he hissed.

'Professor Beaumaris, now he was a man of integrity,' mused Lottie provocatively. 'He was gracious with you when your career surpassed his. It didn't stop him threatening to sack you, when he heard you had been dallying with his wife. Was that why you got me to take over your dig at Douma? Because you thought that you would be unemployed soon and would have to make your home closer to the excavation. Or was it because you wanted to keep your mistresses apart? Either way, Professor Beaumaris died very conveniently for you and your love life—'

'I didn't kill Professor Beaumaris either! What about you? You were meant to have left for Douma that day but I could have sworn I saw you from my office window, hanging around outside the museum that afternoon.'

'You are imagining things Laurence. As I was saying before you rudely interrupted, because of Professor Beaumaris' death you could stay on at the university, you could continue your liaison with his wife and I was successfully running your dig at Douma, oh and producing you an heir. The boy hasn't turned out so badly has he? He is handsome, clever and quite personable. It was such a good idea of mine, for you and Rosamunde to bring up the boy when you couldn't have children together. It left me free to get stuck into my work and I got to see the boy regularly growing up, as his godmother. I was sad to hear that Rosamunde passed away last year. Eric seems to be coping well. He is turning into an excellent young man. He is a dab hand on an archaeological dig too.'

'Stay away from Eric, Lottie. He has changed since Rosamunde's death. He is much more secretive. I don't want you to lead him astray.'

'Well really! I am a much better role model than you Laur—'

'Just stay away from him,' spat Laurence. He turned on his heel and headed for the French windows back into the billiard room.

Lottie snorted with laughter. She waited for a few minutes then followed Laurence inside.

DCI Kydd, returned to the kitchen, via the gardens, pondering what he had just witnessed. His moustache drooped with the amount of water it had absorbed. When Mary Long saw the state of him, she sent him upstairs to have a hot bath and get changed because he was shivering.

'We can't afford for our crime fighting secret weapon to catch a chill!' she said sagely.

***

Eric looked up from the billiard table as his father stormed through the room.

'Father about going to Tarsus with Lottie this summer . . . I think it would really help my studies to work on a 10th century excavation. Lottie's digs are always educational and she is a super teacher. I am sure I'd learn a lot.'

'Absolutely not! You are going nowhere with that woman,' said Laurence Tarleton. 'She is a bad influence on you. You have become secretive since spending time with her last summer. You never respond to my letters and telephone calls. Then you turn up out of thin air, like this weekend, when you want something . . . and her archaeological methodology stinks!'

'But you and Mother always let me go excavate with Aunt Lottie,' said Eric, shocked. 'I thought you and Aunt Lottie were old friends.'

'What do you mean by that? What did your mother tell you?' Laurence was sharp.

'Mother didn't say anything about your friendship with Aunt Lottie. I thought you were her doctoral supervisor, nothing more.' Eric was confused but his brain was working. 'Were you and Aunt Lottie something more?'

'Err no. Definitely not. No,' said Laurence, backtracking rapidly.

Lottie entered through the garden door, letting in a cold blast of air.

'Tell him Laurence,' she said gently. 'He has to know sometime.'

'Yes, tell me Laurence,' mimicked Eric.

Two identical pairs of brown eyes stared at Sir Tarleton, who now resembled a hunted animal.

'I am your father Eric but Rosamunde wasn't your mother. Your real mother is—'

'Me,' interrupted Lottie. 'I hope you can forgive me.'

Eric blanched with shock and then visibly pulled himself together. Choosing his words carefully he spoke with dignity.

'You have kept this from me all this time? I knew there was something odd. I thought the problem was with me, as if I didn't quite belong to our family, like I was a changeling. Well it turns out I am one, but the problem lies solely with your generation, not me and mine. You preach propriety, morality and caution, but struggle with the concept of fidelity. To hell with you both!' He turned on his heel and exited the room without looking back. His chastened parents remained fixed to the spot staring after him.

CHAPTER NINE

Deeds in the Dark

A Concise History of the Curse of the Boniface Psalter by Dr M. Harrison – The Quintrells and the Slave Trade

The Quintrells like many other noble families in the seventeenth and eighteenth centuries, owned sugar cane plantations in the West Indies. These were worked by enslaved people, stolen from West Africa by slave traders. They were transported like cattle across an ocean to undertake forced, manual labour for their enslavers, in horrendous conditions on the sugar plantations that supplied Great Britain with a commodity used by the rich.

The Quintrell's plantations were on islands subjected to frequent attacks, by whoever the enemy of Great Britain was at the time: the Spanish, the French, the Dutch or marauding pirates.

Mark Quintrell the eldest son of the 8th Baronet of Mickering, Sir Richard Quintrell, was sent to the island of St Joanna in 1738 to mind the family's newly acquired sugar plantation. Eventually he married a local heiress and started a family. She gave birth to a son, William Quintrell, but sadly she died a few days later from complications with the birth. Within days of the Quintrell's firstborn son being born, one of the plantation's enslaved women, Elsie, also gave birth to a son whom she named Benjamin. He was mixed race and bore the features of the Quintrell family. Elsie became the wet nurse for baby William. The two little boys grew up together, played together and fought together, unacknowledged half-brothers, one a free man and one a slave. When they were in their twenties, their father died and William was required to run the plantation on behalf of his grandfather, Sir Richard Quintrell, who was back in Britain and had never seen his Caribbean property. Benjamin a good looking lad, worked within the Quintrell household as a footman, trusted with the family secrets but was still not free. He regularly petitioned William on behalf of himself and of his mother to grant them their freedom, as Elsie was suffering from ill health. Even though Elsie had raised William and he was fond of her, he chose not to give the old lady her freedom and she died enslaved.

'I could not set her free because she might have left and I would have missed her,' He remarked to Benjamin.

William Quintrell wed the daughter of the governor of the island, a rich widow ten years his senior. He brought his new bride to live in the plantation house where his father had brought his mother.

Back in Britain, Sir Richard Quintrell died and the baronetcy passed to William, so he made the journey half way around the world to set his grandfather's affairs in order. After many months away, the new 9th Baronet returned home to discover his doting wife eager to share his bed and seven months later, she gave birth to a healthy baby boy, Simeon Quintrell. He was the image of his grandfather and great-grandfather before him. The little boy took a great liking to Benjamin and Benjamin to him. Benjamin stopped asking for his freedom and became like a second father to the child and Sir William Quintrell drew breath.

After a number of years, Sir William appointed a steward to look after the plantation and moved back to his ancestral home at Mickering Priory, with his family, servants and some slaves, including Benjamin.

The aguish conditions of the mosses did not suit Sir William, who was used to the humidity of the tropics and he got sick. The doctors said he would not survive and Benjamin nursed him through his final illness.

'You shall be a free man in my will,' croaked William between coughing fits.

'Thank you sir, but I shall not leave the boy.'

'What about your freedom man?' Sir William was incredulous.

'Simeon is fond of me and he would miss me,' said Benjamin firmly.

'Think of yourself man, the boy will cope.'

Sir William succumbed to another painful coughing attack.

Benjamin gently lifted his master's head and held a glass of water to his cracked lips.

'The boy is my son and he needs me,' said Benjamin very slowly and quietly.

'What?' The dying man's breathing was becoming more laboured.

'Sir William you have always known we were brothers. You wouldn't grant your own flesh and blood freedom when I asked for it. I wanted my children to be free. Everyone in the household knows that your wife is unfaithful, except you. She is probably dallying with the footman as we speak, just as she used to with me, while you were away overseas. My son is a free man, the great-grandson of the 8th Baronet and he will be an excellent 10th Baronet, the first with Africa in his veins. I will teach him well and he will oppose the filthy trade in human lives.'

Sir William Quintrell, 9th Baronet of Mickering, took a turn for the worse in the night and by next morning was dead. Benjamin stayed with Sir Simeon Quintrell, for the rest of his life. Sir Simeon Quintrell studied law, became a judge, then eventually a Quaker and an outspoken member of the abolition movement.

Primary Source: Sir Simeon Quintrell's own Bible which is different to the Quintrell Family Bible. Both are kept at Mickering Priory and the family trees in them do not match.

MURDER BY THE BOOK

Good Friday Evening, 19th April 1935
Upstairs

There was tension in the air after that afternoon's salacious revelations, as the guests assembled in the hallway for dinner. Laurence Tarleton was notable by his absence.

'Poor Laurence is feeling poorly and doesn't want any dinner tonight. He says he will stay in his room and will ring if he wants something,' announced Geraldine Beaumaris to the room in general.

No one offered sympathy. Laurence's dramatic display earlier had convinced those present, that on balance, he had murdered their hostess's brother.

The weather which had been squally all day had taken a turn for the worse, and there was now a full-blown storm hammering down outside. Lightning flickered and thunder rumbled all around them. Any chance that the water levels on the moss would recede soon was wishful thinking. The guests filed into the dining room in silence and uncomfortably sat down to eat dinner. Conversation was desultory. When Jinny dropped a serving spoon everyone jumped and Geraldine Beaumaris gave a little scream.

Just then the lights went off . . . and came back on again after twenty seconds.

'Don't worry ladies and gentlemen it is just the storm. We do have a back-up generator in case of power cuts. My father, the 13th Baronet, was a very, organised man in that respect,' said Theodora reassuringly.

'I'll ask Culthorpe to check that the generator is in order madam, just in case,' said Balvan firmly. To be trapped at Mickering Priory for the foreseeable future without electricity, was not something that Balvan was willing to risk.

'I still can't get over how you have retained such a talented and diverse staff Theodora,' commented Maximilian Harrison. 'If you are ever thinking of selling Mickering Priory, then you know I am still interested and would write you a cheque for whatever amount you asked for.'

'As always it is very sweet of you Max but Mickering Priory is my home and it is not for sale.' Theodora was annoyed but hid it well.

After dinner, Maggie suggested to Geraint, Lottie and Eric that they play bridge in the drawing room. Geraint who was not a fan of the game, tried to decline but the look that Maggie shot him caused him to change his mind.

She has an idea, he thought, *God help me!*

Eric too seemed to be reluctant to play but Maggie chivvied him as well. Lottie and Eric were partnered together. There seemed to be some constraint between them to begin with, which wore off as they became absorbed with the hands that they held. The game started fairly gently, with a slow trickle of bridge related conversation between the players but it soon became apparent that Lottie, Eric and Maggie were all excellent players, adept at calculated risk taking, whereas Geraint was only mediocre and was holding his partner Maggie back.

'You must know everyone here ever so well if you studied with them,' said Maggie ingeniously, to Lottie, as her opening gambit. 'What was everyone like when they were younger?'

'Yes do tell Godmother. Was Max as much of a windbag then, as he is now and did Harold Aldridge spend all of his time glowering?' asked Eric looking up from his hand.

'I shared an office with both of them, when we were studying for our doctorates. Max hasn't changed much. He was all bluff and bluster even then. He would boast to Harold and me about how great his thesis was going to be and all the contacts he made in the most prestigious archives. We never saw him do any work though. Maybe he was different while he was away on his archive trips. He was always off to somewhere rather obscure.

'When he was at the museum, Max spent all of his time chatting, or he was off drinking tea with his girlfriend, who at the time lived in the University Settlement next door. Well, that's what he said they were doing! They did get married in the end but she died young, probably in childbirth poor cow, and Max hasn't remarried. He says that he is still heartbroken for his Phyllis but I think he hasn't yet met anyone who loves him more than he loves himself.

'Harold was always very diligent and quiet. He was so shy that he wouldn't speak to me for my first few months doing doctoral studies. That's segregated education for you! Harold was constantly worrying if his research was novel enough, if he would get it finished in time, if someone might publish before him and if he would mess up his viva.

'The two of them were the epitome of chalk and cheese. In the end, it was Max who had a tough time at viva. It was whispered that his examiners only passed him (with major corrections), because his supervisor had been murdered. Then the war got in the way and he got a cushy desk job at the War Office. Who knows if he actually submitted his corrected thesis?

'Harold put his thesis on hold when war broke out. He ended up in military intelligence, which was the making of him. After the war he returned to Manchester and finished off his thesis with a different supervisor.'

'Was it Laurence Tarleton?' asked Geraint, looking up from his cards.

'No Harold preferred not to work for Laurence.'

'Were you there when "*it*" happened?' asked Maggie carefully. 'Theodora told me a little of what occurred. It must have been simply thrilling to be caught up with a murder.'

'No I had accepted a job offer the day before Professor Beaumaris was murdered, which meant I had to leave England immediately for Syria.' There was a hint of acid in Lottie's reply. 'I managed Laurence's dig for him at Douma while the murder investigation was underway. I had to do a full day's work and on top of that, had to write up my thesis. I was also feeling very queasy at the time I remember.'

'Why was that?' asked Maggie innocently.

'The local water played havoc with my insides,' was Lottie's quick reply.

'Rotten luck Godmother,' commented Eric not looking up from his hand of cards. Maggie noticed Lottie quickly glance at Eric and then away again, before a faint tinge of colour played across her sun tanned cheeks.

'Sir Laurence and Mrs Beaumaris seem to be . . . old friends,' Geraint suggested carefully.

'Geraldine has always been predatory when it comes to men. She managed to catch Professor Beaumaris, whom everyone thought was a lifelong bachelor. Once she had him, she moved on to her next toy, which happened to be Laurence. He was only interested in m— someone else. Geraldine has since had a string of rich gentlemen friends. Seeing Laurence again may have reignited her old passion.'

'I think you'll find that Lottie and I have just won that hand,' exclaimed Eric tallying up. We are beating you two hollow. Do you want another game or do you want to stop?'

Maggie winked at Geraint. 'Absolutely, Geraint needs another chance of proving himself.'

And while being thrashed at cards is painful, we are learning a lot, thought Geraint, resigned to his fate.

***

Upstairs and Downstairs

At ten o'clock Dorothea made two mugs of cocoa and went to find Geraint, who was joining her for the first watch. They sat side by side, companionably underneath the main staircase in the shadows.

'Hunting for murderers isn't all bad is it.' commented Dorothea, 'Even if we are stranded on an island with some very odd people.'

'I don't think your friends are odd,' he teased.

'Oi!'

'Shhh . . . Someone is coming.'

They watched in silence as Lottie came out of the study and climbed the main staircase, her footsteps boomed on the stairs above them.

Geraint waited until Lottie was out of earshot.

'Seriously Dorothea, I've enjoyed all of this . . . sleuthing, amateur dramatics and skulduggery. I'll miss it when life returns to normal, so will Mother.'

'I won't miss making up guests bedrooms every morning, including yours, curtseying, and polishing the silverware. Being a student is a whole lot easier, except when you set an evil essay question.'

'About that, Dorothea there is something I need to tell you,' said Geraint. He paused unsure quite what to say. 'I am thinking of applying for another job. There is a lectureship opportunity at the University of Reading being advertised. The English Department is small but very good. The lectureship is in my area of interest and I'd be nearer to MI5 headquarters for when Mr George wants me to be his golf caddy . . .'

'Oh . . .' was all Dorothea could say.

'A lectureship would give me a good enough income to think about settling down and getting married—'

'But you and your mother have this place. Surely you have plenty of money?'

'Not so I am afraid. When my distant cousin inherited the title of Baronet of Mickering when grandfather died, he got the family money, what was left of it and Mother got Mickering Priory. The mortgages on this place are astronomical and anything my mother has, goes on this place. I wish she would take up Max's offer to buy it. It has been nothing but a millstone around my family's collective necks for generations.' His vehemence startled Dorothea. Geraint noticed her shock and took both her hands in his.

'This house has seen so much unhappiness and I want to be happy, well, as happy as an agent can be, who has to serve two masters. I think I have found the very woman who can make me happy and understands my circumstances.'

Dorothea quickly drew her hands away.

'Is she in Reading?'

'No silly, she is right—' he broke off because there was a soft tread on the stairs above them.

They watched in silence as Theodora descended into the hallway. Her chestnut tresses, unleashed from their restraining pins, tumbled down her back, and her feet were bare. She looked younger in the glow from the candle she was carrying. Running freely down each cheek were rivulets of tears. She walked almost blindly in the direction of the drawing room.

When she returned, she was carrying an ornate, silver picture frame, which she hugged to herself, like it was a comforter.

'It's Uncle Michael's photo. He was her elder brother and she worshipped him,' whispered Geraint to Dorothea. 'The allegations of today have finally caught up with the old girl and opened up that old wound.'

'You need to go after her Geraint, check that she is alright. She looks heartbroken. I'll keep watch.'

Geraint squeezed Dorothea's hand in the dark.

'Thank you darling Dot. We'll talk again soon.'

He left her feeling bereft and elated simultaneously.

He called me darling! But why go to Reading? I don't understand any of it.

***

During the second watch of the night, Simon Culthorpe surveyed the downstairs rooms of the old wing of the house, checking the measurements that Geraint and Eric had made. Studying the plans of Mickering Priory rolled out on one of the tables in the library, he noticed that the measurements for the fireplace in the library appeared to be a little bit bigger than it needed to be, by about the width of a human being. Going over to the hearth, he knelt down and twisted any protuberances around the fireplace but to no avail.

I wonder if there is a hidden staircase going up to an opening upstairs in the room above, thought Simon. *Whose bedroom is directly above me? Laurence Tarleton's perhaps, or possibly Harold Aldridge's.*

Outside in the corridor, he heard stealthy footsteps which stopped outside the door. He grabbed the plans and dived behind some curtains into the alcove of a window seat. The door opened stealthily and through a convenient moth hole, Simon Culthorpe could see a man moving around the room, using a torch to help him navigate. The light gleamed off fair hair and Simon mentally attributed the newcomer's shape to Eric.

Eric began tapping on the panelling by the fireplace, close to where Simon had been working. He too must have noticed the discrepancy between the measurements.

Ten minutes later, Simon was starting to get cold because he was in a draught. Both men were startled when the door began to open, without any other prelude. Eric hurled himself behind a sofa and switched off his torch in one continuous motion.

Maximilian Harrison entered the room and began tapping on a floorboard next to a giant globe. He systematically worked his way over the exposed floor and started to sound the lower panelling on the east wall.

Simon, peeping through his spyhole, saw Max stiffen and then heard feminine footsteps outside in the passageway. Max's reacted quickly and shinned up the intricately carved spiral staircase. He prostrated himself on the upper library platform. Geraldine Beaumaris wafted through the door in curlers, hairnet and a mauve dressing gown, carrying a lamp. She found the section of the library containing modern paperbacks and chose one with a lurid cover, before wafting back out again, obviously looking for a bedtime read.

The three men in the room relaxed. Max came back down the stairs. He decided to finish secret passage hunting for that night, so disappeared off down the corridor.

'Achoo!' Eric sneezed loudly. It was dusty down behind the sofa and he had been holding that sneeze in for a long time. 'Achoo!' He left the room in a hurry to find a handkerchief.

This group of guests are certainly nocturnal, thought Simon.

He left to check with Jinny Moss, who was keeping watch upstairs that all the night time wanderers had returned to their own rooms.

CHAPTER TEN

The Curse Strikes Again

Early Morning, Easter Saturday, 20th April 1935
Downstairs, Upstairs

The weather had improved somewhat by Easter Saturday morning. A wan sun managed to squeeze out a few rays, giving the promise of a warm April day later.

Dorothea and Jinny started to clean the bedrooms while the guests were at breakfast. Laurence Tarleton's door was locked. Dorothea knocked on it.

'Can we come in to make up your room, sir?' she asked. There was no reply. She knocked again, even louder this time. 'Sir, can we come in to make up your room?' There was still no response. She was answered by a deepening silence. She tried the door but it was locked.

'I don't like it.' Jinny was worried.

Dorothea knelt down and looked through the keyhole.

'The room is still dark. Maybe Sir Laurence has been taken ill in the night. Jinny try the master key.'

With trepidation, the two young women opened the door.

'Sir Laurence?'

There was an odd smell in the room. Dorothea made her way to the thick drapes at the window and flung them back. Jinny let out a little scream and clapped her hands over her mouth. At the desk Sir Laurence Tarleton's leggy form was bent over at a strange angle. His revolver was in his hand and there was a dried crimson substance all over the desk.

'Don't touch anything Jinny. Quick get DCI Kydd. I'll wait here on guard,' said Dorothea.

***

Downstairs

DCI Kydd had got up early and had walked down the drive, to

where the water lapped against the road. He looked out over the flood waters. There was no way, except possibly by boat, that they would get back to civilisation at the moment. He had tried the phone line again and it was still out of order.

He heard running feet and his name being called urgently from back up the drive. Clarence Moss came running.

'You need to come quickly sir,' he said between gasps, 'Laurence Tarleton is dead and by his own hand.'

***

Dead Upstairs

Balvan was guarding the door to Laurence Tarleton's room when DCI Kydd and Reverend Moss arrived on the scene. Balvan had relieved Dorothea on Jinny's orders, with much protest from Dorothea and sent her to the kitchen to get a cup of sweet tea "for shock".

'Reverend Moss, please could you break the news to the rest of the household and have everyone gather together in the morning room. I will want to talk with them all shortly,' said DCI Kydd.

Reverend Moss nodded and left.

DCI Kydd entered the room and thoughtfully surveyed the crime scene. He examined the mortal remains of Laurence Tarleton, locked in an unnatural position by rigor mortis at the desk. It appeared he had shot himself in the right temple, with his revolver. He had then fallen forwards on to what, on closer inspection, revealed itself to be a possible suicide note, made illegible with a covering of blood.

'Balvan, please could you fetch Miss Long and Miss Shor. Tell Miss Long to bring her camera and Miss Shor, her medical bag. Have you ever dusted for prints? No? Well now you are going to learn. Please can you borrow some make-up brushes from the young ladies and some fine powders; talc, cocoa, powdered charcoal, even face powder would do at a push.'

'I know what you mean. I'll also find, tape, paper and something to act as a diffuser.'

'Good man!'

DCI Kydd's make-shift scene-of-crime team, was up and running within ten minutes. Mary Long, a little green around the gills, was grimly snapping away with her camera. Mary Short was calmly recording the temperature of the dead man. Balvan was carefully dusting the handle of the revolver for prints.

Wearing gloves, and being careful not to tear the fragile, saturated paper, DCI Kydd extracted it from under the dead man's head. Most of the words were covered in blood but he could read the first line. It said:

"Dear Theodora,
I apologise for leaving in this way. Events have taken a very strange turn—"

'That is an odd start to a suicide note sir,' said Mary Short, looking over his shoulder.

'Yes, it really is.'

In the distance they could hear a rumpus, which gradually got closer and closer.

'I must see Laurence! Where is my dearest Laurence? Something dreadful must have happened . . .' Geraldine Beaumaris had ignored DCI Kydd's orders to remain downstairs.

Reverend Moss and Theodora Hadley-Brown accompanied her, talking slowly and soothingly to her. DCI Kydd came to the door still dressed in his chef's whites and fake moustache.

'Get out of my way, my good man. I want to see Laurence!'

'I am afraid I can't let you enter the incident scene ma'am,' said DCI Kydd. 'It is not a nice sight I'm afraid.'

'You are Theodora's French chef. You can't tell me what to do.'

'I am DCI Kydd of the Manchester City Police Force and in this instance, I am afraid I can. It is for your own good,' he added more gently.

'He really is a police officer Geraldine. He has been doing some sleuthing on my behalf,' added Theodora apologetically.

Balvan Thakkar popped his head around the door. 'Both Marys

have finished what they need to do. Shall I arrange to move the corpse to the bed sir, so that we can photograph and fingerprint the desk?' he said.

'Why are the butler and maids allowed in, when I am not?' asked Geraldine petulantly.

'Reverend Moss can you help Balvan please?' asked DCI Kydd.

'Of course Chief Inspector,' answered Reverend Moss and went to help.

'He is the chauffeur, not a priest.' Geraldine was more and more puzzled.

'Come with me Geraldine and I will try to explain,' said an increasingly desperate Theodora, trying to drag Geraldine Beaumaris away by her hand.

Geraldine attempted to peer around the chief inspector's bulk and caught sight of the two men lifting their gruesome burden carefully from the desk on to the bed.

'Yuck blood!' cried Geraldine. 'Oh my Laurence!' She artistically fainted into DCI Kydd's waiting arms.

'Balvan and Reverend Moss please could you take Mrs Beaumaris to her room and Miss Shor will go with her. Mrs Hadley-Brown can you keep the rest of the guests in the morning room and I'll come and address them shortly,' said DCI Kydd authoritatively.

***

Upstairs and Downstairs Together

The Reverend Moss had gently broken the news to the ill-assorted group in the morning room, of Sir Tarleton's sad accident. Due to shock, all pretences had been dropped and former staff and guests mingled discontentedly, waiting for news.

'That was very crafty of you Theodora, to employ students to staff your house, an excellent economy. I would have sworn that they were all first-rate domestic servants. If any of them want a permanent position . . .' Maximilian Harrison started hopefully.

'They will all be returning to their studies after this.' Theodora broke in firmly, having returned from upstairs. 'They were doing me a favour.'

'It was a good ruse Theodora,' said Lottie thoughtfully, 'If that is what it was.'

'Dot, is that you?' Eric Tarleton was hunched up on the sofa, with his head in his hands, next to Lottie, who had a comforting arm around his shoulders. 'I kept catching glimpses of you hurrying away from me and I thought I was imagining things.'

'I am so sorry about your father Eric,' was all a shaken Dorothea could utter.

Eric stood up, crossed the room, and gave Dorothea a bear hug.

'I am so glad you are here Dot,' he said, kissing the top of her head. 'Everything will be alright now.'

She felt embarrassed to be singled out in front of the room, especially with Geraint Hadley-Brown present, but could see tears in Eric's eyes and felt it would be churlish to push him away.

Geraint noted the embrace and ground his teeth.

As DCI Kydd and his scene-of-crime team entered the room, nervous faces turned towards him.

'Thank you for your patience everyone. A tragic event happened last night. Sir Laurence Tarleton has died and on the face of it, it looks like he took his own life.'

'How dreadful DCI Kydd,' Professor Aldridge was visibly shocked, 'Was it an overdose?'

'No. It appears he shot himself sir, with his own gun.' DCI Kydd didn't mince his words. 'Did anyone hear the gun shot last night?'

Everyone shook their heads.

'The walls of the priory are very thick Chief Inspector,' said Theodora apologetically.

'I have co-opted some of the young people, with expertise in medicine and science, to help me investigate further,' continued DCI Kydd. 'We are cut off from the mainland for the moment, so we cannot call for help. I will conduct interviews with everyone today to help me piece together Sir Tarleton's movements yesterday, to prepare a report for the local police. Sir Tarleton's room is currently locked and is off limits. I would appreciate it, if everyone would agree to have their fingerprints taken too. This is standard police procedure. Dr Thakkar has kindly prepared some fingerprint cards and ink.'

'Did Laurence really kill Michael Quintrell to steal his discovery of Offa's burial place?' asked Lottie, giving voice to the shocking thought that everyone else was thinking. 'Maybe he killed Professor Beaumaris as well? Was there a suicide note?'

'Our investigations are on-going,' was all the chief inspector would say.

'St Boniface's curse has struck again,' said Maximilian Harrison smugly. 'Laurence would never believe me that it was a real phenomenon. Little did he realise that he would be its next victim because of his past crimes. You can't outrun the curse I always say.'

'I think we will leave this "curse" for now sir and focus on the real world.' DCI Kydd was curt. 'Everyone please make your way to the dining room for fingerprinting.'

***

Geraint sidled up to Maggie in the queue for fingerprints.

'Um . . . Dorothea and Eric Tarleton are they close friends?' he asked.

'Well they have been on a couple of dates recently,' she replied.

'Oh . . . Does Dorothea like Eric?' he asked timidly.

Maggie decided to take pity on him. 'He is tall, good looking and pays her attention. Yes she likes him . . . but I don't think she loves him. You are quite safe there. She loves someone else, a stiff-necked, prickly, sarcastic fossil.'

'Who?'

'You, you great, big fossil! For goodness sake, pull your socks up and ask Dot out. She won't wait forever you know.'

'Oh . . . right . . . thanks.'

LIZZIE BENTHAM

Medical Report on the Body of Sir Laurence Tarleton for DCI Kydd by Mary Shor

I, Mary Abigail Elizabeth Shor, a second year medical student at the Victoria University of Manchester, currently residing at Mickering Priory, examined the body of the late Sir Laurence Tarleton at nine thirty one a.m. on Saturday 20th of April 1935.

I checked for signs of life and there were none. He had a bullet entry hole on his right temple, presumably from the gun that was cradled in his right hand. The wound was neat, approximately three quarters of an inch wide and there was no sign of charring to the skin from the firearm (see photographs taken by my colleague Miss Mary Long).

The exit wound was a little lower than the entry wound, by about two inches and came out at the base of the deceased's left ear. It was significantly larger than the entry wound, approximately three inches and had bled profusely.

This suggests to me, that the gun was pointing a little downwards and was not touching the temple, when the deceased pulled the trigger. It seems an odd position for one to kill oneself in, but not impossible.

Sir Tarleton was sat at his desk but had fallen forward on to his left arm that was laid on the desk. He was a tall, thin man (six foot two inches), so had hunched slightly.

Rigor mortis appeared to be fully set in when I examined the corpse (I will continue to monitor its progression over the next day or so). Sir Laurence's internal temperature was eighty four degrees Fahrenheit and his external temperature was sixty four degrees Fahrenheit and the room temperature was fifty seven degrees Fahrenheit. There were the remains of a fire in the grate, so the room might have been hotter when Sir Tarleton died and have cooled down over night. I have extrapolated his time of death to about twelve hours previously, around nine p.m. the evening before, on Friday the 19th of April, using a table from my medical textbook. This is pretty inaccurate so he might have died as early as seven p.m. or as late as eleven p.m. I have tried to record as much information as possible, to allow the police surgeon to reassess my timings, when they examine the body.

In the room with Sir Tarleton was a dirty plate which had contained his dinner. Without doing a post mortem, I was unable to ascertain if it was Sir Tarleton himself who had eaten the food but he did have a piece of broccoli stuck between his teeth, which suggests he probably did eat some, if not all of his dinner.

Signed: *Mary Abigail Elizabeth Shor*
Dated: *20th April 1935*

LIZZIE BENTHAM

Late Morning on Easter Saturday, 20th April 1935

In an old house you can find many things used and then discarded by past generations. Theodora pointed Balvan and Mary Long towards the attic, where she believed there might be some equipment from her father's short lived photography hobby. After some digging, they discovered several boxes filled with crusty lidded chemical bottles and curling paper. Together, they set up a makeshift darkroom in a disused cellar and began to process the material they had obtained.

When DCI Kydd found them, there were pieces of wet paper hung up on a washing line, with faint traces of fingerprints and Sir Laurence's dead face beginning to emerge from the blankness.

DCI Kydd held out an envelope to Balvan. 'Here is the bullet to fingerprint. I have just dug it out of a monstrous wardrobe. I really appreciate both of you helping me.'

'It is no bother sir. Despite the tragic circumstances, we are having a really interesting time,' said Balvan calmly.

'This is so much better than cooking! Jinny, Dot and Theodora are sorting out lunch and Reverend Moss has offered to hold a quiet service in the old chapel for prayer and reflection. What has Shorty said about the body sir?' asked Mary Long, as enthusiastic as a puppy, now she was looking at photographs of the dead man and not the real thing.

'She isn't happy with the angle of the bullet hole and neither am I. We have been crawling around the crime scene with tape measures for the last hour and we can't make the ballistics work. The only way that the bullet could have ended up embedded in the wardrobe, was if Sir Laurence was hovering above his chair with bent knees when he pressed the trigger. Not a comfortable position in which to take one's own life and he was a tall man too.'

'So you think he was in the process of standing up to talk to someone when he was shot?' asked Balvan astutely. 'That would fit with the fingerprints on the revolver or lack of them.

MURDER BY THE BOOK

Look here, it has been wiped clean, then some wobbly faint fingerprints belonging to the dead man were on the gun grip, as if someone had pressed the gun into Sir Laurence's hand once dead.'

'By Jove you are right!'

'Here are the photographs of the letter Sir Laurence was writing.' said Mary. She had been clever with lighting and filters to reveal the hidden message. 'It isn't remotely like a suicide note,'

DCI Kydd read the following:

"My dear Theodora,
I apologise for leaving in this way. Events have taken a very strange turn and I cannot apologise enough that you had to listen to such tasteless and unfounded allegations earlier. I will leave your house as soon as is possible. I remain your faithful serv—"

'It breaks off there, as if he was interrupted halfway through writing it,' added Mary Long.

DCI Kydd stroked his fake moustache thoughtfully. 'On the evidence we have here, I have no other option than to move this forward as a murder inquiry. Would you agree?'

The two young people looked at each other. Balvan voiced what they were thinking.

'We agree too. We would stake our reputations as chemists . . .'

'And photographers!' added Mary Long.

'...And photographers on it sir.'

'How simply thrilling!' added Mary Long.

'We are stuck on an island, with no outside help and with a murderer, who may, or may not have killed more than once,' said DCI Kydd sternly.

'Good point Chief Inspector.'

'For the record, where were you both between seven and eleven last night?'

'I was with you DCI Kydd in the kitchen up until nine thirty playing Rummy. Then I went upstairs to the staff quarters with

Shorty, as we are sharing a bedroom and I was asleep by ten o'clock. I didn't wake up until my alarm clock went off at six o'clock this morning,' said Mary Long.

'I was also with you in the kitchen sir, except when serving the dinner in the dining room to the guests, which I did with Mrs Moss and Mary Short. Then I served drinks in the drawing room, also with Mrs Moss, at eight thirty. I locked up the house with the help of Simon, just before ten o'clock and stayed talking to you in the kitchen until nearly ten thirty, when we both retired to bed. I share a room with Simon, so heard him come and go for his watch shift and then I got up at two o'clock, to do my watch shift with you. Our watch was totally uneventful,' said Balvan.

'Excellent you two,' said DCI Kydd making notes. 'You make very good witnesses. I will start interviewing the other members of the household. Please keep our murder theory under your hats for now. I want Sir Laurence's murderer to believe that we don't suspect anything. Lock up this room when you leave. This is our evidence of murder.'

MURDER BY THE BOOK

CHAPTER ELEVEN

Tactful Questioning

Afternoon on Easter Saturday, 20th April 1935

DCI Kydd sat in the kitchen thinking hard. He had taken statements off all of the staff and was confident that the young people had alibis, for the time period that Mary Short suspected the murder to have been committed. That meant the murderer was on the other side of the green baize door. Hardly surprising when he was already looking for a murderer from within that group.

On this side of the green baize door, most of the daily chores had been accomplished by dinner time yesterday. All of the staff had gathered together in the staff dining hall, when they were not working, to exchange news and to rest. At that time of the night, they also tended to work in pairs, or threes, so no one was ever on their own.

Yesterday Balvan had rung the gong for dinner at six thirty. Prior to that, Mary Long and Dorothea had worked tirelessly in the kitchen plating up starters and getting the main course ready to serve. Balvan, Mary Short and Jinny worked together to prepare the dining room, then served the house party guests their dinner.

While the guests were eating their main course, the staff had sat down to their meal in the staff dining hall. The only person to go anywhere on her own during this time was Jinny, whom Theodora had asked to take a dinner tray up to Sir Laurence Tarleton and she was the last person to see Sir Laurence alive.

When questioned by DCI Kydd, Jinny Moss said, 'I knocked on Sir Tarleton's door and he called out "Who is it?" I said, "Mrs Moss, Sir Tarleton, with a dinner tray for you." He said, "Leave it outside please and I'll be out for it shortly." As I got to the end of the corridor to come down the backstairs, I looked back and his door opened and he picked up his dinner tray and took it back inside, closing the door behind him. I came straight back to the kitchen. It was ten to seven when I got back because I looked at the kitchen clock.' Jinny was adamant that it was Sir Laurence that she had seen. She had got a good look at him in the lamp light.

This sighting at ten to seven was the last fixed point by a reliable witness that DCI Kydd had of Sir Laurence being alive.

I wonder if anyone left the table upstairs during dinner, thought DCI Kydd.

After dinner, Balvan, Jinny and Mary Short had cleared the dining room, while Mary Long and Dorothea cleaned up the kitchen and the men started on the washing up. After the jobs of the day had been finished, they had all sat down together to play Rummy until nine thirty.

The game was paused at eight thirty for Balvan and Jinny to take the drinks tray up to the drawing room, where the guests had retired to after dinner. At the same time, Dorothea and Mary Short had turned down the guest's beds and supplied hot water bottles to those who required them. They had got no answer when they knocked on Laurence Tarleton's door and assumed he was already asleep or ignoring them.

DCI Kydd was thankful, that he had instigated a night watch rota. He could be fairly certain that the murder had happened before ten o'clock when Dot and Geraint had taken the first watch, though Geraint admitted there was a five minute window when he put a distraught Theodora back to bed. That incident raised a whole other kettle of fish, one of motive. Other than the midnight visits of Eric, Max and Geraldine to the library, on Simon and Jinny's watch, there had been no further disturbances that night according to his spies.

What it all came down to, was finding out where the guests were between six fifty, when Mrs Moss saw Sir Laurence alive and ten o'clock at night, when Dot and Geraint took first watch and who had a motive.

Unfortunately all of the guests upstairs, excluding Maggie, had a motive for killing Sir Laurence Tarleton. This was rather grim, because it meant that even people the chief inspector liked were now potential suspects going forward. In his orderly mind, he classified the possible motives:

Revenge: Sir Laurence Tarleton had been accused in a roundabout way of killing Michael Quintrell and had acted like a guilty man, thus giving both Theodora and Geraint Hadley-Brown, Michael Quintrell's relatives, a motive for murdering him.

The jilted lover: Sir Laurence Tarleton had stolen Harold Aldridge's girl, Lottie Ellis, years ago. Dorothea, who had overheard Lottie and Harold's conversation on the first night, had noticed that Harold was still hurting all these years later.

Prevention of academic disgrace: Laurence had threatened Lottie with disclosure for ignoble archaeological practices when funding her digs. He had also banned Eric from joining Lottie's Tarsus dig in the summer. Could thwarted maternal love also be a motive?

To hide a crime: Eric was definitely up to something . . . something criminal? Had Laurence Tarleton found out Eric's secret and would he have given his son up to the police?

A lover's quarrel: Geraldine Beaumaris had made it clear that Laurence Tarleton was hers. Maybe he had told her that their dalliance was at an end and she had killed him in the heat of the moment. Had Laurence Tarleton also murdered Geraldine's husband Professor Beaumaris? Maybe Geraldine had found out and had killed Laurence in retribution.

Fear of Disclosure: Maximilian Harrison had written some rather scandalous things about Sir Laurence Tarleton in relation to Michael Quintrell's death on an archaeological dig. Sir Laurence had retaliated in front of witnesses, with a threat to expose Max for some undisclosed thing.

He decided to interview Maggie first. She was in the unique position of being a spy in the midst of his suspects and DCI Kydd hoped she might have noticed something.

Going through the green baize doors, he headed to the drawing room to begin interviewing the guests. He was about to call for Maggie when Dorothea entered the room, looking anxious.

'Please can I help DCI Kydd? I feel so responsible. It was my idea to hold this weekend. I am sure Laurence Tarleton was murdered. It is too much of a coincidence to be anything else. I thought that since you are without PC Standish I could take notes for you.'

'Miss Roberts, none of this is your fault, believe me.'

'Please may I help?' Dorothea looked pale but determined.

He thought ruefully about the time it would take himself to write up all of the notes on the staff's movements properly and capitulated.

He smiled, 'Thank you Miss Roberts. That would save me valuable time.'

***

Maggie

Maggie told DCI Kydd what Lottie had said about the other members of the house party during the bridge game the previous evening. Her other major news was about Professor Aldridge.

'Chief Inspector, I think the professor knows or suspects something. He was behaving very oddly at breakfast yesterday. He and Dr Harrison disagreed over the number of annotations by St Boniface in the psalter that they are obsessed with. Max said there were more than Professor Aldridge remembered. It made the professor look very thoughtful. I think you need to ask him what he suspects.'

'What were your own movements yesterday please Miss Forshaw?'

'After playing bridge I went to bed early, because Professor Aldridge and I had the final watch of the night, between four and six a.m. I have a room on the ground floor directly under Geraldine Beaumaris' room and I couldn't get to sleep because of her music playing, it went on until after midnight.'

'Did you hear the gun shot?'

'No I did not. I think I would have though, if it had happened after I had retired because my room shares a wall with Sir Laurence's room.'

MURDER BY THE BOOK

'Did anything happen on your watch?' asked DCI Kydd.

'It was a bit odd really. Harold Aldridge could not keep awake. At four a.m. he was pretty groggy and he fell asleep and snored! Normally he seems to be a very lively, active gentleman and he has told me that he was in intelligence during the Great War. I don't think it was old age catching up with him. I think he was drugged!' said Maggie.

***

Geraldine Beaumaris

'Theodora says you want to interrogate me,' said Geraldine, flouncing into the room, 'though why you should is a mystery, because I don't know why my Laurence would want to kill himself and I am simply devastated by it. Anyway, I want to report a theft. Someone has stolen my jewellery box, the contents of which are simply priceless. You should certainly be looking amongst the servants for the class of villain that would be a thief.'

'Firstly ma'am, I want to ask about your movements last night. When was the last time you saw Sir Laurence alive? I want to get an idea of what his mood was like in the hours before his death. Secondly, all of the staff here are university students or graduates, who were posing as servants to help Mrs Hadley-Brown out for the duration of this weekend. They are not part of the criminal underworld. Thirdly, I wanted to inform you as a courtesy, that I am reopening the enquiry into the death of your late husband Professor Beaumaris. You inherited his fortune I believe? Finally, there is a little matter of insurance fraud with regards to the Giant's Tear neckless that we need to discuss.'

Geraldine Beaumaris wilted visibly. 'I have just remembered that I haven't lost my jewellery box after all. I must have misplaced it and I am sure one of the staff . . . err . . . young people will find it for me soon.'

'Beginning with the theft of your necklace Mrs Beaumaris, why did you receive half the value of the Giant's Tear necklace in used banknotes when you arrived here from the Magpie? Perhaps the Magpie or an accomplice is trapped here with us. I suggest you be truthful Mrs Beaumaris. It will help your defence in court if you help the police now.'

'How do you know?' Geraldine Beaumaris's mouth flapped open and shut like a landed fish.

'Dinkworth, Dinkworth and Small, the company that insure your jewels, are very suspicious of so many of its client's heirlooms being stolen and then claimed for all at once. They are employing a very efficient young man, a private detective, to investigate the insurance fraud and he came to see me.'

Geraldine sagged. 'I'll tell you what I know Chief Inspector. Being a patron of the arts is a very expensive occupation. Recently I have been struggling to make ends meet, so when my friend, Tilly Marshall, told me about this scheme I was so desperate I didn't stop to think.

'I made contact with the Magpie through a P.O. Box address and received my orders and a key, back by return of post. At the opening of the Anglo-Saxon Art exhibition at the museum, when a diversion happened, I was to take off my necklace and stick it to some clay under my seat. Then I had to lock myself in the broom cupboard from the inside, which was what the key was for. I was to say that I was attacked by a gun-wielding thug dressed in a rag costume. I did not enjoy being inside the cupboard, as I get terrible claustrophobia, so I really was distressed by the time I was rescued. I checked my seat later and the necklace had disappeared. I then had to wait for the pay-out from the insurance company, who have been very slow, I must say.' Some of Geraldine's normal 'Geraldineness' peeped out for a moment. 'On top of the pay-out, the Magpie sells the jewellery and gives you half of the profits, so as the owner you get one and a half times the worth of the object, a very good return . . .' she caught DCI Kydd's eye, 'If it wasn't illegal,' she sighed.

'Have you kept the message from the Magpie?'

'No, the note said to destroy it once I had memorised what I had to do.'

'Do you have any idea who the Magpie is?'

'None Chief Inspector, except the Magpie must be here with us, because the money was slipped into a drawer in my bedroom on our first day here.'

Which one of us is the Magpie? thought DCI Kydd. Aloud he asked, 'What were you saying about your jewellery box being stolen?'

'The bank is threatening to call in the mortgage on my Didsbury house.' Geraldine looked ashamed. 'I thought I could try the same scheme again, but cut out the Magpie. I didn't put my jewellery case in the safe at the start of the weekend. Instead, I kept it in my room and have hidden the jewellery in the cistern of the bathroom. I am not as creative as the real Magpie.' She sounded so forlorn, that DCI Kydd almost felt sorry for her.

'We would have found them you know. The police are taught to search very thoroughly. Can you please tell me what your movements were yesterday and when you last saw Sir Laurence Tarleton.'

'He went off in a huff after confronting Max with that silly story Max had written about Michael Quintrell. I was absolutely mortified for poor, dear Theodora. What a terrible thing to happen at her house party.'

'Quite. Do you know who stole Dr Harrison's book proofs and placed them on Sir Tarleton's bed for him to find?'

'I did wonder if it was the Magpie. It seems like something they might do. When I tried to follow Laurence out of the room he shut the door in my face and disappeared. I played the piano in the music room but it was terribly out of tune, then I went upstairs to get ready for dinner. I joined my fellow guests at the dinner gong. After dinner I went up to my room. I knocked on Laurence's door on my way but he shouted, "Go away Geraldine," so I did.'

'What time was this?'

'About eight o'clock.'

'And you are sure it was him?'

'I'd know Laurence's voice anywhere,' she dabbed her nose with a handkerchief. 'I borrowed the gramophone from downstairs and listened to it in my room while I got ready for bed and finished reading my book. I tried to go to sleep but I couldn't, so around midnight I got up and went to the library to find myself something else to read.'

'Did you notice anything odd while you were there?' asked the DCI Kydd remembering Simon's account of the incident.

'No nothing.' Geraldine wasn't a noticing sort of person.

'Did you hear the shot from the gun?'

'No Chief Inspector, I was listening to Beethoven's *Für Elise,* such a terribly sad and moving piece.' Tears started to well up in Geraldine's eyes.

'Were you having an affair with Sir Laurence Tarleton?' He asked gently.

'Yes,' she sighed. 'We hadn't seen each other for many years until recently at the museum for the exhibition. After my husband's death, Laurence moved his office back to the main university campus, so our paths no longer crossed.'

'Did you have an affair with Laurence Tarleton, when your husband was alive and did he find out about it?'

She nodded cautiously.

'Your husband had a number of meetings on the morning of his death and some of them weren't cordial. These were with Tristan Hadley-Brown, Harold Aldridge, Maximilian Harrison and Laurence Tarleton. We already know that Professor Beaumaris had discovered that Laurence Tarleton and Lottie Ellis were having a relationship, which was why Lottie was sent to Douma to get her out of the way. To find out that his own wife was also having an affair with his protégé, Laurence, must have come as a shock.'

'My husband was absolutely furious. Someone, one of those other three, must have told him that morning. Probably Max, the world's biggest gossip. My husband summoned Laurence to his office, berated him and sacked him on the spot. He wanted Laurence out of the museum by the end of the day. I was comforting Laurence and helping him pack his things. I totally forgot that I should be helping Theodora to sort out refreshments. When my husband died, it seemed most fortuitous; Laurence and I could finally be together. However Laurence became cold and distant. He left for Douma on sabbatical. On returning, he took over my husband's old role, became a devoted husband and new father to baby Eric, so I didn't see him anymore.'

'Did you kill your husband Mrs Beaumaris so you could be with your lover?'

'No! Absolutely not!'

'Do you suspect Laurence Tarleton may have killed your husband to protect his reputation and to enhance his career prospects?

'I am sure he wouldn't have,' though Geraldine sounded a lot less sure.

'Why do you think Sir Laurence Tarleton killed himself?'

'I don't know! We had only just got back together again after twenty years,' her distress was obvious. 'Please find out why Laurence killed himself Chief Inspector, and who murdered my husband. I don't care what happens to me.'

She walked out of the room with her head held high.

***

Professor Harold Aldridge

Professor Harold Aldridge entered the room and smiled to see Dorothea helping DCI Kydd.

'Do come and sit down Professor Aldridge. I have some questions I would like to ask you about your movements last night and when you last saw Sir Tarleton alive.'

'So it was murder then? I thought as much. I won't tell anyone. What do you want to know?'

He is sharp, thought DCI Kydd, inwardly speculating at the likelihood of the professor having actually killed his love rival. 'There are a few anomalies sir, but we are hoping to clear these up with some routine questions,' he replied.

'Absolutely, mum's the word.'

'When did you last see Sir Laurence Tarleton?'

'I missed the drama about Max's book revelations because I was marking essays in the morning room but I poked my nose out of the door, when I heard shouting. I saw Sir Laurence Tarleton hurtle past and into the billiard room. That was at around four o'clock.'

'Did you see him again after that?'

'I did not. Miss Roberts might be interested to know about the essays I was marking though. I have brought them with me. Here is your essay. B+ my dear, as it was a little ropey around the edges. Here is Eric Tarleton's essay, an A+. It is typewritten but the similarities between the two are plain to see. As if Miss Roberts' one is an earlier draft of Eric's.'

'That's my essay word for word. I had to go back to using an earlier draft when my work got stolen at the inn and I didn't have Dr Harrison's book for reference any more . . .' Dorothea thought hard. 'Eric was the intruder in my room . . . But why?'

'Another facet of Eric's character just fell into place,' murmured DCI Kydd. 'Going back to last night sir, what did you do then?'

'I worked until it was time to change for dinner, a little after six o'clock. I then joined the rest of the guests in the dining room at six thirty. No one left the table until eight when we adjourned to the drawing room. Lottie, Maggie, Eric and Geraint made up a four for bridge. Geraldine disappeared after dinner. Theodora, Max and I listened to a wireless programme, in the morning room, which had a jolly good fire going. Dr Thakkar and Mrs Moss brought the drinks tray in at eight thirty and Max fixed us all a drink. We must all be getting old or it was a very dull programme because all three of us dozed in front of the hearth, until the bridge party finished next door at around nine thirty. I then went to bed, getting up at four o'clock in the morning to share the last watch of the night with Maggie, when not a lot happened. I may have nodded off.'

'Did you take any sleeping pills before going to bed, only Maggie thought you might have been drugged,' asked DCI Kydd.

'No, no I didn't,' Professor Aldridge looked stunned at the idea.

'Or hear the shot fired?' asked DCI Kydd.

'Again no.'

'How was your relationship with Sir Tarleton,' asked Dorothea gently. 'We know about you and Lottie. Surely it must have been odd to meet up again after all these years.'

'The perennial question of motive I see. I did have a grudge against Sir Laurence, many years ago for "stealing my girl" but I did nothing about it then and after all these years I am too old and lazy to do anything about it now. Lottie was right. We would not have made each other happy. Maybe I owe Laurence a debt of gratitude for driving a wedge between us.'

'One final thing, Maggie thought you might have stumbled across something in relation to Dr Harrison and his wretched curse,' said DCI Kydd.

'I studied the *Boniface Psalter* minutely for my thesis. If Max ever stopped to listen properly, he would know that. He told me that there are fifteen annotations in the psalter written by St Boniface, apart from the letter to Æthelbald at the front. He is wrong, there are only twelve. This made me think about why Max had a meeting with Professor Beaumaris on the morning of his murder twenty years ago. Max said it was to talk about his thesis.'

'What are you suggesting?'

'What if Max annotated the *Boniface Psalter* himself, to strengthen his case for the curse?'

'Theodora did say that Professor Beaumaris wouldn't stop to talk to her that day because of a case of "intellectual fraud" he was investigating,' added Dorothea. 'Maybe that is what Sir Laurence meant yesterday when he threatened Max.'

'What would have been the outcome for Dr Harrison if it was proved that he had annotated the *Boniface Psalter* himself?' asked DCI Kydd.

'He wouldn't be "Dr" Harrison for a start. Max would have failed his doctoral studies and have been sent down from the university in disgrace. No one would have employed him in academia and no self-respecting publisher would have published his book.' Harold Aldridge was emphatic.

'So Dr Harrison's life would have been very different, if it was

proved that he had falsified his doctoral thesis.'
'Yes indeed Chief Inspector.'

***

Dr Lottie Ellis

Lottie came into the room with less of her usual *joie de vivre*.

'I suppose you will want to know what my movements were yesterday evening, Chief Inspector,' said Lottie settling herself into the chair.

'Yes please, starting from the last time you saw Sir Tarleton.'

'The last time I saw Laurence was when we were all treasure hunting in the study and he burst in and accused Max of writing libel, which was overly dramatic and very Laurence.'

'I have a creditable witness that overheard you and Sir Tarleton on the veranda at about five o'clock having an argument. He threatened to expose you for malpractice, in regards to selling artefacts from your excavations to fund future excavations.'

Lottie threw back her head and laughed.

'I did see Laurence Tarleton at about that time on the veranda and yes, we quarrelled. We always did when we were together for any length of time. As your witness would have heard, no one would have believed Laurence, because the accusation would have been taken to be sour grapes in our archaeological community. His career is stagnating, whereas mine is blossoming.'

'What did you do next?'

'I had an accidental family reunion in the billiard room, DCI Kydd. Eric wanted to come to Tarsus with me in the summer. Laurence was being a pompous bore. He decreed Eric wasn't allowed to go. Then it all came out that I am Eric's real mother. Laurence and I had an affair when I was studying for my doctorate. Eric was understandably shocked by the news but by later that evening, he seemed to have come to terms with his real parentage.

'Afterwards I went upstairs to get ready for dinner. The guests gathered just before six thirty, minus Laurence. After dinner Eric, Geraint, Maggie and I, played bridge until nine thirty. Then I fetched some work from my room and sat in the study until ten o'clock, after which I gave up and went to bed. I slept like a log until the morning.'

'I saw Dr Ellis going up to bed at ten o'clock,' said Dorothea from the corner.

'Dr Ellis did you see or hear anything odd at all, either of the times you were upstairs yesterday evening?'

Lottie Ellis looked thoughtful, 'No I can't say I did. I definitely didn't hear the shot but then no one would have been able to, over the mournful music that Geraldine was playing.'

'Going back to the veranda conversation, my witness says that Laurence accused you of having been seen near the museum on the day of Professor Beaumaris's death. Tristan Hadley-Brown, Theodora's husband, thought he saw a woman inside the museum, who no one managed to identify. Were you there and were you the unknown woman Dr Ellis?' asked DCI Kydd. 'When I get back to headquarters I will initiate a search of passenger lists for boats that sailed to Syria in the spring of 1914. If you were on a different boat to the one you told the original investigation, I will find out.'

For once Lottie was serious. 'I didn't sail straight away for Syria, from Southampton. I did come to the museum on the day of Professor Beaumaris's death and stood outside for a while thinking. By then I knew I was pregnant by Laurence Tarleton. I thought Harold Aldridge was about to propose and I wondered if maybe I should accept him, to give the child a decent upbringing. I dithered around outside for half an hour but I left at three thirty and I never went inside. I decided against marrying Harold because it wasn't fair to him, so hopped on a train to Southampton and boarded the boat the next day. Laurence Tarleton and his wife raised the boy as their own. Rosamunde Tarleton died last year. Don't tell Harold will you please. He already thinks I am the Whore of Babylon.'

'Thank you for being so candid with me Dr Ellis. Is there anything else that might have a bearing on the case?'

'Not that I can think off Chief Inspector.'

***

In the Morning Room

While he was waiting his turn, Geraint tried to write to the head of the English Department at the University of Reading, in response to her advertisement for a lecturer in English Language. He was struggling because his fellow castaways kept interrupting his train of thought. They were all on edge and bored, in equal measure. Anything that was even remotely a distraction was welcomed.

He had already turned down an offer of an introduction to the head of the History Department at Reading from Maximilian. His mother had volunteered to proofread his application. Geraldine had told him there was a position for a trustee coming up at the museum and that he should apply. Professor Aldridge offered to write him a reference, which Geraint had accepted distractedly and Lottie had read what he had written over his shoulder and then made snide comments about his handwriting.

When Eric Tarleton came over, Geraint braced himself for some more interference with his job application.

'I am sorry for your loss Eric,' began Geraint warily.

'Thank you, I appreciate your condolences. I just don't know what to think or feel. It is all so strange and warped. If it wasn't for Aunt Lottie and Dot, well I don't know what I would do right now.'

'You and Miss Roberts are taking Professor Aldridge's first year Anglo-Saxon course together aren't you?' Geraint asked. 'Miss Roberts has been worried that you would recognise her, since your unexpected arrival, and has taken pains to keep out of sight. Do you know her well?'

Eric chuckled, 'I would have recognised Dot anywhere, so she was sensible to steer clear of me. She is just so damn pretty, even wearing a maid's costume. Did you see her this morning sitting next to Mrs Moss? They make a picture don't they, though my

Dot has the edge.'

'Do you have an understanding with Miss Roberts then Eric?' asked Geraint silently cursing.

'Its early days yet Dr Hadley-Brown but I would consider ourselves to be walking out. I am devastated that I wasn't able to introduce her to my father, as I am sure he would have adored her. It gives me some comfort to know that he did sort of meet Dot, even if it was only to ask her for a clean bath towel or an extra cake of soap . . .'

'Quite,' Geraint was not sure how to reply but had an inkling that Eric was deliberately trying to provoke him.

'I believe that June is a good month to get married. I was wondering how to go about popping the question. How would you woo a girl sir? Over dinner?' asked Eric innocently.

Geraint was saved from having to answer, by DCI Kydd calling Eric through for his interview. Geraint spent the next thirty minutes staring at a blank piece of paper in front of him, wondering how much of an idiot he had been not to declare his love for Dorothea when he had the chance.

***

Eric Tarleton

'Firstly, I wanted to say how sorry I am for your loss Mr Tarleton,' said DCI Kydd, sympathetically.

'I just can't believe Father would do such a thing.' Eric was visibly upset. 'I know that since Mother died last year, he has struggled and I have seen a lot less of him due to my studies and his latest dig. Mother was the glue that held our little family together. Father gave up his academic position at the university a few years ago, to care for Mother when she first got sick. He has only recently restarted his academic career.'

'Can you think of any reason why he might have killed himself?'

'No sir, unless he really did have something to do with Michael Quintrell's death, or the other death which Dorothea told me about.'

He smiled wanly at Dorothea and she blushed. She felt embarrassed for being indiscrete and telling Eric about their investigations at the museum. She wondered what DCI Kydd thought of her.

'What were your movements last night please? When was the last time you saw your father?'

Eric's face clouded. 'We parted with cross words, for which I will never forgive myself. Lottie and I last saw him in the billiard room, before dinner. He told me that I wasn't to go with Lottie on her Tarsus dig in the summer. My parents always let me go and help with Auntie Lottie's digs. The only excuse he gave me was that supposedly Lottie's archaeological methodology is suspect. This seemed odd to me, so I pursued it with him and to cut a long story short, it turns out Lottie is my real mother. Lottie and Laurence had a fling while she was studying under him and well, I am the result. I was shocked and said some things I regret now. I have had chance to reflect and my life makes a lot more sense with this knowledge. I loved my mother, Rosamunde, but we were such different personalities. She always wanted to know what Father was doing and who he was doing it with. I thought she was a wife who was very invested in his work. It turns out she had cause to question his fidelity in the past.'

'What happened next?'

'I was fuming while I got ready for dinner but then I saw Lottie again and realised how lucky I am to have her in my life as a mother figure. I stopped being angry and started to find it funny, that my straitlaced father had such an almighty secret.

'After dinner Lottie, Maggie, Dr Hadley-Brown and I played bridge, then when the game broke up, I played billiards with Dr Hadley-Brown until just before ten o'clock, then I went up to bed.'

'Did you see or hear anything while playing billiards or when you went upstairs to bed?'

'No sir.'

'Did you leave your room once you retired for the night?'

'No sir.'

'Even to go secret passage hunting?'

Eric grinned, 'You've got me there sir. I did go to the library at about midnight. Dr Harrison's stories had caught my interest and I couldn't sleep for thinking about it.'

'Did you see anyone else?'

'Dr Harrison and Mrs Beaumaris came into the library, separately, while I was there. I hid behind the sofa because I was so ashamed of my boyish enthusiasm for pirate treasure,' he laughed self-deprecatingly.

'Eric where were you on Friday the 22nd of March this year?' Dorothea piped up.

'In my spare time I like to explore the local countryside on my motorcycle. The story of the *Boniface Psalter* had got under my skin so I motored over to Mickering Priory to have a look. It was very foggy so I turned around and went back home. That is one of the reasons I invited myself this weekend, because I didn't get to see the priory then.'

Eric's eyes locked with Dorothea's throughout this speech. He seemed so sincere but Dorothea knew he was lying.

'Why you have changed the lock on your bedroom door Mr Tarleton?' asked DCI Kydd.

A shade of annoyance flitted across Eric's face, to be replaced by his normal urbane countenance. 'It is a practice I picked up in Egypt after my hotel room had been robbed by the maid. I have some boxes belonging to Lottie, full of archaeological dig supplies, which I was returning to her and I didn't want any of the staff here tampering with them.' He looked at Dorothea, 'Not that they would of course.'

DCI Kydd gave him a long, hard look. 'Is there anything else you would like to tell me Mr Tarleton?'

'I can't think of anything else sir.'

'Is he a friend of yours?' asked DCI Kydd casually, when Eric had left and Dorothea was tidying up her notes.

'Sort of DCI Kydd, Eric is on my course. We have been out for tea once and the cinema once.' Dorothea felt the need to be stringently accurate.

'He is a bit casual with the truth. He seems honest and open but then he tells great big whoppers. I wonder why? I don't buy his tale about being robbed in Egypt, as the reason for changing his bedroom lock.'

'To be honest, I was surprised that Eric introduced himself to me at all. He and his friends aren't interested in talking to girls, unless the girl is startlingly beautiful and/or wealthy, or they have skipped a lecture and need to copy lecture notes.'

'Do you like Eric, Miss Roberts?'

'I think I am going off him rapidly Chief Inspector!'

CHAPTER TWELVE

Raising More Questions

Late Afternoon on Easter Saturday, 20th April 1935

While the house party were altogether having an awkward afternoon tea, DCI Kydd picked the lock on Eric Tarleton's door, with a skeleton key, while Reverend Moss stood watch.

'This is thrilling Chief Inspector, the law and the church, breaking into the villain's lair. I am sure I could use this to illustrate a sermon.'

'We don't know he is a villain yet, Vicar. We are assuming he is, based on the fact that, no innocent person invites themselves to someone else's house party, then changes the lock on their bedroom door. In my experience everyone is guilty of something; it's just the level of something that differs. You are guilty of enjoying skiving off Easter services more than you should be.

Reverend Moss tried to look contrite but failed.

'I am guilty of trusting absolutely no one, not even you Vicar. Eric Tarleton is hiding something, therefore, he has a guilty conscious which hopefully . . .' he wiggled the skeleton key, 'Ah ha! Will lead us to discover what it is he is guilty of.' The lock clicked and DCI Kydd opened the door and slipped inside.

Eric Tarleton's room was a major anti-climax. It was similar to all the others in this section of the house. There were some clothes thrown over the back of a chair, along with his motorcycle leathers and a battered old suitcase, which held Eric's clean underwear. Poking around under the bed, DCI Kydd found a couple of cardboard boxes. They were labelled as belonging to Lottie Ellis, care of the archaeological dig in Tarsus. Inside there were supplies that an archaeologist might need on a dig; some trowels, paint brushes, bandages for stabilising delicate finds, sticking plaster, solvents for cleaning and first aid purposes, tape measures, drawing materials and a large bag of plaster of Paris. This caused the policeman some excitement, until he tried a few grains on the tip of his tongue to discover it was exactly what the label said it was.

Disappointed, he methodically checked the rest of the room for whatever it was Eric was concealing and found nothing. Sensing defeat, DCI Kydd relocked the door behind himself.

'At lunchtime I went into the coach house to check over the cars. Eric was in there messing around with his motorcycle. I thought it was odd after he had just heard that his father had died. Maybe he moved whatever it is he doesn't want anyone to find, into his vehicle?' said the Reverend Moss helpfully.

'You could have said so earlier Vicar,' grunted DCI Kydd, not best pleased. 'We still have time, let's go and have a look.'

In the coach house they drew a blank with Eric's motorcycle. There appeared to be nothing untoward about the machine at first, until DCI Kydd's prying fingers found that the end of one of the structural metal tubes holding the sidecar in place, had a stopper that unscrewed. Cautiously, he levered the cap off to discover a space inside. Unfortunately Reverend Moss's flash light showed that it was empty.

'This isn't standard for this model. Eric must use it to transport something,' said DCI Kydd thoughtfully. 'So what is this "*something*" and where could it be?'

'Eric did one more thing when he was in here. He patted Lottie Ellis's car on the boot as he was leaving. I irritated me because I had to polish his greasy handprints off it,' said Reverend Moss thoughtfully.

'Good observation Vicar! Let's take a look at Dr Ellis' Bugatti.'

It took them a lot longer to find than the cache on the motorbike, but Reverend Moss eventually spotted a brown paper package under the passenger's seat held in place with sticking plaster. Opening it carefully with a pen knife, so as not to disturb anything, DCI Kydd drew out a sparkling circle of emeralds.

'Ah the ballerina's bracelet if I am not very much mistaken, stolen by the Magpie during the opening night of Swan Lake,' he said.

Lottie Ellis and Eric Tarleton

'You wanted to see us both again Chief Inspector?' asked Lottie Ellis.

She and Eric Tarleton had re-entered the library. Interviews had restarted after the break for afternoon tea. Lottie looked bored, Eric looked wary.

'This bracelet was found hidden in your car, Dr Ellis. Can you explain how it got there please?' Like a conjurer producing a dove from a hat, DCI Kydd placed the stolen emerald bracelet on the desk in front of him.

Lottie eyed it dispassionately. 'I have been looking for that for months.'

'Is it yours Dr Ellis? Think carefully before answering. It is the exact match of the bracelet stolen from the Koning's suite at the Manchester Hotel, last month, by the Magpie.'

'That is definitely my bracelet DCI Kydd. It has nothing to do with the Magpie,' answered Lottie coolly.

Liar! DCI Kydd's subconscious shrieked.

Turning to Eric he asked, 'Reverend Moss saw you in the coach house earlier today and you placed your hand on Lottie's car reverently. Can you explain what you were doing?'

'I make sure that my bike is turned over daily in this weather.' said Eric carefully. 'Lottie asked me to do the same with her car. I checked that her car was working, then left. Nothing more.'

Two pairs of brown eyes, in similar elfin faces looked back at DCI Kydd guilelessly.

'Mr Tarleton we found a modified cache, in your motorcycle, that was empty. What do you normally kept there please?' he said, trying to surprise Eric.

'I don't know what you are talking about. Have you broken my motorbike?' For the first time there was a flicker of fear in those brown eyes.

'Correct me if I am wrong. I think you Mr Tarleton are the Magpie, the notorious jewel thief. Maybe you got into this racket for the kicks, or for the intellectual challenge, or maybe it is purely about the money for you. I believe that you came to this party to deliver Geraldine Beaumaris her share from the sale of the Giant's Tear necklace. I think you hid the money and the prima donna's stolen bracelet in the cache, in your motorcycle, on the drive here. You gave Geraldine Beaumaris her money but kept the bracelet in your bedroom and changed the door lock to stop anyone from finding it. You need to get the bracelet out of the country to your associates in the Middle East, who sell the Magpie's loot to private buyers. Mr Gritty, a private enquiry agent working for an insurance firm, informed me that Mrs Beaumaris' necklace was sold in Ankara for eight thousand pounds. I think you package the jewels up in legitimate supplies that are sent out to Dr Ellis' digs. Once there, one of your associates retrieves the jewels and flogs them for you.

'Your father's death made you worry that your room would be searched, if the police were called in to investigate. You transferred the jewels back to a vehicle but this time to Dr Ellis' car for safe keeping. I think that you are an opportunist, hence the night-time treasure hunting and searching the other guest's rooms. It was you that found Dr Harrison's book proofs, read them and left the most salacious bits to be found by your father, pure mischief making on your part. What do you say to that?'

Lottie laid a warning hand on Eric's arm. 'An interesting theory DCI Kydd, but you are wrong. I am the Magpie and I am willing to sign a statement to that fact,' she said.

'Aunt Lottie . . . Mother—'

'Hush now Eric. I will handle this. Please give me some paper DCI Kydd and I will write that statement.'

Reluctantly DCI Kydd handed Lottie a pen and paper and she dashed off an exciting and highly colourful account of her actions as the Magpie.

'You do know that wasting police time is an offence Dr Ellis.'

'I am brilliant, a good organiser, I have contacts in the antiquities trade in the Middle East, and some would say I am morally reprehensible. You need look no further for your Magpie Chief Inspector! I promise not to run off anywhere until the police are able to get through to us, you have my word.'

And much good will it do me, he thought, as Lottie and Eric exited the room hand in hand. *She makes a plausible case but I wonder...*

***

Dr Maximilian Harrison

'I do hope you have managed to get your book proofs back into some sort of order sir.' said DCI Kydd cordially, as Maximilian Harrison took a seat.

'It has been a slow task but I have made much progress.'

'Do you always travel with so many personal items Dr Harrison? Your typewriter, book proofs and even your own ornaments?' asked Dorothea, who had dusted them all.

'My typewriter is a very superior model and I find it helps the creative juices to flow if you don't have to keep stopping to unstick keys. The deadline from my publisher is a month hence, so I am using every spare moment to finish my manuscript. As for my ornaments, well one has to have a muse...'

'Can Miss Roberts use your typewriter to type up her notes from these interviews, as it is such a good specimen?' asked DCI Kydd.

'Be my guest,' replied Maximilian but he looked unhappy about it.

'Regarding your book Dr Harrison, you wrote a passage about the death of Michael Quintrell, Mrs Hadley-Brown's brother, which happened in 1904 on Professor Beaumaris's archaeological excavation. You seem to suggest that a young Laurence Tarleton had something to do with Michael's death. Have you any evidence?'

'I am a historian, one of the greatest who has ever lived. I did my research. I talked to members of the original dig. Comments were made suggesting there may have been foul play. Some of those I spoke to were also present on Laurence Tarleton's excavation five years later. They mentioned his uncanny sense of where to dig. The first trench he laid out on day one, hit the chapel, where Offa was buried.'

'Presumably you have transcripts of those interviews that I could see please?'

'Alas Chief Inspector they are at home.'

'Would you have actually included that story in your book, Dr Harrison?' Dorothea asked.

Maximilian laughed heartily. 'Of course not, Laurence was correct yesterday when he said it was a libellous accusation. I wrote it merely for completeness and it would have stayed a private matter, except for someone meddling with my things. Have you discovered the culprit yet?'

'My investigations are ongoing,' said DCI Kydd smoothly. 'Could you tell me what your movements were yesterday afternoon?'

'After the scene in the library with Laurence, I took my disarrayed manuscript up to my room to begin the reparation process. After about twenty minutes, Mrs Moss brought me some more pages that had been found under the sofa. I worked on my book until dinner when my mind was more serene. I joined my fellow guests in the dining room for a most depressing meal.

'After dinner Theodora and Harold wanted to listen to the wireless in the morning room. It was all rather dull and I am afraid that I dozed off for a bit. I woke up when the card party broke up and went upstairs at about nine thirty to continue with writing my book. I didn't hear a sound. I certainly didn't hear a gunshot being fired, so can only assume that Laurence was killed earlier.'

'Did you remain in your room for the rest of the evening sir? I have a witness that says they saw you hunting for a secret passageway in the library at around midnight.'

Maximilian Harrison had the grace to look embarrassed. 'Err yes. The romance of hidden treasure was the lure that took me exploring.'

'Did you see anyone?'

'I don't want to get a lady into trouble . . .'

'Geraldine Beaumaris has already admitted to fetching a book from the library.'

'Then I can confirm that I saw Geraldine in the library at that time.'

Trying a different track, DCI Kydd asked, 'I believe that you and Professor Aldridge have some differing opinions on the *Boniface Psalter*.'

'Harold Aldridge and I are old friends. We agree on more than we disagree about.'

'Like the number of annotations in the psalter?' asked Dorothea, innocently.

'Harold's memory is going, poor fellow. It is a long time since he studied the psalter first hand. There are categorically fifteen annotations made by St Boniface himself in the manuscript and three make reference directly to the curse.'

'Professor Aldridge is adamant that there were only twelve when he was a doctoral student and he gives no impression of senility. Did Professor Beaumaris and Sir Tarleton know how many annotations there were in the manuscript? I think the interview that you had with Professor Beaumaris on the morning of his murder twenty years ago, might have had something to do with the annotations in the psalter.'

'You are wrong. It was a constructive meeting about the next steps to writing my thesis. Nothing more, nothing less. If you have finished, I do have a deadline to meet. Especially if the young lady,' he indicated Dorothea, 'is going to be using my typewriter later today . . .'

DCI Kydd nodded assent.

***

Theodora and Geraint Hadley-Brown

DCI Kydd called Geraint Hadley-Brown in next. Geraint was looking more harassed than usual and did not look in Dorothea's direction.

'Can you tell me when you last saw Sir Tarleton alive please, and what your movements were yesterday evening.'

'The last time I saw Sir Tarleton alive was in the library, when he was ticking off Max for writing about Uncle Michael's death. I got dressed for dinner and accompanied Mother downstairs to the dining room when the dinner gong sounded. Everyone was on edge despite Mary Long's excellent culinary skills. Maggie persuaded me to play bridge after dinner until nine thirty. I played billiards with Eric Tarleton for a bit afterwards. He called it a night just before ten. I then took the first watch with Miss Roberts from ten o'clock until midnight. The only thing of note that happened, which I feel obliged to tell you, was that my mother came downstairs at ten fifteen, obviously distressed by the allegations of the day. I went to check up on her and stayed for five minutes, before returning to my post—'

CRASH!

The door flew open and Theodora Hadley-Brown stood in the doorway clasping a handkerchief case to her bosom.

'Chief Inspector I have something that I need to show you and my son.'

'Mother, what are you doing?'

Theodora extracted a letter and key from the cherished handkerchief case and gave them to Geraint. DCI Kydd and Dorothea moved closer to peer over his shoulder and read:

"My Dearest Theodora,

Forgive me, my love, for everything that has happened and for everything that may happen. My mind is in turmoil but looking at your photograph, which I keep in my pocket and thinking of you, comforts me in the day-to-day hell in which I am living. I should have listened to you with greater attention. I let you down as a husband. Rest assured I will always do my upmost to protect you and the children. I enclose my copy of the key to the cabinet of death and entrust it to your guardianship. I found it two days after Professor Beaumaris' murder, replaced in its usual home in my desk drawer. Do with it, what best ensures your peace of mind and safety. I feel so guilty that I am not with you and fear that my luck is running out. I must go now and ready my men. We attack at dawn. No matter what has happened, I will always love you, my very own, sweet Theodora.

MURDER BY THE BOOK

All my love
Tristan"

'Mother! Why didn't you tell us about this before?' asked a startled Geraint.

'Or take it to the police twenty years ago?' added DCI Kydd sternly.

'And have that uppish DI Dawlish attribute the murder to Tristan, when he was no longer here to defend his reputation, close the case and let the real murderer walk free? Absolutely not! I knew my Tristan and he was no murderer. This way the case has remained open all these years and whoever did it, has lived with the niggling fear they might one day get caught. This was my punishment to the murderer for taking my husband from me.' Theodora burned with a white-hot anger, which was painful to watch. In a more normal voice she said, 'DCI Kydd, I think we have found that person. Laurence Tarleton took his own life last night, after being exposed as my brother's murderer. I think he killed Professor Beaumaris too and that guilt mixed with fear of exposure made him take his own life.'

DCI Kydd read and reread the letter carefully. 'What do you make of your husband's letter and key? I remember we turned the museum upside down looking for it.'

'I know Tristan was innocent because in his letter he shows great concern for me. We had no secrets from each other. If he had committed the murder ... which he didn't do, he would have told me. His eyesight without his glasses was poor and he had misplaced them that day. I think that he thought the woman he had seen, might have been me and he tried to protect me. Especially when I said I had seen him in his office when I brought him tea, but in reality he wasn't there. Tristan knew I was lying, so he lied too to protect me. He thought that I had returned the key to his office a few days later. We made a right old mess of it between us,' there was fondness in her voice. 'I think Laurence stole the key from Tristan's office, and used it to kill Professor Beaumaris. He managed to hide it for a couple of days and then returned it to Tristan's desk to throw suspicion on to my husband!'

On the face of it, it makes sense, thought DCI Kydd. *Sir Laurence Tarleton killed Michael Quintrell so that the archaeological find of the century was his, not Michael's. He killed Professor Beaumaris to protect his academic reputation and to carry on his numerous affairs uninterrupted. Then yesterday, when Maximilian Harrison confronted Sir Laurence with his crime, he decided that he could not live with the guilt and committed suicide. It all sounds very plausible except that Sir Laurence Tarleton was murdered. Theodora wants this version of reality to be correct because it exonerates her husband Tristan. Did she or Geraint Hadley-Brown go so far as to murder Laurence Tarleton?*

Out loud DCI Kydd said, 'Mrs Hadley-Brown what were your movements yesterday evening please?

'I saw that dreadful man in the hallway before going upstairs to dress for dinner, just before six. I was tidying up some drooping tulips on the hall table when Eric Tarleton rushed out of the billiard room, nearly knocking me over and stomped up the stairs, without any apology. Moments later, Laurence also appeared out of the billiard room. He totally blanked me and headed upstairs after Eric. I didn't see him again.

'After fixing the flowers I came upstairs to get dressed for dinner. Geraint knocked on the door just before six thirty and we went down together. All of my guests were at dinner, except Sir Laurence. After dinner, I wanted to listen to a wireless programme which was a musical reflection on Easter. Harold, Max and I went to the morning room to listen. At eight thirty I checked on the bridge players and rang for the drinks tray. The morning room was very cosy and I fell asleep listening to the programme. I think Harold and Max did too. I was woken up by the bridge players saying goodnight at around nine thirty. I went upstairs but I couldn't sleep because I was thinking about Michael. I got up in some distress to find his photograph from the drawing room. Geraint checked up on me at about a quarter past ten. I then slept fitfully for the rest of the night.'

'Did you hear the gun shot Mrs Hadley-Brown? Did you Dr

Hadley-Brown?

Mother and son shook their heads.

'Can I hold on to this letter and key for now Mrs Hadley-Brown?'

'Of course Chief Inspector. I'll leave you to continue interrogating my son. So sorry for barging in.'

'Thank you for your candour Mrs Hadley-Brown. Mr Hadley-Brown, unless you have anything else to add you may go too.

***

Dr Lottie Ellis Again

In the silence following the departure of the Hadley-Browns, Dorothea passed DCI Kydd a piece of paper.

'I think that I have spotted a discrepancy between two of the suspect's accounts sir.'

'From last night?'

'No from twenty years ago. Lottie Ellis said she saw no one outside the museum and she was stood outside for half an hour, so she was there from three until three thirty. Well she should have seen someone during that time . . .' Dorothea showed him another statement.

'Let's get Lottie Ellis back in here a third time.'

Lottie Ellis came back into the room looking ruffled and ready to fight. 'Really Chief Inspector, I have already admitted to being the Magpie and promised I would remain here at the law's pleasure . . .'

'Dr Ellis this will only take a minute. Think back to waiting outside the museum on the day of Professor Beaumaris's death. Did you see anyone, anyone at all, come out of the museum by any route?

'No DCI Kydd I did not. Not a soul,' answered Lottie.

'Could you see the main door from where you waited?'

'Yes, I sat on a bench in the grounds. I remember that I shredded my sandwich to pieces rather than eat it. My mind was in such turmoil about what I should do for the best. Well I made my choice and I think it all turned out pretty well considering.'

'Thank you. That is all I wanted to know.'

Sitting back at the desk DCI Kydd said, 'I am starting to get an inkling of how both murders were staged, but there is no evidence at all, nothing that will stand up in court.'

'What do we do now Chief Inspector?'

'Now I put everyone on their guard. I want everyone to get home safely from this island. The best way to achieve that is to make sure that everyone is watching everyone else's backs.'

CHAPTER THIRTEEN

A Murderer Amongst Us

A Concise History of the Curse of the Boniface Psalter by Dr M. Harrison – The Quintrells of the Georgian Period

Lady Quintrell, second wife of Sir Simeon Quintrell the 10th Baronet, was clad in a diaphanous nightgown; her fair curls were bobbing, bare feet padding quietly on the wooden floorboards. She held a dribbling candle in front of her, shielding it with her other hand, as she negotiated the journey back to her own bed chamber, in the early hours of the morning. A satisfied smile played across her lips.

Her husband who was over twenty years her senior was a respected judge and a Quaker abolitionist. He was away at the Lancaster assizes and so could not share her bed. Her nose wrinkled at the thought of him. He had fallen in love with her, married her against the council of his friends and grown-up daughters, and had lifted her out of a state of near destitution. While grateful to him for her new position in society and well-schooled in the role of dutiful wife, she did not love him and was certainly not faithful.

She smiled in remembrance of the energetic love making session she had just enjoyed with the handsome young man staying in the blue suite. The memory of his lithe body made her shiver with pleasure and the candle wobbled dangerously in her hand.

Peregrine Quintrell was the black sheep of the family. Perpetually in trouble with his uncle, Sir Simeon, for gambling and womanising, he was known to be a rake by all of the matchmaking mamas of the elite "ton". He was also heir to the title, after the death of his one male cousin in infancy. Lady Quintrell knew that Peregrine's nose had been put out of joint when his staid uncle married a 'social-climbing guttersnipe' (her stepdaughter Louisa's words), but soon discovered that he and his new aunt, five years his junior, were kindred spirits and the handsome pair initiated a passionate affair at Mickering Priory.

She giggled to herself, let herself into her own chamber and locked the door behind her. She crept across the floor and was about to sit down upon the bed, when a voice from a wing backed chair said mildly; 'Hello wife, where have you been?'

Lady Quintrell shrieked and dropped the candle on the bed, where it set light to the dry bed linen and then her nightgown. Panicked, she ran around the room patting ineffectually at her dress and whimpering in pain, scattering sparks. She ignored her husband's calls to stay still so he could wrap her in a rug. He tried to pour the water jug over her but she could not, or would not stay still. New flames ignited all around the room and smoke engulfed them.

The baroness, now alight like a human torch, crazed with fear and pain, ran and jumped through the window. She disappeared with a splash and a rain of shards of glass into the murky moat. Sir Simeon, unable to find the room key in the inferno, exited the room the same way as his wife, through the window into the moat.

He survived the fire that destroyed the whole of the Tudor wing built by his ancestor the 1st Baronet of Mickering. His wife did not.

History tells us that the Sir Simeon rebuilt Mickering Priory in the regency style. He got married again to a young widow and had three sons with her. His adulterous nephew now disinherited, died of cholera in a debtor's prison.

Primary Source: The prison doctor's report of the fevered ramblings of Peregrine Quintrell on his death bed.

MURDER BY THE BOOK

Evening of Easter Saturday, 20th April 1935

After dinner, DCI Kydd asked that the clearing up be left for the moment and everyone withdrew to the drawing room. It was rather a squeeze, with all the young people and guests but they managed it, with some perching on arm rests and five people squeezed on to the sofa. It was certainly a lot warmer than the dining room.

Geraldine Beaumaris took umbrage to Maggie, the film star, sitting on the knee of Simon the undergardener. For the umpteenth time, it was explained to her that neither Maggie nor Simon were who they said they were and they were engaged to be married in less than a weeks' time.

'During my investigations today I have come across some unsettling evidence that leads me to believe that Sir Laurence Tarleton did not take his own life, as we were led to believe, but instead he was murdered,' began DCI Kydd.

There was a collective intake of breath around the room.

'This means that the murderer must be in this room with us now. As most of you have guessed, the reason for this weekend party was to reinvestigate Professor Beaumaris's death. That means that there may be more than one murderer present. I also believe that the jewellery thief known as the Magpie is here with us too.'

Lottie put up her hand. 'DCI Kydd, what happened to Bertram Pickles the museum watchman? Surely he should be here too. He was a suspect under the original investigation.'

'Yes Dr Ellis, he should be. Unfortunately he was killed in December 1914 in a supposed street mugging. I believe he had been blackmailing the murderer, so had to die.'

'My apologies for asking an indelicate question Theodora, but Tristan Hadley-Brown was rather in the frame for murder back then. We all thought he had done it. Was he innocent? asked Max.

'Bertram Pickles' murder proves that Tristan Hadley-Brown was innocent because it happened after Tristan was killed in action at Ypres.'

LIZZIE BENTHAM

Theodora dabbed her eyes with a handkerchief.

'Could Sir Laurence have killed Professor Beaumaris? Someone might have killed him as revenge for Professor Beaumaris's death or Michael Quintrell's death,' said Reverend Moss, thinking aloud.

'Laurence didn't kill anyone. He was a very sweet hearted man,' declared Geraldine.

'He was a letch,' whispered Theodora slightly too loudly, to Geraint beside her.

'There is at least one very real and malevolent killer here. We don't want any more of our number to die while we are cut off from civilisation. I propose that from now, on we stay together in groups of two or more and make sure that other members of the group know where we are going at all times. That way we can protect each other.'

The lights flickered and went out, plunging the drawing room into darkness. Someone shrieked and there were rustlings and complaining.

'Someone go and see to the backup generator and someone fetch some candles please,' DCI Kydd shouted into the darkness.

Balvan magicked some candles out of thin air. Suddenly little lights began to spring up around the room, little islands of comfort in a gloomy space. Simon Culthorpe took one and headed off to the boiler room in the basement.

'Is everyone accounted for?'

Geraint did a quick head count.

'We are one short Chief Inspector. Let me check again. Yes with Simon in the basement there are only fourteen of us in here.'

'It's Maximilian Harrison,' said Theodora. 'Max is missing.'

'When did he disappear?' queried DCI Kydd.

'He asked that stupid question about Tristan, so he was definitely here ten minutes ago,' she replied.

'Dr Hadley-Brown and Professor Aldridge can you check his bedroom and the lavatory. The rest of us will stay here.'

The two men went off together and were gone for five minutes before returning without Max.

'No luck DCI Kydd.'

MURDER BY THE BOOK

'We'll give Simon time to get the generator up and running and then go looking for Dr Harrison,' said DCI Kydd grimly.

They waited in silence, candles flickering in phantom drafts. Simon was gone a further ten minutes but when he returned his face was grim.

'That wasn't a power cut sir. Someone has disabled the electrics. The main generator has been smashed. The back-up generator has been operating without my knowledge for the last few hours. It has now run out of fuel and someone has poured the remaining fuel down the drain. Everything was in working order when I checked this afternoon. It will take some time to get the main generator working again.'

'No power, no telephone, one of our number missing and there is a murderer amongst us. This is grave indeed,' DCI Kydd was worried.

Reverend Moss put up his hand. 'I can give Simon a hand with the generator and it seems expedient to me that we attract the attention of the mainland. I propose that I try and make a radio transmitter to send out an SOS distress call. We could also try signalling from the top of the house towards the nearest village with candles or a lantern.'

'Thank you Reverend. That seems eminently sensible.'

'It is a pity we don't have a boat of some sort like a punt with a flat bottom to get over the mosses,' said Maggie.

'First we need a search party to find Dr Harrison,' said DCI Kydd decisively. 'Simon and Reverend Moss please work on the generator. Balvan and Maggie you take the ground floor. Professor Aldridge and Mary Long check the basements. Jinny, Theodora and Geraldine search the first floor. Dorothea, Eric and Mary Short please take the staff quarters on the top floor. Geraint, Dr Ellis and I will search the grounds and outbuildings. We will meet back here when we have thoroughly searched our allotted areas. Share out torches between the teams. Watch your backs everyone and look out for each other. That way, we will all make it off this island.'

***

Geraint opened the door of the old coach house which was now used as a garage. Clarence Moss had parked the four cars and one motorcycle neatly side by side. Geraint's footsteps on the cobbles echoed loudly around the building as he made his way to the Crossley. He was sure he had a spare lantern in there, which the vicar might find useful for signalling with. On opening the boot he could not find what he was looking for, so opened one of the doors to check if it was on the back seat. There he confronted a pair of boots that were attached to a pair of legs, which were attached to a very damp man who was wrapped in Geraint's picnic rug and shivering uncontrollably.

Geraint and the stranger became aware of each other and startled at the same time.

'Aaah!'

'Eeek!'

Geraint shone his torch in the man's face. 'Who the hell are you and how did you get here?' he asked.

'I can explain. I am a journalist, I overturned my boat.'

Geraint looked closer. Underneath the mud and sludge there were some vaguely familiar features.

'You're that journalist fellow from the student magazine *The Worm*. What are you doing here? Where is your boat? No, never mind that now. You are soaked and freezing. Let's get you inside.'

***

A little while later, David Simpkins dressed in some dry clothes belonging to Geraint, was wrapped in swathes of blankets in front of the fire. The searchers gradually came back to the morning room to report failure to locate Dr Harrison and were surprised to find a stranger in their midst.

'How did you get here Mr Simpkins? We are surrounded by water,' asked DCI Kydd.

'I borrowed a rowing boat from a friend who lives in Formby. It was out of the water on a trailer. He helped me tow it to Downholland Cross and I rowed over from there. The boat grounded and got stuck in the mud a couple of hundred yards away from Mickering Priory, out on the moss. I fell in and got soaked. I was so cold and wet and Mickering Priory was in darkness. I headed for what I thought was a barn but was actually the garage. I found that Dr Hadley-Brown's car was open. I curled up inside and waited for death to take me.'

'When was this?'

'I set off from Downholland at just after five thirty when it was still light. I don't know what time I got here as my watch stopped when I got soaked.'

'Can you show us where the boat is in the morning? We might be able to use it to get news to the mainland.' Geraint asked.

DCI Kydd gave Geraint a pointed look. 'All in good time Dr Hadley-Brown. Is there someone that can vouch for your movements David? There have been some very odd events happening here.'

'My friend saw me off from Downholland and thought I was crazy for attempting the journey. Mary Shor can vouch for me here.'

'Humph!' Mary Short was still not speaking to David. She had however checked him over thoroughly and had tenderly tucked an extra blanket around him.

'Have you seen Dr Maximilian Harrison since you arrived? He has unfortunately gone missing,' asked DCI Kydd.

'The famous historian? Wow is he here too? No I haven't seen him.'

'Why did you want to come here anyway?' asked DCI Kydd.

'I am a journalist sir and I am always looking for a story. My friends have been acting very oddly for the past month, coming here each weekend. This is the ancestral home of the Quintrells, who were once the keepers of the *Boniface Psalter* and Mrs Beaumaris' necklace was stolen at the recent exhibition of the psalter, so I thought they might be investigating something interesting again without me—'

'You always put journalism above friendship,' said Mary Short, furiously interrupting him. 'If you had asked, we would have told you what we were doing. Instead you spied on us and half drowned yourself in pursuit of a story.'

'Yes I know that was stupid.' He looked so repentant that she relented enough to pour him out another cup of tea.

The electric lights flickered back on momentarily but then went off again, leaving the group in the morning room in the gloom.

***

Mary Long was pottering around the cavernous kitchen of the priory, by candlelight, making an inventory of what supplies they had left. Jinny had accompanied her and was making high tea by the light of a torch. They were both startled from their tasks by a muffled banging sound coming from the other end of the kitchen.

Knock, knock.

'Is it a rat?' squealed Jinny.

'It's coming from the pantry,' said Mary Long thoughtfully.

Cautiously they pushed open the pantry door and the knocking grew louder. Jinny put her ear against the cupboard at the back, where Geraint had showed the party the location of the priest hole.

KNOCK, KNOCK.

'I think that there is someone in there. We need Geraint or Theodora here quickly.'

'I'll go,' Mary Long volunteered. She did not want to be left alone with a potentially possessed kitchen cupboard.

'Let's go together,' replied Jinny, who did not want to be left behind either.

The tale of the ghostly knocking caused a stir with the others and there was a mass exodus to the kitchen, apart from Mary Short and her patient.

Geraint Hadley-Brown entered the kitchen at a jog, with DCI Kydd puffing along behind. Geraint showed Jinny where to press so that the false back of the cupboard sprang open.

It disgorged a groggy Maximilian Harrison, bloodied and bruised, gagged and bound. He had been in there a good while and was shivering. They cut his cords with a bread knife and supported his large, wilting frame back to the safety of the morning room.

DCI Kydd hung back for a moment to have a thorough look in the priest hole for any clues, using one of their precious torches.

MURDER BY THE BOOK

Between alternate sips of brandy and rubbing his abraded wrists and ankles, Maximilian told his story. 'I was in this room with all of you when I began to feel quite unwell, so I left to use the bathroom. As I was coming out, I sensed a presence in the darkness, and then felt a pain in my head. The next thing I knew I had woken up inside that priest hole. I have been tapping away in there for what seems like hours.'

They assured Max that he had only been gone for two hours. Looking over towards the fireplace he saw David Simpkins for the first time and did a double take.

'Who is this and how did he get here? He must be my assailant. Why isn't he under lock and key?' asked Max.

'He is the editor of a student magazine, sir. It is highly unlikely that it was him that knocked you out, because he was rowing across the mosses and falling in, just when you were attacked. Dr Hadley-Brown found him shivering in the garage.' Mary Short answered firmly, protective of her erstwhile boyfriend. 'Now Dr Harrison, I want to patch up your cuts and bruises. Professor Aldridge and Dr Hadley-Brown will help you upstairs.'

'I have never been attended by a lady physician before,' said Max, despite his injuries he looked almost happy.

'Professor Aldridge and Dr Hadley-Brown will also stay to chaperone,' said Mary Short, even more firmly.

Lottie Ellis had been conferring with Geraldine and Theodora.

'Chief Inspector, we think the best way for all of us to make it through the night is to stick together. We would like to propose that the ladies take this room and the gentlemen take the drawing room and we'll camp downstairs. We can take it in turns to keep watch.'

'An excellent idea ladies and one I was about to suggest myself.'

The lights came back on and stayed on as everyone was ferrying pillows and blankets downstairs from their rooms to their makeshift basecamp.

'Well done Simon! Well done Vicar!' they cheered.

This small victory gave the besieged group the boost they needed to survive the night on the cold, hard floor.

LIZZIE BENTHAM

First Light, Easter Sunday, 21st April 1935

On Easter Sunday morning, a little group gathered on the driveway looking over the expanse of submerged fields to watch the sunrise. Reverend Moss recited the familiar words of the Book of Common Prayer Communion service. This was a diversion. A more covert group were trying to rescue David Simpkins' rowing boat from the flood waters, which had ever so slightly receded. Geraint, Simon and DCI Kydd were on a reconnaissance and recovery mission.

They spied the boat stuck against a hedge some hundred yards from dry ground. The water was not very deep here, about ankle depth, but there was a lot of sucking mud under the calm surface. Geraint remembered a pair of snow shoes in one of the attics, left over from a Victorian Quintrell who liked alpine sports. He attached these to a pair of gum boots, to spread his weight across the marshy ground. Simon Culthorpe tied a rope around Geraint's waist and tethered the other end to a fence post on dry land.

'So we can recover your body,' he said reassuringly to Geraint.

Geraint set out walking stiffly, penguin like, across the waters towards the boat. He made it there without mishap and managed to untangle the boat from the flotsam caught in the hedge. He righted the boat with lots of cussing and a lot of getting soaked. He then attached the end of the rope from around his waist to the prow of the rowing boat and attached himself to the boat with a smaller length of rope.

'Okay, start hauling lads.'

The idea was sound in principle, however while Geraint had been stationary his snow shoes had settled into the silt and had got stuck. The two men back on dry land gave an almighty tug and the boat shot forward yanking Geraint off his feet and out of his gum boots, headlong into the waterlogged moss. He floundered around like a trout on a line, dripping and covered in mud and weeds. He ended up flopping over the stern of the boat and being dragged back to shore, cold, shivering, and a little bit rank smelling.

Whilst Geraint traipsed a soggy trail of silt through the kitchen to get changed, Simon and DCI Kydd examined their catch.

'It isn't too badly bashed around. Obviously the oars are lost but I can bodge something together,' said Simon.

'You have one hour. I want you and Hadley-Brown to set out while the rest are at breakfast. The sooner the police are here the better. I don't want anyone else to die.'

'Right you are, sir.'

'Do you know which way you are heading?'

'Easterly. From the roof I've spotted a couple of farms which might have a telephone or access to transport.'

'Good man!'

'Another thing sir,' Simon fished his hand drawn plans of Mickering Priory out of his jacket inner pocket. 'Can you keep these safe. I think Dr Harrison is correct, there is a secret passageway but I think it starts in one of the upstairs rooms, either Laurence Tarleton's or Professor Aldridge's. I think the chimney stack hides a narrow set of stairs, so my best bet would be to start looking by the fireplace.'

'I doubt that I'll have time to go hunting secret passageways Culthorpe, with a murderer on the loose.'

'Perhaps not sir but both Eric Tarleton and Maximilian Harrison are looking for it. If there really is a priceless treasure hidden inside, well, that could be a motive for murder.'

LIZZIE BENTHAM

Easter Sunday Morning, 21ˢᵗ April 1935

At eight a.m. Geraint and Simon set off in the rowing boat with makeshift oars, one an actual oar from an ancient Oxbridge boat race, the other a shovel from the garden potting shed. They tried to row where the water was deepest, in the ditch on one side of the road, heading back towards Aughton and civilisation.

They could see that the flood waters were starting to recede and the low lying land around Mickering Priory had kept their watery covering proportionally more than to the east. It took a while but eventually the boat scraped the bottom and finally grounded. They abandoned it and waded the last few hundred yards to lush green pasture. They could see some farm buildings up ahead and followed the sound of lowing cows to a shed, where the morning milking was just about finished. A dour figure in overalls approached them.

'Can I help you gentlemen?' asked the farmer.

'We are sorry to bother you, but there has been an accident at Mickering Priory and we desperately need to use a telephone to call for help. Can we use yours?' asked Geraint.

'It is out of order. The exchange at Holt Green was flooded, so this whole area is without telephone at the moment. You'll have to go to Town Green and maybe try at the station.'

'Thank you for your help, sir.'

Dejectedly the two men started to trudge along the road in the direction of the village. They had gone perhaps a half mile, when behind them they heard the noise of a horse clip clopping along the road pulling a wagon of turnips. It was the same farmer that they had spoken to earlier.

'Thought you two might need a lift and I am going your way. Would you like a ride?'

Geraint and Simon gratefully accepted his offer and clambered into the wagon with the turnips. Slowly but surely they were getting nearer to civilisation.

MURDER BY THE BOOK

After Lunch on Easter Sunday, 21st April 1935

Dorothea was ensconced in Maximilian Harrison's room typing up her notes, at what she could only describe as the crème de la crème of typewriters. She was flying through the witness statements without the usual amount of cussing and pen wiggling, to unstick stuck keys.

Her eye was drawn to a plaque on the mantelpiece directly in front of her. She had noticed it when dusting and thought it was an odd object to bring to a weekend in the country. The plaque made from plaster of Paris, was of impressions of some rather uninspiring Anglo-Saxon coins. She got up, stretched and wandered over to the mantelpiece for a closer look.

Turning it over, she noticed that in just one spot the back was coated in a substance, which turned out to be wax. Curiously she gave it a poke and a section crumbled off revealing a small piece of metal.

Intrigued, she prodded it again and a larger section broke away to show that it was a key and one she recognised too. It was the twin of the one that Tristan Hadley-Brown had given to Theodora to look after.

Why is that here?

She was so focused on the objects in her hands, that when someone grabbed her from behind, it came as a complete surprise. Before she could scream, a hand held bandages over her face, covered in the sickly smell of chloroform. She fought as hard as she could but her assailant was terribly strong and slowly she was overwhelmed by the fumes and drooped.

In the struggle she dropped the plaque which shattered into a thousand pieces.

CHAPTER FOURTEEN

Buried Alive

A Concise History of the Curse of the Boniface Psalter by Dr M. Harrison – The Victorian Quintrells

Sir Bartholomew Quintrell, the 11th Baronet of Mickering, invested heavily in a prospective diamond mine in South Africa. It seemed a fool-proof investment to him. He had been shown maps and diamond samples that the mine had already produced by a friend of a friend. He was promised even bigger and better quality diamonds, still to be mined. He sunk five thousand pounds into his friend's, friend's company and waited to become a rich man.

He waited a long time. Nothing happened. No telegrams, no letters, no money, no diamonds. The friend's friend had disappeared.

Undeterred, Sir Bartholomew Quintrell took a boat to South Africa to see his diamond mine for himself. His friend Fred Appleby went too, as a penance for introducing him to a potential rascal and near-do-well.

They travelled to a tiny settlement north of Durban and found that Sir Bartholomew had purchased a mine, abandoned years previously, that had only produced quartz.

Sir Bartholomew Quintrell was undaunted. He financed an exploratory survey and his mining engineers and geologists found a miniscule amount of gold. This was all the encouragement that he needed to reopen the mine.

Because he had used most of his savings on the mine, the passage to South Africa and the survey, after a few months there wasn't much left to pay the mine workers, so corners were cut with safety. An accidental explosion left three miners dead. What with their wages in arrears and a rock fall closing one section of the mine, only a few miners would continue working. Sir Bartholomew Quintrell and Fred Appleby took turns themselves to dig.

One day, a jubilant miner came to find Sir Bartholomew Quintrell.

'We think we've found it boss.'

'Gold?'

'Yes a huge seam.'

In all the excitement, prop shafts were not placed to shore up the ceiling with the accuracy or regularity that they should have been.

Sir Bartholomew Quintrell had forged ahead of the other miners following the gold seam, so when the roof of the mine collapsed, he was cut off from the rest of his men. They could hear him tapping behind the wall of rock and debris. The tapping gradually got weaker and weaker over a number of days. The miners struggled to reach their boss in time without causing another cave in to occur and eventually the tapping stopped.

It was thought that Sir Bartholomew Quintrell had not left a will, until his friend, Fred Appleby, produced one that left the mine to himself, signed six months previously on the voyage over from Britain. No one questioned the will too closely and the mine thrived under Fred Appleby's ownership and produced much gold and precious metals.

One day the miners broke into the blocked up section and came across Sir Bartholomew Quintrell's remains. They discovered a piece of paper in his pocket on which was written in shaky handwriting:

'I saw Fred Appleby move one of the prop shafts an hour before the cave in.'

Nothing could be proved.

Primary Source: An interview with the son of one of the miners, when he himself was an old man. His father told him stories of the collapse of the mine and the change in ownership.

LIZZIE BENTHAM

A Little Later Again on Easter Sunday, 21st April 1935

Eric hoisted his fair burden over his shoulder and carried Dorothea down the backstairs, through the courtyard, and to the old stable block where his motorcycle was waiting.

With a few bumps and knocks, he managed to insert his unresponsive load into the sidecar and strapped a spare driving hat tenderly on to Dorothea's lolling head. Eric then put on his own hat, goggles, and gloves before realising that he had forgotten something. He jogged back towards the house. A scene unfolding through an upstairs window caught his attention and made him flee.

He mounted the motorcycle and kick started the engine. Carefully he manoeuvred out of the garage and headed down the drive towards the junction with the road. The lane was still submerged but Eric had been out earlier with a measuring stick and checked the depth. He rode the motorcycle and sidecar slowly but confidently through the floodwater leaving two wakes trailing behind.

***

DCI Kydd had forgotten about the plans that Simon had given him while writing up his report during the morning. After Sunday lunch, he remembered them, got up from the table without apology and headed towards the kitchen. There he found Mary Long and Balvan Thakkar congratulating themselves on a culinary job well done. He took out the plans and showed them.

'Simon says that the most likely place for an opening into a secret passage is from Sir Tarleton's or Professor Aldridge's rooms,' began DCI Kydd. 'If someone used a secret passageway to enter his room unseen and kill Sir Tarleton, then we need to find it. Simon thinks there is a flight of stairs incorporated into the chimney. Do you want to go secret passage hunting with me?

'Absolutely! It is definitely not our turn to do the washing up,' said Mary intrigued.

MURDER BY THE BOOK

They began in Laurence Tarleton's bedroom. Mary could not bring herself to look at the human-like shape on the bed shrouded by a blanket. Carefully they went over the whole chimney breast pressing, prodding and twisting every inch. Nothing happened, until DCI Kydd used an iron bracket to haul himself stiffly to his feet and the metalwork shifted slightly.

Mary Long ran downstairs to get some butter to grease it. They stuffed butter into any available crack they could find and DCI Kydd gave the bracket an experimental wiggle. It definitely did wiggle, so DCI Kydd gave it an even bigger wiggle but nothing happened.

'Allow me sir,' said Balvan switching places with him. He heaved downwards putting all of his weight on to the spike. There was a scream of tortured metal and the bracket broke off in Balvan's hands, causing him to continue in a downwards motion and strike a small hearth stone at the back of the fireplace a glancing blow. A section of panelling high on the wall slid open a crack, then stuck.

'Well done Balvan! Which stone did you knock?' asked DCI Kydd. 'Let's mark it with some chalk before we forget.'

They clustered around the opening. DCI Kydd managed to push the panel open enough to get his head through and have a look around.

'I can't see a thing. Mary, can I borrow your torch please and the butter.'

He worked industriously greasing the ancient mechanism, then with the help of Balvan, pushed the hatch fully open to reveal an aperture of three feet squared, at about five feet off the ground.

'That is the silliest place to have a secret passage, hanging in mid-air,' commented Mary, busily snapping photos.

'There may have been something under it all those years ago which made it a lot easier to enter,' said Balvan.

'Can you give me a leg up?' asked DCI Kydd, keen to have a look.

It took some shoving to get him through the hole. Once inside, he fumbled with his torch and let out a shout of surprise. He had come face to face with a skeleton, sprawled on the floor of the passage, which ran behind the panelling for the full length of the room. The skeleton grinned at DCI Kydd and after he had recovered from the shock, Kydd grinned back, as the skeleton was partly clutching, partly squashed by, an old fashioned sea chest.

'Grab some sheets to put on the floor. Mary can you photograph this? I am going to hand out something that looks very heavy.'

Huffing and puffing, they lowered the chest on to a sheet.

'Let's wrap this up and get out of here before we disturb this room anymore,' said DCI Kydd.

Carefully they carried their burden downstairs and into the morning room. The house party guests had drifted there after lunch, not sure of what to do with themselves. The terrors of last night's dark, foreboding house had abated in the light of day.

There was a hush of expectation, as the treasure hunters lowered their burden on to an occasional table and carefully peeled its bedsheet wrappings away.

'You've found it! The secret passageway and Guy Quintrell's treasure,' Maximilian Harrison's voice was reverential. 'Where was it?'

'In Sir Tarleton's room,' began Mary Long. 'There is a flagstone on the hearth that acts a butto—'

'We found it as part of our investigations into the death of Sir Tarleton,' interrupted DCI Kydd. 'Now let's see what we have got here.'

Cautiously, he tried the leather straps but they disintegrated at his touch, which meant the lock was the only thing holding the lid shut and tenaciously it was still doing its job. By now a crowd had gathered around, with Maximilian Harrison the historian, Lottie Ellis the archaeologist, David Simpkins the journalist and Geraldine Beaumaris the art collector, hogging the best positions.

DCI Kydd took out his trusted skeleton key and hummed tunelessly under his breath whilst fiddling with the lock. There was a clunk and something broke. On applying some pressure, the lid of the chest opened stiffly to reveal, under a layer of grime, the tell-tale gleam of gold doubloons and precious jewels.

'This will be the find of the year! Please let me write this up for *History Monthly*?' pleaded Max.

'This is an archaeological find! I'll write it up for the *Journal of Archaeological Interest*,' Lottie was adamant.

'*The Worm* needs this as a scoop. It will be picked up by all the national papers,' David Simpkins piped up.

'As an important cultural item, I think I am best placed to find the right museum to exhibit this hoard to its best advantage,' added Geraldine.

'This is going nowhere except in the safe for now. It is potentially a motive for murder and either the property of Theodora as the last of the Quintrells, or the current baronet.' DCI Kydd raised his voice above the hubbub.

'Where is Dot? She wouldn't want to miss this,' asked Mary Short suddenly.

'Typing up statements in Dr Harrison's room,' answered DCI Kydd.

'By herself? Is that safe? I'll go and get her,' said Mary Short. She was back almost immediately. 'Dot has gone! There is a broken plaque on the floor and a very faint smell of chloroform.'

'Are you sure?' DCI Kydd asked.

'I know what chloroform smells like. I have done a surgery placement,' she said.

There was a stampede out of the morning room and upstairs to Maximilian Harrison's bedroom. DCI Kydd cautioned everyone to stay back. They clustered around the doorway while he walked carefully into the room sniffing. He knelt to examine the chunks of plaster of Paris on the floor and uncovered a key covered in plaster dust.

'Hello . . . what do we have here?' he said.

Theodora gasped, 'That looks identical to the museum key that Tristan gave me to look after. Why would Max have a key to the cabinet where Professor Beaumaris died?'

'Because he murdered Professor Beaumaris,' said DCI Kydd matter-of-factly, finally voicing his unspoken suspicions.

'Yes I did kill Professor Beaumaris,' Max's voice boomed

from behind them. 'And Laurence Tarleton and Bernard Pickles too. Hands up in the air everyone please. I am holding a gun and I am willing to shoot any of you, if you try something silly.' The gun in Max's hand covered them all very efficiently.

'But why?' Theodora burst out. 'We have all lived under this cloud for twenty years. Tristan died under suspicion. Why did you murder them?'

'To save my academic reputation of course. Professor Beaumaris found out that I had annotated the *Boniface Psalter* to give the impression that the curse is a bigger deal than it actually is. "Defacing a priceless manuscript," was what he called it. I started my doctorate with the premise that throughout the ages St Boniface's curse had influenced all who owned the book. It turns out no one really cared tuppence about the curse, so I had to make up sources and evidence to support my hypothesis. Laurence suspected that it was me. He examined the psalter on the day that Geraldine's pearls were stolen and had noticed the three new annotations. I had to get rid of him too because he would have talked. How was I to know that this weekend party was a blind for an undercover detective investigation?'

'So *A Concise History of the Curse of the Boniface Psalter* is all made up? Your book is all lies?' asked Lottie Ellis incredulously.

'Some of it is made up, some of it is embellished to appeal to a mass audience but a lot of it is true, the Quintrell treasure being a case in point. The links I draw to St Boniface's curse are purely fictional.'

'What happened with Professor Beaumaris?' asked DCI Kydd, stalling for time.

'He read a copy of my thesis and realised that I had added the annotations to the book. He asked me to meet him in the cabinet containing the *Boniface Psalter* at three thirty on the afternoon of the opening of the original exhibition to, "See how bad the damage was and whether it could be repaired". He railed against me and said he was going to get me sent down from the university. I lost my temper and said that if he had been a better supervisor, I wouldn't have had to resort to cheating. Why did he let me start a doctorate which had nowhere to go? I picked up the psalter and attacked him with it in rage.

'Apparently I don't know my own strength. Before I knew it, he was lying dead at my feet with his head caved in. I had an enlightened thought and set the stage by propping his body against the glass of the cabinet and using his finger to write the Persian symbols "Mene, mene, tekel, upharsin," as a nod to the Bible story that St Boniface quotes in his letter to Æthelbald. I left the cabinet and locked it with my own key. It was my practice to make copies of any key I needed to use.'

'Hang on a minute!' interjected Harold Aldridge. 'You are making this out to be a crime of passion. I was really sleepy after you gave me a cup of tea that day in the doctoral office. You never normally made me tea. You used to go and hang out in your girlfriend's room and get her to make you tea. You knew that you would need to come and go without someone watching you that day so you drugged me, *ergo* . . . the crime was premeditated. Both Theodora and I nodded off after we drank cocktails that you made us on Friday night. I think you drugged us because you again needed to come and go unseen to kill Laurence.' Harold Aldridge was irate.

'What about the woman that Tristan Hadley-Brown saw on the day of Professor Beaumaris' murder?' asked DCI Kydd.

'That was me disguised in Phyllis' clothes. Poor Phyllis, she became such a liability. I know that you are trying to keep me talking until help arrives. I saw Geraint and the undergardener chap set out in the reporter's boat from my window. I will have to get rid of rather a lot of witnesses pretty sharpish, won't I? Luckily I have thought of that. You are all going to disappear. That hidden passageway has held secrets for over two hundred years, so will make a fitting mass grave for you lot. I can then deal with your amateur forensics laboratory full of evidence, when you are all out of the way.'

'So you are going to bury us alive?' Reverend Moss asked the question calmly, so as not to antagonise the desperate man further.

'That is the general idea. Then I will turn up the heat.'

'Aren't you forgetting something Max,' Professor Aldridge's voice was strangely triumphant. 'You tampered with St Boniface's own psalter. You changed the words of the saint himself. The curse will fall upon you Max. The annotated manuscript is a signpost straight to you. You shall never be free while the psalter is on display. Some bright spark will go digging in the archives and realise you have defaced it. History will show you for what you are, a liar, a faker and a murderer.'

Dr Harrison blanched as this new thought sunk in. 'I am quite capable of dealing with the curse thank you Harold but you are correct, the *Boniface Psalter* will have to be destroyed. No more chattering, get into Laurence's bedroom one by one and don't try anything.'

They filed past the once genial man, who was now holding his gun with ruthless indifference. He indicated that each of them should climb through the hole in the wall. One by one, they disappeared into the secret passage and the darkness engulfed them. When Geraldine who was last had scrambled through the opening, Max touched the flag stone that Mary Long had helpfully drawn around in chalk, and the ancient mechanism slowly closed behind the party.

***

The panelling slid shut behind the group and everything went dark. Harold Aldridge lit a match and the darkness receded to show a large group of very frightened people, tightly packed into a tiny space. By its light, they could see they were in a recess behind the panelling that led to a narrow flight of stairs that hugged the chimney.

They also saw the other inhabitant of the secret passage, the skeleton of Sir Philip Quintrell, slumped against one wall in all his mouldy frippery. His wig and hat were askew on top of a skeleton face; his eyeless sockets stared right at them. Jinny screamed and Harold Aldridge dropped the spent match.

They started to talk at once and banged on the panelling in the hope of discovering a way out, but DCI Kydd hushed them.

'Quiet. Listen. Dr Harrison is up to something?'

They heard the muffled sounds of Max tramping around Laurence's room, the splashing sound of some sort of liquid, then a match striking, and an odd crackling noise.

'What is he doing?' asked Theodora anxiously.

The first few tentacles of smoke found their way through microscopic gaps in the woodwork.

'I think that he is planning to burn down the priory with us inside,' said DCI Kydd grimly.

This produced a renewed frenzy of banging on the panelling. Harold Aldridge struck another match and conferred with Lottie Ellis.

In his best lecturer voice he called across the panic, 'Settle down everyone. Lottie thinks she has found a way out. There is a draft coming from down the staircase making this match flicker.' The match went out and he struck another one. 'Let's follow the passage and see where it leads.'

The temperature in the confined space was becoming uncomfortably hot and the smoke was sufficient to set everyone off coughing.

'I'll go first,' said Lottie, already starting down the stairs, 'I am used to working underground in confined spaces. Harold, please come next with some light.'

'Reverend and Mrs Moss please can you help Maggie. I'll bring up the rear with some more matches,' DCI Kydd organised them.

One by one the squash of people lessened, as they picked their way down the staircase into the bowels of the earth. Geraldine Beaumaris had been very quiet up until this point and was the last member of the party remaining in the passage.

'I don't think I can do it Chief Inspector. I am claustrophobic. What have I got to look forward to anyway? You are going to arrest me for insurance fraud, if we get out of here alive,' she whimpered.

BANG!

Something exploded in Laurence's room blowing out part of the panelling wall of the secret passage, in a shower of sparks and splinters. Geraldine suddenly found the desire to live and was down the stairs like a shot, with DCI Kydd hard on her heels. They found that the passage opened out into an old, walled up wine cellar, which had been used for storing contraband by eighteenth century smugglers.

'We must still be underneath the old priory,' called Professor Aldridge. 'We can't stay here too long if the place is alight.'

'There is a tunnel over here,' called Lottie who had been exploring. 'It must be the passageway that Max was talking about, that leads to the grounds. This would be jolly fascinating if it wasn't a life or death situation.'

Reverend Moss was poking around in some old crates. He reverently drew out a bottle of port, two centuries old, and carefully wiped off some of the grime with his handkerchief.

'Come on Clarence,' called Jinny with one arm around Maggie's waist.

Reluctantly he left his discovery but not before slipping a bottle into his pocket.

'Coming love,' he called and followed the group into the engulfing darkness of the new tunnel.

MURDER BY THE BOOK

Easter Sunday Afternoon, 21st April 1935

At around lunchtime, the farmer dropped Geraint and Simon off at the railway station. From there they telephoned the local police station. They got through to a very young sounding constable, who on hearing that they were reporting a murder at Mickering Priory was rather flustered. He said he needed to speak to his inspector at Ormskirk for reinforcements. He told them to wait where they were, until he cycled over to meet them.

The constable arrived fifteen minutes later, hot and radiating excitement. He took their statements in the station master's office, borrowed hurriedly for the purpose. A little later, three dark police cars drew up outside and spewed out eight police officers, including the local superintendent and the familiar face of PC Standish.

'DCI Kydd wanted some information urgently but the phone lines were down. I got to Ormskirk to find that Mickering Priory was an island. I was at the local nick asking for advice how to get there, when your call came through, so I hitched a lift.'

It did not take Geraint and Simon long to convince the superintendent that a sensational murder had happened at Mickering Priory and that they were worried about their friends left behind. The superintendent asked them to accompany the police and the three police cars departed in convoy towards the mosses.

As they were turning off Turnpike Road, a motorcycle and sidecar, with a lolling passenger inside, cut the corner and whizzed away in the opposite direction.

'That was Eric Tarleton! I didn't see who his passenger was. The goggles and hat obscured their face. At least we now know that the roads are passable for vehicles,' called Simon, his nose pressed to the car window.

The convoy travelled down progressively narrower roads, until they came to the edge of the lapping water where the road disappeared. The lead car carefully drove into the silty waters, trying not to splash too much, while the other two cars followed cautiously.

LIZZIE BENTHAM

As they were nearing their destination, a car careered around a blind corner almost hitting the lead police car. It swerved just in time and drove away at speed. A massive bow wave hit the three cars in turn and the superintendent, who had his window open, got a face full of water.

Geraint noticed something familiar. 'Hey that's my Crossley! Who was driving it?' He strained to see from the passenger side.

'Maximilian Harrison,' answered Simon who had a better view. 'He is going to crash it if he continues to drive like that.'

The overgrown hedges on either side dropped for a section and they got their first glimpse of Mickering Priory sitting serenely in its temporary lake, except for the black smoke pouring from the old wing, and a hint of red flames dancing high above the water.

'Mickering Priory is on fire!' shouted Geraint.

'Step on it Jones,' called the superintendent sharply.

***

The police cars came to a sudden halt on the gravel outside and disgorged their passengers in front of what had once been the old wing of the house. Flames leapt and licked the brick work and the temperature was hotter than hell.

'Maggie would have struggled to get out!' cried Simon, in distress.

He had to be restrained by Geraint and PC Standish to stop him plunging head first into the raging inferno.

'Use your head Simon. We need to look for places the group might have taken refuge.' Geraint was equally horrified but tried to remain calm.

The superintendent dispatched one car back towards Town Green to telephone for the fire brigade. He then sent volunteers to scout around the grounds looking for any survivors. Those left behind formed a bucket chain, stretching to the old well shaft in the middle of the courtyard, passing buckets of water backwards and forwards.

The men returned unable to find any members of the house party. Together they worked to fight the fire with grim determination, fearing the worst, but still hoping for a miracle.

CHAPTER FIFTEEN

Daylight

Easter Sunday Afternoon Continued, 21ˢᵗ April 1935

The tunnel was just tall enough for a short person to stand upright. It led the group nearly due north, down a very slight incline for two hundred yards, before they had to halt because the roof had collapsed.

'We are doomed. Fire behind us and earth in front of us . . . I am a dead woman walking. We'll run out of air, I shouldn't wonder, before we dehydrate or starve to death,' said Geraldine Beaumaris, fatalistically.

'Oh Geraldine don't!' Theodora was distressed.

There was a conflab happening between Lottie Ellis and Harold Aldridge.

Lottie's cheerful voice floated back down the tunnel. 'Hang on in there Geraldine! This is not like the air in the tombs of Egypt or Syria. It is fresh. See, the flame is flickering in the breeze. We think there may be a rabbit hole or badger set ventilating the tunnel. Harold is going to blow out the match to see if we can see any natural light.'

The tunnel was plunged into darkness except for a tiny shaft of dim light, probably only the size of a sixpence.

'We'll be out of here by tea time.' Lottie was ecstatic. 'We will need something to dig with and something to shore up the tunnel roof and walls. Can someone nip back to the cellar and grab some of those bottles that the vicar was fascinated by? We can bash the ends off the bottles to use them as scoops. The wood of the crates might still be good enough to use as supports.'

Reverend Moss with a wry expression on his face pulled the bottle of port from his pocket and smashed the bottom against the wall. The tunnel was filled with a rich, alcoholic smell and the vicar tried a little bit on his finger.

'Turns out that this port was an exceptional vintage,' he sighed and passed the new shovel to Lottie.

DCI Kydd and the Reverend Moss were nearest the back so retraced their steps. It was a lot warmer in the cellar and some smoke wisps had managed to sneak in from up above.

'We don't have much time.' DCI Kydd was worried. If this chamber collapses, then smoke and flames will shoot up the tunnel like a chimney and we will be grilled.'

They hauled some of the crates into the tunnel and yelled for their friends to come and help. The crates were broken into planks, which were then passed along the tunnel like a bucket chain.

Lottie was in her element. She shored up the tunnel walls with wood and rocks, directed Harold, Mary Long and Balvan where and how to dig, instructed Jinny, Mary Short and Theodora how to make a spoil heap and ignored David Simpkins questions about her past excavations. Part of the roof gave way and Harold was half buried in a deluge of earth. They yanked him out by his ankles, coughing and sneezing up soil but he was otherwise unhurt.

Balvan taking a turn at excavating called back that he was through and could see daylight. 'It looks like we have come up into some sort of building. I can peep through a crack and see wood and brick in a round shape.'

'That sounds like the old ice house,' called Theodora. 'The roof fell down when I was a little girl and my father banned Michael and I from playing there.'

'I'll keep digging. Please pass me some more planks of wood.'

'The tunnel is starting to fill with smoke and the roof of the cellar has cracked in a number of places,' DCI Kydd called up to Balvan. 'We don't have much time.'

'Right you are, sir. I'll dig fast,' he said.

***

Soon there were four fire engines on the scene using hoses and pumps to douse the flames.

The men from the original bucket chain were told to desist and

MURDER BY THE BOOK

move away from the building. They sat exhausted on the damp grass, as far from the house as the floodwater would allow them, happy to relinquish the job to their fire brigade colleagues.

Geraint head-in-hands and Simon prostrated on the ground, were a little way removed from the superintendent's men, cocooned in a fog of exhaustion and despair.

PC Standish, looking more like a St Bernard dog than normal, paced up and down worrying about his missing boss. His trudging took him towards what looked like a derelict, brick-built igloo encased in a mound of earth. A young tree was growing through a hole in its roof. He heard a noise. It sounded like a small animal scrabbling around inside. He was about to beat a hasty retreat, when his keen ears heard a muffled expletive followed by coughing.

'Hello is anyone there. This is the police. Show yourself.'

'*Cough*, the police? *Cough*, help us! We are trapped,' the muffled voice shouted.

'Sir! Everyone! Over here! I've found someone,' yelled PC Standish to his colleagues. 'They are trapped in this old structure.'

'Please could you hurry up? I am stuck, the tunnel is filling up with smoke and the others are behind me,' called the voice.

Police officers were sent to find spades and two of the burliest broke down the rotten, locked door with their shoulders. Inside they found some ancient wooden steps leading down into the ground, which came out into what had once been a cavernous chamber, built in the eighteenth century to store ice for year round use.

'I am over here,' the disembodied voice called again. 'I appear to be stuck in the staircase.'

Carefully, PC Standish descended into the grotto, mattock in hand.

'Please be careful on the stairs. You just knocked a load of earth on to my head,' complained the voice.

'Stand back!' shouted PC Standish.

'Crawl back you mean,' said the voice.

PC Standish hit the step hard with the mattock. Old rusty nails sheered, wood splintered and soon there was a gap about three feet high showing a void behind the staircase.

A man in traditional Indian clothing, covered in dirt and grime, crawled out blinking into the light, coughing from the dust and smoke which curled round his ankles.

'There are eleven more people down there,' he spluttered. 'Dr Ellis is just behind me.'

The police officers worked like fury to excavate the house party. One by one, they popped out of the hole in the ground, filthy, coughing and blinking in the daylight.

The last one out was DCI Kydd, who was a little bit bigger than the others and had got slightly stuck.

'Don't worry sir. We'll have you out in a jiffy,' called a deliriously happy PC Standish.

'I am going to get trim,' grumbled a floundering DCI Kydd. 'No more French food for me!'

***

Geraint was distracted out of his own personal hell by the sudden activity focused on the ruined ice house. He watched languidly for a few minutes before fully realising its significance.

'Simon get up, I can see Balvan.' He shook Simon by his shoulders. 'Look there is Lottie too and Harold Aldridge. They are safe Simon. They are alive!'

Simon was pale, with eyes red from the smoke and crying. He half rolled over and looked up uncertainly. 'What?'

Geraint hauled him to his feet. 'Simon I can see Maggie. She is being carried out of the ice house by a smitten police officer.'

'Maggie!'

Simon was on his feet and sprinting across the grass. Geraint followed hotly after.

'Hello Simon darling!' called Maggie serenely.

The police officer sensibly placed his fair burden on the ground and stepped away quickly, as Simon caught Maggie in a hug so strong, it spun her around and then he kissed her with abandon.

'I've missed you too darling,' said Maggie, laughing.

The sense of being at a wake disappeared ushering in a jubilant, party atmosphere. People mingled, hugged each other and spread congratulations around wildly.

After making sure that his mother and godfather were in good health, Geraint looked around for Dorothea but could not find her anywhere.

'Where is Dot?' He called out anxiously. 'Where is Miss Roberts?'

DCI Kydd, emerging last from the ice house, was met by a very worried young man.

'DCI Kydd where is Dorothea?' asked Geraint.

The chief inspector's only focus for the past few hours, had been to stay alive and keep everyone else alive. He was rudely jolted back into the present.

'Damn it! I quite forgot. I think she has been abducted,' he said.

***

'You let Eric Tarleton kidnap Dorothea . . . We have to rescue her!' cried Geraint. After a trying day, finding out that the woman he loved had been abducted by his rival, was the final straw and the usually composed Geraint was beside himself.

'Try and be calm Dr Hadley-Brown. We don't know where Eric will have taken her,' said DCI Kydd.

A crowd of eavesdroppers had begun to collect around the two men.

'Eric is the Magpie,' said Lottie, sheepishly. 'He might do anything and go anywhere.'

DCI Kydd raised an eyebrow. He knew that Lottie had been lying to protect her son.

'Actually, I think we might be able extrapolate where Eric might go.' Professor Aldridge spoke up. 'We now know that Eric is the Magpie, therefore he has a predisposition towards shiny, expensive things. He has shown an inordinate amount of interest in the *Boniface Psalter*. I remember that he asked in a lecture how much it was worth. I foolishly said it was priceless and that certain collectors would pay a fortune for it. He even submitted an essay about it which is very out of character. My hypothesis is that he is on his way to the museum to steal the *Boniface Psalter*. Lottie to your knowledge does Eric know anyone who collects valuable things?'

Lottie Ellis nodded shamefacedly. 'He does. I introduced him to some of the biggest names in the antiquities black market when they visited my dig last year . . .'

'The museum is where Max is heading as well,' piped up Geraldine Beaumaris.

'Max killed Laurence Tarleton, Professor Beaumaris and Bernard Pickles and he tried to kill us too, before setting Mickering Priory on fire,' added Theodora Hadley-Brown, for Geraint and Simon's benefit.

Geraint was stunned. 'Not only has Dorothea been kidnapped by the most notorious jewel thief of our time, her path may well cross with a deranged killer . . . again.' He turned tail and sprinted across the grass towards the coach house.

'We had better help him rescue Miss Roberts,' called Professor Aldridge to the rest.

'Never mind the girl, I am going to rescue my son,' called Lottie, galloping after Geraint.

Geraint had forgotten that Max had stolen his car. Upon reaching the garage, he paused momentarily nonplussed, which was enough time for the others to catch up with him and pile into their cars.

Lottie Ellis was first out of the blocks. In one elegant manoeuvre she backed out her two-seater from the garage and turned it around. Harold Aldridge nimbly jumped over the door to land beside her and off they shot tooting the horn.

Jinny, the Reverend Moss, Mary Long and Balvan scrambled for the old Ford and followed them at a smart pace. Maggie, Simon and Mary Short headed for Maggie's Riley. Geraint wavered then followed them into Maggie's car. He had heard of Maggie's driving reputation and was terrified, but speed was of the essence.

DCI Kydd hung back and gained permission from the

superintendent to borrow one of the police cars. PC Standish climbed into the driver's seat and DCI Kydd stiffly lowered himself into the passenger seat.

'Wait for me. This is the biggest scoop of my career!' David Simpkins threw himself into the back of the car.

'If there is a burglary at the museum then I, as a trustee, should be there. Besides I have a key, so you'll struggle to get in without me.' Geraldine followed on David's heels.

'I want grandchildren,' was Theodora's cryptic remark, as she settled down in the back seat next to Geraldine.

DCI Kydd was about to argue but realised there wasn't time. 'Step on it Standish!' he said.

***

Dorothea partly woke up. She was groggy, had a splitting headache and felt like she wanted to be sick. She had the impression that she was flying, moving fast about a foot off the ground. There was a silent knight, wearing strange armour, on a silver and black horse that made a lot of noise next to her. She did not like the noise, or the smell of fumes, or the taste in her mouth. She decided that her best course of action would be to go back to sleep.

When I wake up again I'll feel better. I won't be flying anymore and the smelly, noisy horse will have gone, she thought. She passed out again.

***

Waking up fully was painful. The feeling of flying had gone, to be replaced by the solidness of a cold, tiled floor pressing against her cheek. The room was dark and shadowy. The only light came from high up on the wall, through the grimy basement windows and was the orange colour of the setting sun.

Dorothea wanted to use her arms to push herself up but for some reason they were stuck behind her back. Her hands felt full of pins and needles, as did her feet, which would not do as she commanded.

Dorothea took stock of her surroundings. She seemed to be in a storeroom full to bursting with stuff. There were cabinets lined with pinned insects, ancient books and Neolithic hand tools, standing next to a moth-eaten, stuffed bear and a rocking horse with mad staring eyes. A real human skeleton was strung up on a stand, next to a public health poster telling people to remember to brush their teeth daily and bathe once a week.

Looking down at her feet, she saw that her shoe laces were tied together tightly so that she could not separate them. Presumably her hands were bound too.

A noise over by the door caused Dorothea to stiffen in terror. It opened on oiled hinges and a tall man entered, dressed in black. In the light of the setting sun she thought it was the ghost of Sir Laurence Tarleton and her horrified gasp drew the spectre's attention.

'Dot, are you alright?' Eric's voice full of concern relieved Dorothea that he was not a supernatural visitor.

'Eric is that you? I don't know where I am, or how I got here, or who tied me up.'

He knelt down and started to unknot her bound feet and hands.

'We are currently in the basement of the museum, hiding from the night watchman as he does his rounds.'

'He is called Alfred,' murmured Dorothea.

'Ah is he? I don't know how to explain this and please don't be cross with me, but I tied you up and brought you here,' he paused, fearfully awaiting Dorothea's response.

'You hit me over the head, tied me up, and kidnapped me!' Dorothea was livid.

'No I chloroformed you. By accident I managed to hit your head on a beam coming down the servants stairs at Mickering Priory – it was a right old bump. Then I had to tie your arms and legs up because they kept lolling everywhere and I was frightened that you would fall out of the sidecar . . . I know that doesn't sound good.'

'No it does not,' said Dorothea grimly, attempting to massage her swollen wrists. 'Why on earth did you kidnap me?'

MURDER BY THE BOOK

'I wasn't going to leave you at Mickering Priory with a murderer about was I? I have checked the floodwater level every day and thought that if I could get the motorbike as far as Causeway Lane, the worst of the flooding would be past. It was Max that killed Father. When I managed to get you strapped into the sidecar, I went back to see what the others were doing. Max had them held at gunpoint in Father's room, so I turned around and got the hell out of there.'

'You left the others at risk of danger from a desperate criminal? Lottie Ellis is your mother! What kind of person are you?' Dorothea was simultaneously incredulous, disgusted and terrified for her friends' safety. 'You are a coward and a thief. You stole my essay!'

'Aunt Lottie . . . I mean Mother, can take care of herself. Besides, my sidecar can only fit one passenger and I couldn't leave you behind.'

He offered Dorothea a hand up, which she refused. Her feet were leaden and she clutched at the table instead, making the skeletal rib cage rattle disconcertingly.

'You should have left me behind Eric. Maybe I could have helped my friends, or prevented Dr Harrison, or—'

'But I love you Dot. I am totally head over heels for you. I have been all around the world and never met anyone I cared half a carat for. Then I saw you working on your Anglo-Saxon translation in this very museum and I knew I had to have you.'

'Is this some kind of weird date? If so, it is the least romantic gesture anyone has ever made.'

'No it's not a date. I was hoping to steal the *Boniface Psalter*.'

'Eric, are you mad?'

'No, I am the Magpie actually,' he sounded rather pleased with himself. 'This will be the pinnacle of my very successful career to date.'

'Lottie said she was the Magpie. How on earth did you become the most notorious jewel thief in Britain?' Dorothea was incredulous.

'Well I am rather a bright chap and Father used to keep a tight hold on the family purse strings. I saw how Aunt Lottie used unorthodox methods to fund her digs. I was inspired to hunt around for a wheeze that would be lucrative and not hurt anyone that mattered much. Then I thought of this scheme,' he said smugly.

'You recruit well-to-do people that have a reputation to uphold and that are strapped for cash. They own an heirloom that is too distinctive to sell at an auction house in this country. Instead, you ask them to hide the piece in a place of your choosing. They pretend to find their heirloom stolen by the supposed Magpie, act upset, and call the police in distress with a made up story. You pick up the artefact from its prearranged hiding place, at a time that suits you. Hang on, there was a bracelet stolen from the Manchester Hotel when we went dancing. Was I your alibi?' asked Dorothea.

'Exactly and a beautiful alibi you were too! My clients then call their insurance companies to receive the full value of the artefact from them. I smuggle the object out of the country and sell it to some contacts in the antiques trade. I give the owners half of the price that I receive from my buyer and I keep the other half. Everyone is a winner!'

'Everyone accept the insurance company you are swindling!'

'That is what I love about you Dorothea, your morality. I do believe you could make an honest man out of me. Your attention to detail is pretty good too. The map and notes you made of this museum that I, *ahem* . . . borrowed, along with your essay, came in very handy for breaking in tonight. I congratulate you my dear,' said Eric, giving Dorothea a mock bow.

Choosing her words carefully because she was obviously in the company of a madman, Dorothea answered, 'Look Eric, I like you, you are brilliant company but I don't think we would suit each other.'

'Don't you think I would make a good husband?'

'I think DCI Kydd has a strong suspicion that you are the Magpie, so a husband behind bars isn't much of a husband.'

'I am smarter than DCI Kydd, Dot.'

'Eric, I don't love you.'

'If I turned over a new leaf could you learn to love me?' Eric looked like a large puppy, albeit with suspected rabies, that she had kicked.

She shook her head sadly. 'I am pretty sure I am in love with someone else and I might be about to lose him.'

'Hadley-Brown?'

'Yes.'

'I shouldn't worry. He is totally bowled over by you,' said Eric, surprisingly magnanimous in defeat.

'He is? Thank you Eric!' Dorothea was so delighted, that she forgot Eric was a deluded madman with dubious morals and gave him a hug.

'Oh Dot. You don't know what you are missing. I could have shown you the wonders of the ancient world and we would have lived the high life.'

'On the proceeds of insurance fraud!'

'You are so picky my love.'

***

Maximilian Harrison pulled up outside the museum in the Crossley. He walked purposefully towards the main entrance and rang the doorbell. Alfred opened the door cautiously, surprised by an Easter Sunday visitor. When faced with an eminent academic on the doorstep who wanted to have a look at the psalter, Alfred acquiesced readily. The night shift was very tedious and he looked forward to having a cosy gossip.

As Alfred turned to lead Dr Harrison to the South Gallery, Max grabbed a bust of the Duke of Wellington and brought it down with all the force he could muster on Alfred's head, causing "Old Nosey" to shatter and Alfred to crumple in a heap. Dusting off his fingers, Max sauntered into the South Gallery to claim his prize.

***

In the basement Dorothea and Eric heard a crash, a muffled cry of pain, followed by a dull thud, and then brisk footsteps receding into the distance above their heads.

'What was that?' Dorothea was visibly shaken.

'It sounds like someone else is in the building and that they have just knocked out the watchman,' answered Eric.

'Poor Alfred! We need to go and help him.'

'Not a chance. If this is an amateur break in, there'll be coppers swarming all over this building in less than twenty minutes. We need to get out fast.'

'I am going to investigate. I won't abandon an injured person to their fate. You can do whatever you please,' said Dorothea, scathingly. She pushed past Eric to get to the doorway.

'Aren't you forgetting our companions at Mickering Priory? There is a possibility that our murdering friend is upstairs, returning to the scene of his earlier crime.'

Dorothea paused at the door. 'Maximilian Harrison murdered your father. Help me stop him,' she said, trying to appeal to Eric's better nature.

'Those that thieve and run away, live to thieve another day,' he chanted.

'You are a coward,' spat Dorothea, incensed. 'I never want to see you again.' She turned and headed towards the stairs.

Eric stood looking after her. 'Damn. Apparently I do have a conscious after all.' He quietly headed after Dorothea.

CHAPTER SIXTEEN

Museum Break In

Evening of Easter Sunday, 21st April 1935

Lottie Ellis and Harold Aldridge were the first to arrive at the museum as night was falling. Harold, with his military intelligence training reconnoitred the museum's grounds, much to Lottie's impatience. They spotted Geraint's Crossley parked on Palmerston Street and Eric's motorcycle more discretely hidden in an alleyway off Every Street. With a mirthless smile, Harold used a pocket knife to slash each vehicle's tyres. He hoped that Geraint would forgive him for mutilating his car.

Looking inside the Crossley's boot, they discovered the Quintrell treasure lying there gleaming in the street lights. Together Harold and Lottie moved it to a hiding place behind a tree in the museum grounds.

'Theodora will thank us for rescuing this,' Harold said.

The museum side of Ancoats Hall was in complete darkness. The wing containing the women's hall of residence was lit up like a Christmas tree. There was a jazzy number playing on the wireless and laughter could be heard coming through an open window. Not all of the students had gone home for the holidays. Those remaining had decided to throw a party, while the warden was away.

Lottie stiffened. 'We need to get into the fun half of this building. I wonder if they have replaced the fire escapes in the last twenty years.'

'I shouldn't think so, but how will that help us?'

'Wait and see.'

She led Harold to the hall of residence side of the building and in the shadows gazed up at the ladder attached to a protruding metal platform, hanging too high out of reach for either of them.

'Ok Harold, I'll have to climb onto your shoulders.'

'But Lottie . . .'

'No buts Harold.'

He braced himself against the wall. Nimbly, Lottie stepped

on Harold's knee, then his cupped hands, and with one foot put her full weight onto his shoulder while simultaneously stretching up and grabbing the bottom rung of the ladder.

'I learnt to do this in a souk in Egypt,' said Lottie chattily. She gracefully descended to earth, with a squeak of metal on metal, as the ladder slid down to the ground.

There was an '*Umph,*' from Harold Aldridge as Lottie landed on top of him.

'Do stop messing around Harold.'

She was up the ladder and on to the platform ten feet in the air, before Harold could even dust the grime off his already ruined trousers. He followed behind her stiffly. He found Lottie with her eye pressed to a crack in the warped wood of the fire door.

'The party is happening on the ground floor. There doesn't seem to be anyone about.'

'Yes, but how are we going to get in?' puffed Harold.

Lottie had already spotted an open bathroom window three feet away. She climbed over the safety railings to lean out over the drop. She pushed up the sash and wriggled through the gap and disappeared.

She was gone a while. Harold who was feeling rather exposed up a girls' dormitory fire escape, was just wondering if he should try to follow her, when the fire door opened. Lottie stood there, clothed in a dress that did not belong to her, with her hair brushed neatly and wearing makeup.

'What the devil?'

'Shhh!'

Lottie whisked him inside and into the girls' bathroom. She then locked the door behind them. The bathroom was strewn with washing lines and someone had recently hung up their wet laundry, against hall regulations. Lottie grabbed a nearly dry blouse and skirt.

'I have reccied downstairs. The young people are all three sheets to the wind. A young gentleman who was obviously sozzled even asked me to dance. Go and put these on,' she commanded. 'We will be able to sneak past the revellers and get in to the museum.'

'Lottie I must protest!'

'Do you want to rescue Eric and what's-her-name from a murderer?'

'I want to rescue Dorothea, yes.'

'Then put these on. There's a cubicle to change in over there. I'll pass you in some lipstick and head scarf.'

'But I have a beard!'

'Those students are too tipsy to notice.'

A short while later Harold sheepishly exited the cubicle wearing the borrowed clothes.

'Lottie I feel so stupid.'

'Nonsense Harold you make a fine figure of a woman. Let's go and see if we can get through the throng downstairs.'

They found around thirty young people crammed into the common room and spilling out into the corridors; dancing, drinking and talking loudly over rhythmical music.

Someone handed Harold a highball glass as he nervously passed by, which smelt like a fruit punch laced with sherry. He tried a sip and it was rather good. Lottie grabbed his hand and yanked him through the melee, towards the interconnecting fire door into the museum.

'Stand there and give me some cover while I get this door open,' ordered Lottie.

Harold obliged by standing with his back to the fire door, sampling his drink.

An inebriated male student meandered towards Harold. He leaned against a wall and looked bleary-eyed at what he imagined to be a seductive temptress.

'You are the most beau . . . beautiful lady I have ever seen. Give me a hug, darling!'

'Hurry up Lottie,' called Harold, fending off the young man. He succeeded in distracting his amorous suitor by yelling, 'Look over there. It's Greta Garbo!'

The drunk wandered off in search of the famous actress.

'Quick thinking Harold,' said Lottie approvingly and dragged him through the now opened door to safety.

***

Dorothea climbed up the stairs from the basement as swiftly

and silently as she could. In the foyer she discovered Alfred's prone body. There was a bloody wound on his bald pate which oozed slowly. She paused to check his pulse. It was faint and fluttered like a butterfly.

She headed to the office where there was a telephone. She lifted the receiver and asked for police headquarters in hushed tones.

'There is a break in at the Ancoats Art Museum. The watchman is hurt, he might be dying. Please send an ambulance. I think the assailant is still in the building,' she whispered to the police constable on duty. 'Someone is out in the corridor. I have to go,' she hung up and dived for cover under the desk.

The door to the office opened and Maximilian Harrison entered. From his hand, dangled a large bunch of keys which he must have stolen from the unconscious guard. Max went straight to the open wall safe and rummaged around inside. With an exclamation of triumph, he removed a smaller set of keys and exited the room. The sound of his feet in the corridor gradually receded.

Dorothea drew a breath of relief then berated herself. *This is no good. I am the only person who can stop Dr Harrison. Eric won't help, the police won't be here in time and the others are all back at Mickering Priory. What I need is some form of weapon.*

Casting her mind back to the evening when they reconstructed Professor Beaumaris' murder, she remembered the suit of armour that Mary Short had worn. It stood outside the long gallery upstairs. There were a number of swords, spears and maces hung on the wall next to it.

I wonder, she thought, *it is ridiculous but it might just work.*

Quietly she left the office and headed upstairs.

***

Once inside the museum, Lottie and Harold spotted the prostrate figure of Alfred some way off. Lottie, who arrived first, began tucking her borrowed cardigan under Alfred's head and then yanked a priceless tapestry off the wall, to use as a blanket for the sick night watchman.

As they knelt by Alfred, a rag tag knight dressed in mismatching armour descended the main stairs, dragging a sword that was nearly as long, as the short knight was tall. It entered the South Gallery. Listening, they heard Maximilian Harrison cry out in fear.

'That must be Dorothea. Max is in there with her. We need to help her,' whispered Harold.

'What we need is a diversion Harold. Let's bring the party in here.' Lottie jumped up and ran back to the fire door. She opened it and yelled, 'Party in the museum!' to the befuddled revellers inside.

***

Maximilian Harrison was feeling the pressure. On his drive to the museum he had noted the police cars heading towards Mickering Priory. While he felt confident that there was no one left to testify against him, Max was worried that someone might have spotted Geraint's Crossley on route to the museum. He wanted to steal the *Boniface Psalter*, blame it on the Magpie and be out of there in the shortest time possible.

Max was thwarted in this by Alfred, his latest victim. The key to the psalter's cabinet was on a different fob to the watchman's everyday bunch of keys attached to his belt. Max had tried each key on the first bunch, before extracting a second set from the safe. He tested each in turn before finally finding the correct one. All of this was done by torch light, as Max did not want to alert a passing bobby on the beat, to his presence in the museum.

He now gazed at the leather-bound, vellum tome held in his hands and tried to balance the desire to possess the book, with the fear it would betray him. He wondered if he should destroy the manuscript and put an end, once and for all, to the curse. Nevertheless he could not even bring himself to rip out the pages, on which a younger Max had rashly forged the saint's handwriting.

His train of thought was broken by a heavy footstep behind

him and he spun around to see the eerie spectre of a medieval knight, clunking towards him across the marble floor. Involuntarily he gasped in shock.

'Who are you? What do you want?' He asked, backing up against the display cabinet.

There was a sudden drop in temperature. The drapes at one window at the back of the gallery began to billow dramatically in the cold night air. Goosebumps rose on Max's skin.

Slowly raising the sword she was carrying, with both hands, Dorothea began her performance, speaking in deathly tones.

'I am Boniface, Æthelbald, the monks of Nhutscelle and Mickering, members of the Quintrell family throughout the ages, Professor Beaumaris, Tristan Hadley-Brown, Bertram Pickles, Laurence Tarleton and all of those whose timelines you have tampered with for your own advancement. Listen to me Maximilian Harrison! The curse has fallen upon you. You have been weighed upon the scales and found to be wanting. Your fame and fortune shall pass away to others and you will die. Mene, mene, tekel, upharsin.'

A tall book case shook, then toppled over, disgorging all of its treasures on to the floor, as if to demonstrate the ghost's point.

This startled Dorothea and her sword gave a lurch as her muscles grew tired. With some skill she turned it into a Damoclesesque jab towards her target and hoped it gave the artistic impression of divine judgement.

'What say you Maximilian Harrison in your defence?'

'I . . . I . . . I can explain.' Max managed to gasp in fear.

There was a closer cold blast of air and another set of drapes began to billow in time with the first set.

'Explain then Maximilian Harrison. Your victims are all in this very room, waiting to hear you speak. Speak then Maximilian Harrison! Tell them why you changed their histories.'

Max was pressed up against the wall, as far from the phantom as was possible and moaned in terror. His shaking hands searching for a weapon, found the revolver in his coat pocket. He fired wildly at the ghost three times, before the gun jammed and the spectre seemingly disappeared. The bullet's trails sparked red in the dark and ricocheted off metal, creating more sparks.

Max scrabbled to find a light switch. His need to exorcise the ghost was now more pressing than his need for caution. He flicked on every switch, fully illuminating the room. His tormentor was lying on the floor, clutching at its left shoulder. He raised his gun again and pathetically the onetime apparition tried to weakly scramble out of his line of sight.

A number of things happened simultaneously.

A rhythm that had been just on the cusp of hearing for a few minutes, suddenly got a lot louder. A cacophony of sound hit Max as the main doors to the South Gallery were flung wide open. A line of conga-dancing, drunk students stormed the room, with gramophone in tow, to continue their party in a grander venue.

'What the hell?' cried Max.

A tall man dressed in black, detached himself from what remained of the shadows and grabbed Max from behind and swung him off balance. The gun fired again above the heads of the dancers causing screams to ring out and pandemonium to ensue.

A loud *CRASH* shook the building. There were more screams from the revellers and the fire alarm began to sound as someone broke the glass in panic.

***

Outside the basement door of the museum, there was a whispered conversation happening between the members of the vicarage carload.

'How are we going to get in?' asked Balvan, thoughtfully.

'We could climb up a drain pipe to enter from the roof?' Mary Long gave the cast ironwork a hefty tug, to see if it budged.

'You might be able to Longy, but the rest of us would slip and die!' said Jinny firmly.

Reverend Moss took decisive action. He took off his shoe and hit a pane of glass in a nearby window. It broke with a satisfying crack. Then reaching in, he turned the latch and lifted the sash.

'I saw that in a film once.' he said with relish, climbing over the sill.

Jinny was shocked but a little impressed with her husband's new found lawbreaking streak.

CRASH

They heard a muffled noise in the distance that seemed to shake the whole building. Hurriedly they scrambled through the window and made off in the direction the sound had come from.

***

As Maggie's car approached Ancoats at speed, there was a discussion going on about how best to enter the museum.

'Why don't we park up, then sneak into the museum by the basement,' suggested Mary Short from the back of the car, whose only show of nerves was the white of her knuckles holding tightly to the seat in front.

'We don't have a key for the basement door,' answered Geraint, clutching his seat as Maggie took a corner very fast, using the racing line.

'Maybe there is a window we could break down there,' this was from Simon in the front passenger seat who was serenely map reading, apparently unconcerned by Maggie's speedy driving.

The car left the ground for a moment, as they went over a hump in the road and Geraint thought his stomach had been left behind.

'I think a more direct approach is needed. Let's try the main door,' said Maggie.

'The main office is there, so we could alert Alfred to the potential break in,' conceded Mary Short.

'What if Dr Harrison has nobbled Alfred first?' asked Simon.

The shape of the museum hurtled out of the twilight towards them at a great rate.

'Where are you thinking of parking Maggie?' Geraint whimpered from the back.

Maggie turned the car into the museum drive at twenty miles

per hour.

'I wasn't thinking of parking,' called Maggie, 'We are going to ram the main door. The element of surprise and all that! Brace yourselves people!'

'What the hell?'

'Ahhhhh!'

CRASH

The car hit the main doors of the museum, which burst open under the impact of the now braking car. They came to a halt in the hallway of the museum surrounded by wreckage, watched by a gaggle of rapidly sobering student merrymakers.

***

In the police car there was bickering going on in the back seat.

'Are we nearly there yet?' asked Geraldine Beaumaris.

'Don't fuss the police constable, Geraldine. I think we took a wrong turning at Eccles. Don't you agree Chief Inspector?' asked Theodora Hadley-Brown.

'Can't you drive any faster PC Standish? This is the biggest story of my career. It might be a stepping stone to the nationals!' said David, breathing down PC Standish's neck.

'No one cares about your career you annoying, little man. We would be there by now, if your "short cut" hadn't added extra time to the journey,' said Geraldine Beaumaris acerbically.

'Take that back!'

'No . . . because it is true.'

'Are there any public lavatories on route PC Standish? I am sure we would all feel better for a break and some fresh air,' suggested Theodora, trying to distract the combatants.

'And some tea and cake,' added Geraldine.

'I wouldn't object to a convenience break either,' said David Simpkins begrudgingly.

DCI Kydd and PC Standish remained woodenly silent throughout this conversation. As they were driving down Great Bridgewater Street, PC Standish spotted the Victorian public toilets and pulled up outside. The three passengers all alighted, still bickering.

'I think a penny is extortionate.'

'It's extremely reasonable if you really need to go.'

'Could one of you ladies lend me a penny? I only have notes.'

'I have a threepenny bit in my pocket somewhere. I can treat us all . . .'

While Geraldine, Theodora and David sorted themselves out, DCI Kydd looked pointedly at PC Standish. PC Standish nodded. He put the car into gear and drove off, leaving their three annoying passengers behind.

'Thank goodness they are gone,' DCI Kydd breathed a sigh of relief. 'To the museum Standish!'

***

In the basement, Mary Long, Balvan Thakkar, Clarence and Jinny Moss could hear a commotion above their heads.

'We need to get up to the South Gallery quickly,' shouted Mary, leading the way through the bowels of the building.

'Let's use the trap door Mary,' called Jinny, tugging on a door to the stock cupboard. 'It will give us the advantage of surprise.'

They piled into the tight space, then realised they could not all fit on to the lift platform.

'You three get on and I'll work the controls to raise you, then I'll join you in a minute,' suggested Mary Long.

Balvan kissed her, then joined the Mosses on the platform, squeezing together to fit through the hole that had appeared in the ceiling. They disappeared upwards into the unknown.

***

In the back footwell of Maggie's car, Geraint groaned and untangled himself from Mary Short, who was cursing and holding a handkerchief to a cut above her eyebrow but otherwise appeared to be uninjured. Simon Culthorpe also uninjured, was already hopping out of the car to get Maggie's wheelchair out of the boot.

'Everyone ok in the back?' asked Maggie cheerfully. 'The old bus has stood up to being a battering ram rather well. Simon thinks it is still drivable. Come on you two slow coaches, we are the centre of attention. Would you all like a weapon? Simon be a lamb and give everyone one of my golf clubs please.'

Together they advanced in a square formation - rather like roman soldiers, wielding their golf clubs in front of them. Mary Short peeled off from the rest of the cohort, when she noticed Alfred's body on the floor and went to try and help him.

Inside the South Gallery, some enterprising students had thrown together a barricade to protect themselves from the war that was raging at the other end and were singing songs about taking back the museum for the good of the people, but were doing very little about it.

As Geraint watched, Max smashed a chair over the head of a figure dressed in black. In retaliation, Lottie jumped on Max's back and clamped her hand over his nose and pulled hard. While trying to shake her off, Max tripped over the deliberately placed hairy leg of a lady with a white beard and was sent sprawling. There was plenty of kicking, biting and other dirty tactics, that would not have been allowed by the Marquis of Queensbury.

Jinny, Reverend Moss and Balvan appeared through the floor squashed together on the trap door and joined in the brawl. Simon and Maggie charged into battle too waving their golf clubs. Geraint saw Max, who had just regained his feet, tripped over again by a precision, hit and run, golf club attack.

Geraint could see that Max was tiring, so left his capture in the capable hands of his colleagues and went looking for Dorothea.

***

When Maximilian Harrison had shot at the Ghost of Easter Present, Dorothea had been hit by a bullet which dented the antique steel and had ricocheted off again, leaving her right shoulder in agony and right arm drooping and useless. She did her best to wriggle out of Max's line of fire, supporting her injured arm with her good one. She ended up propped up near the open window, gratefully breathing in the fresh, night air, to prevent herself feeling nauseated.

She watched in a haze of pain as her black-clad rescuer, Eric Tarleton, wrestled the gun from Max's hand and threw it out of the nearest open window. It whistled near to Dorothea's ear and she flinched.

Eric momentarily distracted, was rugby tackled by Max to the floor. Dorothea watched as the two men scrabbled around, one, then the other, gaining the upper hand. So engrossed in the life and death struggle happening in front of her, she had ignored the blaring beat coming from a gramophone and the drunken students partying. Two particularly dishevelled students broke away from the main gaggle and joined in the fray, apparently trying to help Eric but half the time getting in each other's way.

A loud crash out in the foyer caused Dorothea to wince.

Harold Aldridge, wearing very odd clothes, intercepted an evil right hook thrown by Eric but meant for Max. It lifted Harold off his feet and knocked him out cold.

Dorothea was suddenly aware that more of her friends had appeared all resolutely trying to stop both Maximilian and Eric from escaping. At one point, Jinny hit Lottie with a Turner painting because Lottie had tried to prevent Reverend Moss from stopping Eric escaping, by squirting him with a fire extinguisher.

A dishevelled Eric appeared at Dorothea's side. He raised Dot's uninjured hand to his lips.

'Was it you adding the creepy effects to my performance?' whispered Dorothea. 'Thank you for coming to my aid.'

'Anything for you, dearest Dot. I shinned up the dumbwaiter's rope while Max was busy picking the lock on the psalter's cabinet. It was the quickest and quietest option I could see to enter the gallery. Your performance was masterful, my love. Ah, I see my rival approaching. I am sorry for abducting you. Really I am. If you ever need me, you only need to ask and I will come.'

He kissed her hand again, hopped over the window sill and was away into the night.

***

Geraint spotted Dorothea huddled beneath the window cradling her damaged arm, and a chap that he assumed was Eric, looming over her. Already sorely tried, he finally lost all self-restraint and ran over waving his golf club and hollering blood curdling war cries. Eric saw him coming and exited through the window, into the night.

Geraint stood half in and half out of the window, bellowing to the now empty street. 'Come back here Eric, you slimy, thieving coward. I want a word with you! When I catch you, you'll be sorry that you were even born.' Remembering himself and the reason for his own presence here, he knelt by Dorothea's side. 'Are you alright?' He asked brusquely, placing a hand tentatively on her injured shoulder.

'Absolutely fine,' she said, through teeth gritted with pain. 'It just my arm . . . Max shot me.'

'I am sorry,' he removed his hand rapidly. 'Can I get you anything?'

'A doctor, please.'

'Hang on.'

He was back in a moment with Mary Short, who had liberated the museum's first aid kit.

He stood by impotently not knowing what to do, while Mary Short checked over her friend.

'I think that you have a broken clavicle Dot, but we will need to get you to the hospital.'

Near the *Boniface Psalter* display, Balvan and Simon had finally managed to wrestle Maximilian Harrison to the floor. Jinny was sitting on his legs and Lottie was tying his ankles with the vicar's belt.

Exhausted but jubilant, an uninjured Mary Long stood up and surveyed the battle scene. It was less than ideal. Maggie was trying to right her wheelchair that had tipped over when she had side slammed Max, to stop him beating the vicar's head repeatedly on a table. Jinny was hobbling because she had tried a flying kick at Max, that she had seen at the cinema, but had unintentionally kicked Balvan, who was precipitously catapulted into Lottie and Simon, knocking them down like skittles. Harold Aldridge was still unconscious on the floor.

'We did it everyone, we captured the killer!' She stepped backwards into the gapping chasm of where the trap door should have been.

'Aaaaaaaaaahhhhh!'

CRUNCH!

While Mary Long's friends were distracted by her accident, Max saw his chance and took it. With one massive heave, that great bear of a man broke away from his captors. He managed to hop with his ankles tied across the South Gallery towards the door.

Geraint leaping into action strode across the hall and punched Max full in the face.

'That is for shooting Dot,' he yelled.

Max reeled but kept on hopping. Geraint punched him again.

'That is for framing my father!'

Max punch drunk, face distorted, aimed a fist at Geraint which he easily side stepped.

'And this is for stealing my Crossley!' bellowed Geraint and punched Max one last time.

Dr Maximilian Harrison, best-selling author of *The Curse of the Boniface Psalter* and notorious killer, was felled like a log.

***

DCI Kydd and PC Standish pulled up outside of the museum just as a number of stretchers were being carried out through the main doorway into a fleet of waiting ambulances. Hurriedly they left their borrowed police car and rushed up the museum driveway. They past a whimpering Mary Long on a stretcher with her legs in makeshift splints made of broom handles. Balvan was at her side, holding her hand and tenderly whispering reassurances in her ear.

As they came to the main entrance, Dr Maximilian Harrison was being escorted out of the door by Geraint Hadley-Brown and Clarence Moss.

Walking straight up to the group, DCI Kydd made the arrest. 'Dr Maximilian Harrison I am arresting you for the murders of

MURDER BY THE BOOK

Professor Beaumaris, Sir Laurence Tarleton and Mr Bertram Pickles and the attempted murder of myself, Miss Mary Long, Miss Mary Shor, Reverend and Mrs Moss, Miss Maggie Forshaw, Dr Balvan Thakkar, Dr Lottie Ellis, Professor Aldridge, Mrs Geraldine Beaumaris, Mrs Theodora Hadley-Brown and Mr David Simpkins. PC Standish here is going to caution you and then we will arrange for your transfer to a cell at police headquarters, where our police surgeon will patch you up.' To PC Standish who was glowing with pride, 'Handcuff him Standish and load him into the car.'

CHAPTER SEVENTEEN

Confession

Dr Harrison's Confession to be Published Posthumously as an Addendum to the Second Edition of A Concise History of the Boniface Psalter

By the time you read this dear reader, I, Maximilian Harrison will be dead. The officers of his majesty's judicial system will have taken me to a place of execution and will have strung me up by the neck, until I am no more. Do not weep for me dear reader because even though I am gone, this book will remain, maybe as long as the *Boniface Psalter* itself. It is a very good book after all!

You are probably wondering just how I came to be in this predicament. I graduated from the Victoria University of Manchester in 1911 with a Bachelor of Arts degree in history. Due to my natural scholarly ability, my tutors suggested I progress to doctoral studies. I settled on Professor Beaumaris as my supervisor because he was very highly regarded in academia. Little did my younger self know that he wasn't a very good doctoral supervisor.

He suggested that I come up with a research project on the *Boniface Psalter* and immediately I was drawn to the idea of the curse. I suggested to Professor Beaumaris that I entitled my thesis, *The Curse of the Boniface Psalter throughout the Ages*. He wasn't very supportive and even suggested multiple other projects, all of them vastly inferior. He eventually said, "If you must, but I can guarantee that you will be back here in six months asking to change direction."

I began my research with energetic fervour but soon found that Professor Beaumaris was correct, there was very scant information available about the curse. I was too proud to go back cap in hand to him. Instead, I made up sources where the curse of the *Boniface Psalter* was mentioned. Sometimes I started from scratch; other times I adapted stories to fit my theme. I pretended to go on archival trips all around the world, when in reality I use to book into a boarding house in Blackpool for a holiday. I also added one or two little annotations of my own to the manuscript, copying the saint's handwriting of course. I flatter myself that St Boniface himself wouldn't have been able to tell the difference.

My girlfriend at the time, Phyllis Peters, later my wife, resided in the hall of residence next to the museum. It was my usual custom to take a tea break with her. I had procured the key to the fire door between the women's hall and museum and had made a copy of it, so I could visit Phyllis's room without getting cold and wet in winter.

On the day of the original exhibition of the *Boniface Psalter* in February 1914, Professor Beaumaris's secretary had asked me to attend a meeting with the professor that morning. When I got there (a little late), he railed at me. He had finally read a draft of my thesis and had become suspicious of some of my "sources". I had forgotten that he had studied the manuscript himself as a postdoctoral researcher, therefore my own little additions could not slip past him unnoticed. He threatened me with every punishment under the sun.

Eventually he calmed down enough to agree to meet me at three thirty that day, "to see what damage my reckless vandalism had wrought," in the cabinet, a freestanding museum case specifically made for exhibiting the *Boniface Psalter*.

There were only three official copies of the cabinet key. One was kept by Bertram Pickles, the museum watchman, in the safe, one was kept by Professor Beaumaris in his office for his students to use, and one was kept by Tristan Hadley-Brown, the museum's curator. I had secretly made a fourth copy of the key for my own use. I had even copied the main museum key so I could come and go as I pleased, though Bertram Pickles was becoming a little suspicious of my ability to enter the building unnoticed.

I laid my plans. I went home to get some things I needed but was back in the museum by lunchtime.

At two forty five I offered to make my office mate, Harold

Aldridge, a cup of tea. Fortuitously the other student, Lottie Ellis, had been having an affair with Sir Laurence Tarleton, who was Professor Beaumaris's protégé and had got herself into the family way, so had been sent to manage a dig in Douma, to hide the growing evidence. I overheard all the salacious details while waiting for my own morning interview with Professor Beaumaris. Professor Beaumaris berated Laurence Tarleton at the top of his voice and sacked him on the spot because he had also been dallying with Professor Beaumaris' wife. What a troubled love quadrangle!

I made the tea in the staff kitchen in the basement, making sure I had a chat with Mrs Theodora Hadley-Brown, who was there helping to prepare the refreshments for the exhibition opening. I put laudanum in Harold's cup because, by that point, I knew what I must do and didn't want any witnesses.

I took my own tea over to the hall of residence, leaving by the front door and waving to Bertram Pickles. I let myself into Phyllis's room and changed her clock back by half an hour. I then put on some of her clothes over the top of my clothes, including a head scarf and let myself back into the museum through the fire door with my illicit key.

The museum was closed to visitors that day so I knew there were fewer people around to see me. Tristan Hadley-Brown caught a glimpse in the distance, but no one believed him, as he had the biggest motive of all for wanting Professor Beaumaris dead.

The South Gallery was quiet. The cabinet already had the red velvet curtains drawn around it, for later that evening. I quickly took off my borrowed feminine apparel and entered the cabinet which was unlocked.

Professor Beaumaris was there reading the psalter and began to chastise me for defacing a priceless artefact. He would not listen to my side of the story. I got so angry that I snatched the manuscript off him and beat him with it around his head. A twelve hundred year old leather-bound, illuminated manuscript is rather heavy and I managed to stave his skull in.

When my anger had subsided, I realised I had killed him and I knew I needed to set the scene in a theatrical manner if I wanted to walk away scot-free.

I propped up the dead man against the glass of the cabinet and used his finger to write "Mene, mene, tekel, upharsin," in blood on the glass, a direct nod to the saint's message to King Æthelbald in the preface of the psalter. I left, locking the door behind me with my own key, donned my women's clothes and past unseen into the hall of residence, via the fire door. A nice little locked room conundrum for the local police!

I had time to change out of my girlfriend's clothes before she returned to her room for tea at three thirty. Because I had changed the clock in her room by thirty minutes, she was able to give me an alibi for the crucial time, though the police weren't very good at narrowing down the time of the crime so I wasn't totally out of the woods.

I returned to the office through the internal door from the hall of residence to the museum, with my own key, to find my fellow PhD student sleeping like a baby, as I had planned. I had time to hide my copy of the cabinet key in a plaster of Paris mould I had been making of some Anglo-Saxon coins for a diagram in my thesis. I woke up Harold in time to help with the exhibition opening and was present when the grisly discovery was made of Professor Beaumaris' body. I offered to telephone for the police and used Tristan Hadley-Brown's office. While there, I spotted his key to the cabinet, so I stole it and hid it in the soil of a plant pot for a couple of days, to throw suspicion on to Tristan and away from me. Once the police lost interest, I dug it up and placed it back in his desk drawer. Tristan Hadley-Brown supressed its return for reasons of his own.

Over the next few weeks my girlfriend, started to think a bit too much. She noticed that her clock had lost time, before I had a chance to correct it. As a distraction I proposed and she accepted me. We had a whirlwind marriage a couple of weeks later.

Then the blackmail began. Bertram Pickles had become suspicious that I had my own key to the women's hall of residence. He guessed that I had a key to the psalter's display cabinet too. He was troubled that he couldn't remember seeing me return from the hall of residence via the main door. Pickles confronted me about it late one night and said he would go to the police if I didn't give him a hundred pounds. It was a massive sum for a poor postgraduate student to find, but somehow I managed to scrape it together.

That was the first of many requests for money, politely made but threatening me with exposure. After six months, with a new wife and a position to uphold, I was desperate.

Luckily for me, the continent was plunged into war, which meant that men from all walks of life enlisted to help the war effort. The police were understaffed and were unable to focus on an unsolved murder investigation.

Through my uncle's connections I had got a desk job at the War Office so I put my doctoral studies on hold for the good of the country. Bertram Pickles' demands had increased with the pay packet of my new job and I needed to stop him.

I had some leave booked for Christmas 1914. I travelled north from London to see my wife and I intended to sort out Bertram Pickles once and for all.

I set up a rendezvous with him at a public house in Salford, where neither of us was known. I watched him go into the pub to wait for me but I deliberately didn't go in. He waited for me for three hours and had become drunk in that time. As he left, I waylaid him and manoeuvred him into a nearby alley. I struck him with a knife, beat him up and took anything valuable he had. I left him to die in the snow. The incident was investigated by Salford's police and they did not make the connection between the death of Bertram Pickles and the murder of Professor Beaumaris, so again I got away with it.

Then Phyllis fell pregnant. She became moody and difficult. The time difference of the clock in her room had been playing on her mind. She had a trick of turning all the clocks back in the house by half an hour, whenever I was there. She never openly accused me of murder but she knew it was me.

She was a liability and she had to go. I put aconitine in her toothpaste and left for London. She was admitted to hospital with gastrointestinal difficulties and vomiting. There she and the baby died. I feel remorseful that the child didn't get a chance of life but it was probably for the best. I would have been a terrible parent!

After the war, I returned to university to finish my doctorate. I nearly came unstuck in my viva, as it was so long since I had written some of the chapters of my thesis, that I couldn't remember what I had made up.

My examiners took pity on me given that my PhD supervisor had been murdered and passed me with major revisions. I never submitted them. In my own mind I had done enough for a doctorate, so I started using the honorific title doctor and never looked back.

I wrote my best-selling book, *A Concise History of the Curse of the Boniface Psalter* which brought me fame and fortune. On the back of it, I gained a lectureship post at a prestigious university and lots of offers for further books which I have enjoyed writing in my own unique style. So the years passed and I thought I was safe.

Every year I visit Mickering Priory, the ancestral home of the Quintrells, the keepers of the *Boniface Psalter*. I call it a research trip and Theodora Hadley-Brown, née Quintrell, has indulged me in my little eccentricity.

Some of the stories in my book are based on fact. One in particular, the tale of the missing Quintrell treasure, caught my imagination and annually I search for the secret passage. When Theodora invited me down for a weekend party over the Easter weekend of 1935, I jumped at the chance. Little did I know it was a devious plan on Theodora's part, to clear her late husband's name.

I was surprised when I arrived at Mickering Priory to see that Theodora had smartened the old place up. I should have been suspicious when an entire staff lined up to greet the weekend guests. It has been at least twenty years since the Quintrells could afford a full staff. "The staff," was Geraint Hadley-Brown's friends all playing detective, under the watchful eye of PC Kydd, now DCI Kydd, pretending to be of all things, a French chef! Obviously his disguise was so good, I didn't recognise him at first. I was a little disconcerted to find out that all the suspects from 1914 were back together.

The spring weather was atrocious. A major storm and localised flooding meant that Mickering Priory, became an island and we were trapped there for the Easter weekend.

Other than that, everything had been going smoothly and I had even managed some secret passage hunting. Out of the blue someone stole my working copy of the second edition of *A Concise History of the Curse of the Boniface Psalter* from my room, which I kept under lock and key in the bureaux there. Then I realised that my experimental sections had also been taken. I had written an updated chapter on the ill-fated archaeological dig led by Professor Beaumaris, where Michael Quintrell, an exceptionally talented archaeologist and surveyor, sadly died. I had interviewed members of the original team and had come to the conclusion that Laurence had a hand in Michael Quintrell's death but I knew my editor wouldn't let me keep it in because it was libellous. That chapter reappeared on Laurence Tarleton's bed of all places.

He was furious and rightly so, but my little tale had hit a nerve because never have I seen a man protest his innocence so strongly. In his anger, he hinted that he knew something about me that could ruin me. This was alarming, as I had assumed that by now I was safe.

Laurence Tarleton retired to his room and wouldn't leave it. This posed me a logistical problem but with my major intellect, I knew I would prevail.

He had brought a gun with him to Mickering Priory. He took it on excavations as a precaution against looters and marauders, so kept it in a draw next to his bed. I learnt this when Geraint Hadley-Brown offered to put anything of value in the safe for the guests on the first night but no one took him up on his offer.

After dinner, half of the party began playing bridge in the drawing room and the rest of us: Theodora, Harold and I, sat in the library listening to the wireless. When the drinks tray arrived, I mixed Theodora's and Harold's cocktails with a splash of laudanum.

When they had fallen asleep, I went upstairs unseen and knocked on Laurence's door. He told me to go to hell. I said if he didn't open his door and let me in, I would tell Geraldine that he was having another affair with Lottie. It made him open the door pretty sharply I can tell you!

Laurence let me in and I closed the door of his room. He sat down at his desk and returned to writing a letter.

'What are you doing?' I asked.

'Writing to Theodora to say that I am leaving,' he replied.

I surreptitiously positioned myself near to the bedside table, where I assumed he had hidden his gun. My plan was to get hold of it and shoot him from point blank range, making it look like he had committed suicide.

Suddenly he laughed at me nastily and said, 'It's not in there Max. I suspected you might call in to see me, so I moved it.' He drew his gun from his desk drawer and pointed it at me. 'You killed Professor Beaumaris, didn't you Max. He had found out that you defaced the *Boniface Psalter*, to fit your own research hypotheses. I noticed your annotations at the opening of the new exhibition last month. I didn't say anything about my suspicions because I benefitted from Professor Beaumaris' death myself.'

'What about you? Did you kill Michael Quintrell?' I asked merely out of academic interest. Laurence inclined his head ever so slightly. He began to stand up from the desk.

BANG!

I shot him with my own revolver that I had hidden in my pocket, just in case of accidents. Even office-based officers in the Great War had fire arms and we knew how to use them. Laurence toppled forward on to the desk.

I now had a dilemma. There were two guns; one with his fingerprints on but which hadn't been discharged, and one that had been fired but which didn't have his fingerprints on. In the end I left mine, which I wiped clean and then superimposed with Laurence's fingerprints. I pocketed Laurence's gun, set up a very touching scene and left the letter Laurence had been writing on display. It was very apt.

It came as a horrible shock to discover that there was a chief inspector of police marooned with us at Mickering Priory, with sidekicks with the necessary scientific expertise to mount a full forensic investigation. I knew it wouldn't take them long to prove that the bullet that killed Laurence Tarleton was from a different gun. I was banking on being cut off from civilisation for at least a week. DCI Kydd pretended quite convincingly during interviews, that he believed Laurence's death was suicide, but I was taking no chances.

The short power cut on Friday at dinner had given me an idea of how to divert suspicion away from me. This became increasingly necessary, when DCI Kydd announced to everyone that Laurence death was murder, rather than suicide. During the afternoon I disabled the main generator. As I hoped, the backup generator started up automatically. I got rid of any spare fuel down the drain. When the backup generator ran out of fuel, in the subsequent blackout, I headed to the priest hole in the pantry to hide. I had already made bonds out of clothes line and had stashed them in there. My knowledge of knots is exceptional! I used some raw steak from the kitchen to fake a head bump. I was discovered in the priest hole covered in blood, tied up, moaning, and incoherent. It was a fine performance but I was still worried that DCI Kydd was starting to be suspicious of me.

I had hoped that I could make use of the miraculous appearance of the journalist in some way and had thought he would make a jolly good scapegoat, but apparently he had a decent alibi.

I knew then that I would have to kill everyone in the household. My mind at once hit upon the idea of burning Mickering Priory down, but how to keep everyone locked up in the house?

I was annoyed to learn that Geraint Hadley-Brown and his friend had managed to use the journalist's boat, to escape from Mickering Priory to find help. In hindsight this was where my plan ultimately started to unravel.

An idea came to me just as DCI Kydd and his lackeys brought the Quintrell treasure into the morning room. They had finally managed to locate the secret passageway in Laurence Tarleton's room on the first floor, (obviously they wouldn't have found it without my input!). The Quintrell treasure, a trophy of smuggling and piracy, was a sight to behold. I knew then that I wanted it and that I would take it with me.

Suddenly the rest of the party got distracted by the whereabouts of the housemaid, in reality Hadley-Brown's bit of fluff. She appeared to have disappeared along with Eric Tarleton. She had been typing up DCI Kydd's interview notes using my typewriter. Good riddance I thought.

Everyone dashed upstairs to discover that there had been a scuffle and my plaque of imprints of Anglo-Saxon coins had been broken, exposing my copy of the incriminating key from the cabinet of death. I should have got rid of it but keeping it was rather a thrill. Theodora recognised it straight away. I knew the game was up, so drew out my gun (Laurence Tarleton's gun) and encouraged the whole party to enter the secret passageway in Laurence's room, which I closed behind them. I proceeded to set light to the drapes around the bed and anything else that looked flammable. Laurence got a funeral pyre worthy of any Viking lord!

I quickly made my exit, collecting my typewriter, my manuscript and the Quintrell treasure. I borrowed Hadley-Brown's Crossley and drove hell for leather to the museum. Why to the museum you ask? Something that Harold Aldridge had said had sparked an idea in my brain. The *Boniface Psalter,* with my annotations in it, would always point towards my guilt. I decided to steal it and either destroy it, or keep it with me always.

Gaining entrance to the museum was easy enough. The new night watchman is a gullible, lonely fool and welcomed me in to see the psalter after hours. When his back was turned, I hit him over the head with a bust of Wellington. Historical sacrilege, but needs must. I couldn't find the correct key on Alfred's keyring, so had to go rooting in the safe to find it.

Just when I had finally got the cabinet open and was staring at my Nemesis, Geraint's fancy bit popped up, dressed as a spectral knight. I wasn't fooled for a second and I took aim and shot at her.

Then the world went crazy. I had to fight off a whole host of people, who I thought were dead. Later, I found out that that my prisoners had dug through the collapsed smuggler's tunnel and were rescued by Geraint Hadley-Brown and the undergardener, bringing with them the police and the fire brigade. Fair play to them, I commend their desire to live.

How was I, Dr Maximilian Harrison, finally captured you ask? I fought like a lion, but eventually weight of numbers prevailed and Hadley-Brown finished me off with a tremendous right hook. He hit me so hard that he broke my jaw in three places. The police surgeons have had to wire my jaw shut. When questioned by the judge at my trial, I had to write everything down and have my council read it for me. Alas, I shall go to the gallows unable to speak!

So my dear readers let these be my final words to you and all of humanity: I am no different to you. All men have a pivot point about which they rock to and fro, between light and dark, scales going up and down. My pivot stuck in the dark and the dark consumed me – supernatural interference perhaps. I am a modern day example of the curse at work. Beware of staying too long in the dark, or the saint's curse will fall on you too.

Postscript from the Editor: Dr Maximilian Harrison was executed at nine fifteen on the morning of the 25th January 1936. At no point in his trial or sentencing did he show any remorse for his crimes. He requested that his body be donated to science, "As an exceptional specimen for study."

CHAPTER EIGHTEEN

Blessings Bestowed

Monday Morning, 22nd of April 1935

Harold Aldridge had been one of the casualties kept in hospital overnight for observation, with suspected concussion. He was discharged the next morning. Feeling somewhat sore and disorientated, he made his way slowly to the main desk to ask someone to phone for a taxi.

When he gave the porter his name, he was told that there was a lady waiting outside to take him home.

Bemused, Harold made his way out of the hospital and walked straight into Lottie Ellis, who was waiting for him and whose car was parked in an ambulance bay.

'In you get Harold. I am here to take you home.'

'I thought you would go straight back to your dig.'

'Yes I am. I am heading to Southampton this afternoon, to catch a ferry to France. Then I'll take the Orient Express from Paris to Istanbul.'

'It is very good of you to pick me up from the hospital,' said Harold stiffly.

'I couldn't leave again without saying goodbye, could I?' Lottie was embarrassed. 'I enjoyed getting reacquainted with you and I thought that perhaps I might miss you, just a little bit.'

A big smile erupted on Harold Aldridge's bruised face. 'I don't wish to presume Lottie, but might I in future, write to you occasionally at your dig?' He asked tentatively.

'Yes Harold you may . . . I'd like that. I'll give you my forwarding address.'

Emboldened Harold Aldridge asked, 'Next time you are back in the country may I take you out to dinner?'

'No Harold, next time I am back in the country, I will take you out to dinner.'

'Capital!' *It is now or never,* he thought and cleared his throat,

'I was thinking that it might be fascinating to visit Turkey during the long vacation. Could you possibly recommend someone who might act as a tour guide?'

'Someone does come to mind,' she said. 'They are a highly regarded field archaeologist and the foremost expert in the post-Roman to early middle-ages period for the Middle East and they really need a holiday too.'

They grinned at each other, both elated at the twist of fate that had given them a second chance.

An ambulance coming up behind them beeped its horn and Lottie had to move her Bugatti rapidly out of the way.

MURDER BY THE BOOK

Tuesday Morning, 23rd of April 1935

'Did you have a relaxing Easter weekend, Chief Inspector? How was your French cookery course?' asked Miss Grimstead casually, as DCI Kydd entered his office.

Word had obviously not reached Trafford, where Miss Grimstead lived, about the dramatic happenings of the previous few days.

'It was very . . . informative,' he answered cautiously.

He noticed that Miss Grimstead looked different. She was wearing lipstick and eye make-up and she had styled her hair differently, which was most becoming.

'Did you have a good weekend Miss Grimstead?'

'Why yes, DCI Kydd. I went to the pictures with a new friend.'

'Oh . . . anyone I know?' He asked casually.

'Mr Gritty from Dinkworth, Dinkworth and Small Insurance asked if I would like to go with him. I was sceptical at first, but it turns out that he is very good company and a perfect gentleman. He had lots of exciting stories to tell and it turns out he was newly back from Turkey of all places. We are going to the pictures again tonight.'

DCI Kydd congratulated Miss Grimstead on her blossoming romance and said she could leave half an hour earlier that evening, to get to her date on time.

'Thank you very much DCI Kydd, but I won't leave until you have gone to your meeting with the chief superintendent at a quarter to five,' said his perfect secretary. 'I feel it is my job to prevent anyone bothering you with anything unnecessary.'

After solving three murder cases, a string of notorious burglaries and insurance fraud, all in his weekend off, DCI Kydd positively welcomed the unnecessary!

***

PC Standish bounded into DCI Kydd's office, the visit having been sanctioned by Miss Grimstead.

LIZZIE BENTHAM

'Congratulations sir! The newspapers are full of the arrest of Dr Harrison this morning. Dinkworth, Dinkworth and Small are offering a reward for the capture of Eric Tarleton – the Magpie.'

'I am just glad it is over,' said his boss. 'You came just in the nick of time Standish. I am eternally grateful.' DCI Kydd had been so happy to see Standish's face peeping into the tunnel, wielding a mattock, he had nearly cried but he was not going to admit that. 'How are the patients doing?'

'I spoke to Matron first thing and all patients are out of theatre and are comfortable on the wards. It was touch and go with Alfred for a while but it looks like he will pull through. Mary Shor and Professor Aldridge have been discharged home already. There should be no lasting damage, but the young people will be uncomfortable for a little while.'

'So what was it you found out at Somerset House Standish?'

'What you suspected, sir. Dr Maximilian Harrison married his girlfriend, Phyllis Peters, in a registry office wedding, secretly, two weeks after the murder of Professor Beaumaris in May 1914.'

'I knew it! A wife can't be forced to testify against her husband. It was in Dr Harrison's best interests to keep Phyllis loyal and a wedding might have stopped her thinking about what happened on the day Professor Beaumaris died. When and how did she die?'

'The 5th of March 1916. She was pregnant with their first child and the death certificate says gastroenteritis, or stomach flu, during pregnancy. It presents as nausea, vomiting, and diarrhoea. I have talked to her doctor, who is coming up to retirement but he still remembers the case. Mrs Harrison had a normal pregnancy but had been suffering from low spirits. He attributed this to being on her own, while her husband worked in London. The doctor was called in to see Mrs Harrison by the Harrison's housekeeper, who was extremely worried about her mistress. He arrived to find Mrs Harrison in a very bad way. He rushed her to the hospital himself, on the brink of life and death. She died before even getting to theatre and they weren't able to save the baby either. The doctor said that Mrs Harrison deteriorated very quickly, quicker than he would have expected and he was surprised no post mortem was carried out at the time by the hospital.'

'Max poisoned his wife and unborn child too because she was on to him. He very nearly told us he had done it at the priory.' The realisation hit DCI Kydd like a blow to his stomach.

'Will they hang him sir? Is he mad?'

'No he isn't mad Standish. They will hang him alright.'

LIZZIE BENTHAM

The Evening of Tuesday 23rd April 1935

David Simpkins and Mary Short were at the theatre. David was writing a review of a new play *Island Ho!* and had tentatively asked Mary Short if she would accompany him. He had enjoyed himself hugely. He had got some pithy quotes from the retired naval captain sat next to him. He had also had a lovely chat with an older lady about growing peculiar shaped vegetables and had promised to cover the local vegetable growing competition in the summer.

During this time, Mary Short had become increasingly reserved. Her head hurt and she self-consciously rubbed the stiches on her forehead covered in sticking plaster.

At the end of the evening while they walked back to the tram stop, David said, 'This was a good evening wasn't it? We met some interesting people and the play was excellent, "a real peach," to quote Captain Porter sat next to us.'

'David you spent so much time talking to other people, you didn't speak to me once. You didn't ask about how my day has been. It was awful. I still started my new placement after everything that happened this weekend. My new consultant is a narcissist, my registrar is suicidal and my houseman spent the evening chatting up the matron. I had to cover three wards on my own and two of my patients died of pneumonia.'

'I didn't know. Would you say staffing levels are endangering patient safety and the government should step in to better fund this country's hospitals, rather than rely on charitable donations?'

'This is off the record David! I am fed up of having to watch everything I say with you. That is not how a relationship should work. I need to be able to trust you not to quote me as an anonymous source.'

'But I won't do it, if you don't like it,' he said sulkily.

'You do it without even thinking. Your mind is always on the next big story. David, this isn't going to work between us. Thank you for taking me to the theatre tonight, but tonight will be our last night out. I wish you every success with your career going forward and I hope that in time we can be friends.'

'But Mary . . .'

'Here is my tram back to halls now. Goodbye David.'

She climbed into the tram, showing her ticket to the conductor. At no point did she look back.

LIZZIE BENTHAM

Saturday Morning, 27th April 1935

The sun shone down on what was shaping up to be a gloriously mild April day. The hedgerows were alive with blossom and bird song. There was the promise of new life and fresh starts in the air.

At St Bartholomew's church, Lower Heaton-in-the-Marsh, the flower arrangers had surpassed themselves with window and pedestal displays filled with white, blue, yellow and pink flowers that filled the air with fragrance. The congregation had assembled to support the young couple. The groom had arrived with his supporters, looking suitably nervous and very smart in his best suit. The only thing that jarred in this expectant scene was that the vicar had two puffy, black eyes and was struggling to read the order of service.

The organist struck up Mendelssohn's *Wedding March* and the vicar asked the congregation to rise.

First, Jinny the matron of honour, immaculate in her pale green dress but clutching a posy in her teeth, hopped down the aisle on crutches and took her place on the left of the church with the bridal party. Next Mary Short also immaculate in pale green walked down the aisle, posy held demurely, still sporting a sticking plaster on her forehead. Following her, Mary Long in a wheelchair with two legs in plaster, wearing a slightly rumpled pale green dress, was pushed down the aisle by Balvan Thakkar, who radiated pride in his charge. Then came Dorothea, with her arm in a sling and the buttons of her green dress done up incorrectly at the back.

Bringing up the rear was Maggie Forshaw, the bride, dressed in satin and tulle and looking beautiful. She held on to her father's arm and teetered down the aisle to a spontaneous round of applause and quite a few tears.

MURDER BY THE BOOK

Monday Morning, 13th May 1935

A tall, bespectacled, young man with flaming red hair, the colour of henna, got off the boat at Mersin, in Turkey and sniffed the hot, dry air spiced with the scent of the orient.
It is good to be back, he thought.
He was dressed in a slipshod manner, wearing a crumpled linen suit with a large sunhat shading his face and keeping the sun off his head. With him, he had a battered suitcase and some cardboard boxes of equipment.

'Derek Ellis?' queried the immigration official peering at his shiny, new passport.

'Yes that's me. I am the nephew of Dr Lottie Ellis, the archaeologist, and I am joining her on the dig at Tarsus this season. I am so looking forward to trying my hand at some excavation. I have never been to Turkey before. I have never even been outside of the United States of America before either,' he said excitedly, in a transatlantic accent.

The immigration official smiled indulgently. He had heard of the crazy English lady who liked to dig up his country's heritage and had no difficulty imagining that this was her nephew. He leisurely stamped Derek Ellis's passport and waved him through. The young man vigorously shook the immigration official's hand, picked up his luggage and wandered, somewhat absentmindedly, out towards the dockside, a veritable cauldron of hawkers, beggars and tourists.

A battered, old Austin tourer pulled up on the quayside, with the recognisable profile of the Middle East's most famous and occasionally, infamous, female archaeologist sitting in the driving seat, who waved and "Cooeed" to get his attention.

Derek Ellis sauntered over to the car, loaded his luggage into the back and joined his "aunt" in the front.

Lottie put the car into reverse and cumbersomely turned the vehicle around, trying not to run over anyone.

'It sure is lovely to see you again Auntie Lottie. It's been ever such a long time,' he drawled, grinning wickedly and chastely kissing Lottie on the cheek.

Lottie grinned too. 'Did you have any trouble getting through customs my dear nephew?' she asked.

'None whatsoever.'

'Was the voyage eventful? No jewels went missing I hope.'

'No it was terribly tedious Auntie.'

The car slowly weaved in and out of local traffic, animals and street vendors, until the suburbs gave way to fields and the fields gave way to wilderness. The two people in the car visibly relaxed.

'I am not sure I like your red hair dear.'

'I am sure the sun will bleach it back to its old colour soon enough. I just have to establish the persona of Derek Ellis for a year or two and no one will remember Eric Tarleton, or the Magpie. Thank goodness you live a peripatetic lifestyle Mother.'

'Well I for one am very glad to have you here with me dear. Let me show you the dig and your new home.'

MURDER BY THE BOOK

Wednesday Morning, 15th May 1935

'Miss Long and Dr Thakkar are here to see you Chief Inspector,' a cheery Miss Grimstead popped her head around the door.

'Please send them through.' DCI Kydd sent up silent prayers of gratitude that Miss Grimstead was currently so happy. She had even baked her colleagues some biscuits the other day, though the chief inspector deduced that Mr Gritty was partial to a Viennese whirl and that the police were merely guinea pigs for Miss Grimstead's culinary experiments.

'Do come in Balvan, Mary, it is lovely to see you again and looking so much recovered.'

Mary was still hobbling a little bit from her injuries but was now down to one crutch.

'I wanted to thank you for your help with the Mickering Priory case. It was invaluable and I was very impressed by your professionalism. You both made excellent scene of crime experts. While Mary was teaching me to cook Balvan, she mentioned that you are struggling to find a permanent academic position at a British university and that you might be forced to return to India. The chief superintendent wants to expand our forensic division so I recommended you. There is a position as a police chemist available, if you would like it.'

The young couple looked at each other in surprise and joy. Mary squeezed Balvan's fingers tightly.

'Thank you Chief Inspector. I enjoyed working with you too. Applying my scientific skills to fighting crime is something that I really got a taste for. I would be delighted to accept,' said Balvan.

Mary bounced out of her seat and impulsively threw her arms around DCI Kydd's neck.

'You are an absolute lamb DCI Kydd. We can get married now. You shall be the guest of honour at our wedding. Head bridesmaid or best man or whatever you want to be.'

Chuckling indulgently he said, 'Thank you Mary. If it is all the same to you, I'll happily sit in a pew with Mrs Kydd, sing some hymns and throw rice at you at the end. I'd enjoy that a lot.'

'In that case Chief Inspector, that is precisely what you shall do!'

MURDER BY THE BOOK

Tuesday Morning, 4th June 1935

Theodora looked thoughtful. She had come from an interesting meeting with her solicitor. The finding and subsequent sale of the Quintrell pirate horde of gold, had captured the public's imagination. A prestigious British museum had stepped in and bought it for the nation, at an eye watering price. Theodora was now a very wealthy woman indeed.

On top of that, the insurance company had paid out on the fire damage to Mickering Priory. The old part of the building was beyond repair and would have to remain as an interesting garden folly going forward. The Georgian box however, was salvageable and she had asked a local architect, to draw up plans for a much improved Mickering Priory.

Theodora's solicitor had just told her, that a company that ran a chain of well-known country hotels had been in contact to ask if she would be willing to sell Mickering Priory to them, for a very generous price.

Buses do all come at once, she thought nipping into a teashop off Ormskirk's high street for a celebratory cream tea.

Part of her was tempted to buy a modern, little house near the seaside at Southport perhaps, to enjoy a leisurely retirement. She could go on some holidays; a coach trip or two, or a cruise to somewhere exotic. Her children definitely supported this plan and had told her to go and razz it up as much as she wanted, however Theodora had other ideas.

She was about to start out in business. Theodora had instructed her solicitor to decline the offer from the hotel company and had instructed the architect to make sure there were lots of bedrooms in his plan, plus a couple of secret passageways.

Theodora had enjoyed herself so much with a house full of young people investigating a murder, that she was going to run murder mystery weekends for paying guests. Dorothea had put her in touch with the drama society at the university and they were going to supply a constant stream of budding actors. The punters would come with the triple publicity of the capture of a now notorious mass murderer, the discovery of the Quintrell horde and the unmasking of the Magpie. Theodora had enough money to hire a real French chef, even if it was just for weekend parties and a small, but permanent staff to look after the improved Mickering Priory. Mrs Barns was thrilled by this idea.

Theodora thought Tristan would have approved. He had always thought the priory should be enjoyed by a wider circle of people than just the Quintrells. She was so pleased that Tristan had been vindicated. She thought that leaving a healthy business to her children and hypothetical grandchildren would be a good legacy from them both.

Now what am I going to do to get Geraint and Dorothea together? She thought. They were so well suited but totally hopeless.

She had an idea and quickly wrote one of two postcards, then popped it in the letter box while she waited for the bus to take her back to Mickering Priory. Task complete, she spent the way back home daydreaming about owning a motor car and decided that she would look into purchasing one forthwith, a red one.

MURDER BY THE BOOK

The Magpie Insurance Freud Case, Summer 1935

The Magpie was never caught, so Messrs Dinkworth, Dinkworth and Small, the insurance company, brought a fraud case against the accomplices of the Magpie. Geraldine Beaumaris was allowed to turn King's evidence, which was an embarrassment to many of her erstwhile well-to-do but hard up friends. She sailed through the trial and out the other side as a free woman but with her reputation in tatters. The trustees of the museum politely requested her to step down from the board and she had to pay back the money she had received from the insurance company. Geraldine ended up having to sell her mansion house and many of her treasured artworks.

Retiring to the obscurity of the Lancashire countryside to lick her wounds, she hit upon a plan that would revive her ailing fortune.

If Max can do it, Geraldine thought, *then so can I.*

She sold her idea to a well-known publisher and knuckled down to write her memoir. Sitting back at her second-hand typewriter, in her two up, two down cottage, she read the first draft of what she had written and was disappointed.

'How have I made something so infamous, so boring?' she exclaimed in disgust.

With nothing to lose, she reinvented the Magpie as a romantic older gentleman figure and imagined a steamy affair between herself and him. She called it, *The Curious Affair of the Magpie in the Night.*

Her publisher was delighted. The public lapped it up. Geraldine became a famous author with a string of bestselling books. They even made a film of the book with a famous actress, playing her.

Geraldine married an American shipping tycoon and emigrated to America. Her new husband doted on her and indulged her passion for art.

LIZZIE BENTHAM

Saturday Morning, 8th June 1935

The summer exams were over for the year and students all around the city waited impatiently for their results to be announced, to see if they had passed or needed to do resits during the long vacation. The residents of Rose Cottage had managed to do their exams despite their injuries and waited hopefully to hear what their course grades were.

On results day, Dorothea hurried to her pigeon hole to find two missives. One was her results. Despite everything, she had passed the year, averaging an upper second class degree result!

The other was an invitation with strangely familiar handwriting:

"Dr Hadley-Brown requests the pleasure of Miss Robert's company at Heaton Park, on Saturday at 10 am. Meet by the band stand. RSVP to Mickering Priory."

On Saturday morning dressed in her best, Dorothea made her way to Heaton Park both excited and terrified simultaneously. She had not seen Geraint since Maggie and Simon's wedding and even then it was fleetingly, because she was taken up with her bridesmaid duties.

The park was alive with the colour and fresh scents of summer. Dorothea positioned herself near the bandstand, where the Salvation Army band was preparing to play a concert to raise funds for good works.

Dorothea's heart felt full to bursting, when she saw a familiar figure walking towards her carrying a bunch of flowers.

'Hello Dr Hadley-Brown . . . Geraint! Thank you for your invitation. The park is so lovely this time of year. Are these for me? I love peonies.'

This drew him up short. 'Yes, they are indeed for you but you said "my invitation". I thought that you had invited me?'

'I received a postcard from you and I had to RSVP to Mickering Priory,' she took the cherished postcard out of her bag, to show him. He reciprocated by pulling a near identical postcard from his coat pocket. His postcard said:

'Miss Robert's requests the pleasure of Dr Hadley-Brown's company at Heaton Park, on Saturday at 10 am. Meet by the band stand. No RSVP needed.'

'I think my mother may have been doing some match making,' he said with a wry smile. 'She really took a shine to you.'

Dorothea's heart was disappointed but her head said, *You came Geraint Hadley-Brown because you thought I had invited you and you bought me flowers . . .*

'Come on, let's go for a walk. It is a lovely day,' he said offering her his arm which she took gladly.

They fell into step, walking without aim while enjoying the warm summer sunshine and being near each other.

Geraint broke the silence. 'I have accepted the lectureship at Reading Dot,' he said almost shyly.

'Oh, um, very well done, congratulations,' Dorothea tried to sound pleased for him but couldn't quite pull it off.

'Whatever is the matter?'

'Nothing,' she turned away from him and pretended to be interested in some roses planted artistically around the base of a lime tree.

'Something is the matter.'

'Well I'll miss you . . . a bit . . . if you move to Reading.'

'Will you?'

'Yes,' there was a break in her voice. 'Especially if you get married to whoever it is in Reading that you think is so special.'

Suddenly he was very close and gently turned her around to face him, so he could see the silent tears sparkling in her eyes. He kept hold of both of her hands.

'Dot you goose. Look at me. Don't you understand why I need to go to Reading? I love you. I think I've loved you since our very first meeting in that train carriage back in September. You are beautiful, smart, courageous, and funny. Whenever you are near me I can't take my eyes off you.

'You are . . . I mean you were my student. I handed in my resignation yesterday. I am not one of these academics that are comfortable with dallying with one of their students. I am too impatient to walk out with you, to wait until you graduate. This way I am no longer your tutor.

'Please Dorothea Roberts will you walk out with me? Let me court you like we are a normal couple and not the Mancunian answer to Holmes and Watson. I want to take you to the cinema and go dancing with you at the Ritz. I want to eat fish and chips with you, in the rain, on Southport pier and go on the fairground for fun and not because we are chasing a murderer. I don't know what lies ahead. Some people say that we could be at war again within the next few years, but whatever happens I want to face it with you by my side. Hell Dot, I know I am a grumpy, boring fellow but do you think you could love me just a little bit?'

'Yes I do, I do love you! Much, much more than a little bit!'

He wrapped her in a massive bear hug and lifted her off her feet.

'Darling Dot!'

'Geraint!'

They kissed under the lime tree, blissfully unaware of everyone and everything else going on around them.

A little while later, they were sat on a bench with Dorothea snuggled under Geraint's arm talking happily together.

'I was so worried that you liked Eric Tarleton better than me, when I saw you together at Mickering Priory. When I found out that he had kidnapped you, I didn't know what to think.'

Dorothea stroked his cheek affectionately. 'I was flattered by Eric's attention. He could be excellent company when he chose to be charming, but there was a part of me that never really trusted him.'

'So will you come and visit me every few weekends in Reading?'

'Only every few?'

'I'll come up here some weekends to visit you and you will need some time to write your essays. I've seen your usual standard.'

'Oi! I got an upper second this year, I'll have you know! Will you write me long, romantic love letters every week?'

'Yes absolutely. They will be more than ten sheets of paper long, containing at least three poems to your sparkling eyes.'

A thought assailed Dorothea.

'Geraint I want to make it quite clear, if we are the Mancunian Sherlock Holmes and Dr Watson . . . then I am Holmes. You are my side kick.'

'I will always be your side kick darling,' he said and kissed her again.

LIZZIE BENTHAM

Extract from the Worm, 2nd July 1935

In light of the recent debacle surrounding the *Boniface Psalter* and the dramatic events played out at the Ancoats Art Museum and Mickering Priory, about which *The Worm* has reported on in a previous special edition, the university has decided to donate the psalter to the University of Bavaria, in Germany.

In a statement our provost said, 'After much deliberation, the trustees and senior leadership of the university, with the permission of Mrs Theodora Hadley-Brown, the last surviving member of the Quintrell family who gifted the *Boniface Psalter* to the university in 1914, have decided to donate the psalter to a sister institution in Germany, as a gesture of friendship. St Boniface is the patron saint of Germany and the University of Bavaria is delighted to receive the *Boniface Psalter* as a generous gift.'

The *Boniface Psalter* will go on display at the University of Bavaria's library next month. Let's hope the infamous "St Boniface Curse" doesn't have an international reach . . .

(David Simpkins – Journalist)

MURDER BY THE BOOK

Annex 1

The Family Tree of the Quintrells of Mickering Priory as researched by Dr Maximilian Harrison

Sir Timothy Quintrell 1st Baronet of Mickering b1504 - d1541 (Jousting accident) Enobled in 1536 by King Henry VIII	m 1538	Mary Howard b1514 – d1569 (remarried a jousting champion)
Sir Henry Quintrell 2nd Baronet of Mickering b1539 - d1558 (Protestant, burnt at the stake by Queen Mary I)	m 1557	Ellen Martin b1537 – d1583
Sir Frances Quintrell 3rd Baronet of Mickering b1557 - d1599 (Involved with a Catholic plot, died in prison awaiting execution by Queen Elizabeth I)	m 1577	Margaret Beresford b1550 – d1612
Sir Matthew Quintrell 4th Baronet of Mickering b1588 - d1647 (A roundhead, died in battle fighting for Parliment, died without issue)		
Sir James Quintrell 5th Baronet of Mickering b1588 - d1649 (Twin brother of Sir Matthew, a cavalier, died in battle fighting for the King)	m 1613	Lavinia Sutton b1589 – d1671
Sir John Quintrell 6th Baronet of Mickering b1620 - d1665 (Contracted bubonic plague at a theatre in London)	m 1644 m 1650	Alys Robinson b1619 - d1647 (Killed as a witch) Harriet Johnson b1630 – d1665
Sir Philip Quintrell 7th Baronet of Mickering b1660 - d1737 (In league with smugglers, disappeared in 1730 declared dead in 1737)	m 1692	Francis Alsworthy b1674 – 1753 (Shot her husband)
Sir Richard Quintrell 8th Baronet of Mickering b1693 - d1779 (Died of old age)	m 1717	Sofia Coniston b1699 – d1780
Mark Quintrell b1719 - d1772 (Died of typhoid on St Joanna)	m 1748	Teresa de Bellis b1718 – d1749

LIZZIE BENTHAM

END NOTE

This book is dedicated to members of the Friday Club past and present, at St Boniface's church, Nursling. They gave me the idea for this story, after some fascinating discussions about where the location of the original Nursling, or Nhutscelle Monastery might have been, which is where St Boniface studied. They also let me spend many fun hours flower arranging with them.

St Boniface was a Benedictine monk, an archbishop, a missionary, a church reformer, and a martyr and I am sure he would never have cursed anyone. The *Boniface Psalter* is imaginary. What I find fascinating is that St Boniface really did write to King Æthelbald to tell him off for his immoral lifestyle. I found *The Life of St Boniface by Willibald* translated by George W. Robinson and *The Kings and Queens of Anglo-Saxon England* by Timothy Venning really useful.

I have loved setting this novel at Ancoats Hall, at the University Settlement and Art Museum, which jointly did amazing charitable work in Ancoats. The building was demolished in the 1960s. The following books were helpful to learn about the Victoria University of Manchester and University Settlement in the 1930s: *Little Wilson and Big God* by Anthony Burgess and *Portrait of a University 1851-1951* by H.B. Charlton. The Manchester Art Museum Online website was great for helping me picture what the museum at Ancoats Hall would have looked like.

I made up Mickering Priory on the mosslands, near Aughton, as a good place to strand my characters and to indulge my *Downtown Abbey* fantasies. I have thoroughly enjoyed making up Geraint Hadley-Brown's Quintrell family history.

Dorothea Roberts and Geraint Hadley-Brown will be back for more adventures in *Dying to Get to The Truth*.

Many thanks are due to the fabulous team at Sharpe Books for bringing this book to life, particularly to Richard and Tara. Thank you to my wonderful boys Ian, Nathanael and Samuel for all your love and support. Special thanks are due to Alan, Jean, Ian, Alex, Diana, Tracey, Kerri, Dave and Ags for helpful conversations, reading early versions, support and encouragement throughout.